A SPINSTER AT THE HIGHLAND COURT

THE HIGHLAND LADIES BOOK ONE

CELESTE BARCLAY

OLIVER
HEBER
BOOKS

GNARLY WOOL PUBLISHING

0 9 8 7 6 5 4 3 2 1

Published by Oliver Heber Books

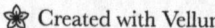 Created with Vellum

"Wherever I wander,
wherever I rove,
The hills of the Highlands forever I love."
~ Robert Burns ~
To the bonny lasses and braw lads who hear the Highlands
calling them home.
Happy reading, y'all,
Celeste

SUBSCRIBE TO CELESTE'S NEWSLETTER

Subscribe to Celeste's bimonthly newsletter to receive exclusive insider perks.

Have you read *Their Highland Beginning, The Clan Sinclair Prequel?* Learn how the saga begins! This FREE novella is available to all new subscribers to Celeste's monthly newsletter. Subscribe on her website.

Subscribe Now

THE HIGHLAND LADIES

PREFACE

The Highland Ladies series is a spin off to my first series, *The Clan Sinclair,* and follows the lives of ladies-in-waiting at King Robert the Bruce's court. If you are a fan of Highlander romances, then you've surely encountered the time period that spans the Wars of Scottish Independence, along with the rise and reign of Robert the Bruce.

While I was intentionally vague about the time period and royal couple in *The Clan Sinclair,* there is little way to avoid the history of Robert the Bruce when this series takes place predominantly at Stirling Castle after he was crowned king. I have taken creative license in a number of areas, especially the creation of characters such as our hero, but the events and clan dynamics are true to history.

Robert the Bruce's family shared a claim to the throne with at least twelve others, and the most notable was John Balliol, who some historians have dubbed the "pretender king." Initially, he was favored by much of the Scottish nobility, but once he ascended to the throne, he demonstrated an unforgivable, in the nobles' estimation, tendency to do the English King Edward I's bidding. The nobles argued that he was little more than Edward's puppet. Longshanks, as was Edward's moniker, had ambitions to rule all the British Isles and focused strongly upon the Scots intending to hammer them into submission. This earned him the other moniker The Hammer of the Scots. As his power and influence grew during the reign of John Balliol, so did the seeds of rebellion. Robert the Bruce came to the forefront of the rebellion and those claiming a divine right to the throne.

The Clan Comyn was among the most powerful at the time and became one of the Bruce's major impediments to ousting John Balliol. They had branches throughout the country and occupied many strategic castles. History tells that Robert the Bruce killed John "the Red" Comyn (there were many Johns and Douglases at the time, and many were give nicknames of "the Red" or "the Black"; it can be quite confusing) within the church at Dumfries. Shortly thereafter, Isabella MacDuff defied her husband John Comyn, the Earl of Buchan and cousin to the murdered John "the Red" Comyn, to crown Robert king, as was her hereditary right, at Sconce. The Earl of Buchan plays a strong role in *His Highland Surprise, The Clan Sinclair* book five. Robert ascended to the throne in 1306 and ruled until his death in 1329. It is during that time span that *The Highland Ladies* takes place.

Queen Elizabeth de Bourgh was Robert's second wife after the death of Isabella of Mar who was the mother to Robert's oldest legitimate child, Marjorie (mentioned in the companion to the series, *A Spy at the Highland Court: De Wolfe Connected World*). She was the daughter of a powerful supporter of King Edward, and there are thoughts that she was married to Robert to serve as a spy. Three months after their marriage, in 1306, Robert sent his wife, daughter Marjorie, Mary and Christian Bruce (his siters), and

Isabella to safety escorted by his brother Niall. Elizabeth was kidnapped by order of King Edward I and spent eight years under house arrest. Isabella (another popular name) was seized alongside Elizabeth but was imprisoned in a suspended cage exposed to the elements at Berwick Castle.

The other women in their party were sent to various convents and castles while Robert's sister, Mary Bruce, was imprisoned in a cage at Roxburgh Castle. During the attempted escape, Niall (also referred to a Nigel, a younger brother) was captured and later drawn and quartered. Elizabeth's imprisonment is mentioned briefly in *His Highland Pledge* and *His Highland Surprise* but plays an important role in this novel. During this same period, two other brothers, Thomas and Alexander, were captured and executed.

The Edward Bruce that is the hero of this story is an entire work of fiction. There is no historical record of an adopted distant cousin. But the actual Edward Bruce, mentioned in this story as a secondary character, did fight the English in Ireland and was crowned High King of Ireland shortly before his defeat and execution by the English. It had been the Bruces' ambition to create a united Gaelic partnership to diminish the English power within the British Isles.

Clan Gregor, which plays a part in the political intrigue within this novel, originally sided with the Balliols but eventually came over to Robert the Bruce's camp. However, Robert awarded a substantial part of Clan Gregor's land to Clan Campbell as reward for their unwavering support of his cause. Clan Campbell was another immensely powerful and influential clan at the time and harried the Gregors off the land. The animosity grew over the next three hundred years, escalating to the point where King

James VI, in 1603, abolished the clan entirely and made it a crime to associate with the Gregors or to bear their surname. An event the precipitated this banishment is mentioned toward the end of this story. While Clan Grant assisted Clan Gregor in reclaiming a castle from the Campbells, they were loyal to Robert the Bruce, complicating the alliances. They did little or nothing to defend the Gregors once they were pushed off their land.

The MacAdams clan was a sept of the Gregors and originated from the larger clan. They did not grow in prominence until several centuries later when the Gregors were outlawed. They were not a powerful clan in comparison to the Comyns and Campbells, but they were well known at the time of this novel.

Clan Baird held sway in Lanarkshire County, and in 1308, three members were convicted and executed for conspiring to assassinate Robert. However, the clan returned to Robert's favor when he granted them a barony. This is where I took some creative license in the timeline. While the story takes place after Queen Elizabeth's release in 1314, elements of the event in question play a part in this story.

The locations named in this story are, in fact, real and the estimated time for travel is based upon traveling by horseback along Medieval roads. The locations belonged to the clans mentioned, and some still exist, mostly in a ruinous or rebuilt state.

I hope you enjoy *A Spinster at the Highland Court* and come to love Elizabeth Fraser and Edward Bruce as much as I have.

Happy reading,

Celeste

CHAPTER ONE

Elizabeth Fraser looked around the royal chapel within Stirling Castle. The ornate candlestick holders on the altar glistened and reflected the light from the ones in the wall sconces as the priest intoned the holy prayers of the Advent season. Elizabeth kept her head bowed as though in prayer, but her green eyes swept the congregation. She watched the other ladies-in-waiting, many of whom were doing the same thing. She caught the eye of Allyson Elliott. Elizabeth raised one eyebrow as Allyson's lips twitched. Both women had been there enough times to accept they'd be kneeling for at least the next hour as the Latin service carried on. Elizabeth understood the Mass thanks to her cousin Deirdre Fraser, or rather now Deirdre Sinclair. Elizabeth's mind flashed to the recent struggle her cousin faced as she reunited with her husband Magnus after a seven-year separation. Her aunt and uncle's choice to keep Deirdre hidden from her husband simply because they didn't think the Sinclairs were an advantageous enough match, and the resulting scandal, still humiliated the other Fraser clan members at court. She admired Deirdre's husband Magnus's pledge to remain

1

faithful despite not knowing if he'd ever see Deirdre again.

Elizabeth suddenly snapped her attention; while everyone else intoned the twelfth—or was it thirteenth—amen of the Mass, the hairs on the back of her neck stood up. She had the strongest feeling that someone was watching her. Her eyes scanned to her right, where her parents sat further down the pew. Her mother and father had their heads bowed and eyes closed. While she was convinced her mother was in devout prayer, she wondered if her father had fallen asleep during the Mass. Again. With nothing seeming out of the ordinary and no one visibly paying attention to her, her eyes swung to the left. She took in the king and queen as they kneeled together at their prie-dieu. The queen's lips moved as she recited the liturgy in silence. The king was as still as a statue. Years of leading warriors showed, both in his stature and his ability to control his body into absolute stillness. Elizabeth peered past the royal couple and found herself looking into the astute hazel eyes of Edward Bruce, Lord of Badenoch and Lochaber. His gaze gave her the sense that he peered into her thoughts, as though he were assessing her. She tried to keep her face neutral as heat surged up her neck. She prayed her face didn't redden as much as her neck must have, but at a twenty-one, she still hadn't mastered how to control her blushing. Her nape burned like it was on fire. She canted her head slightly before looking up at the crucifix hanging over the altar. She closed her eyes and tried to invoke the image of the Lord that usually centered her when her mind wandered during Mass.

Elizabeth sensed Edward's gaze remained on her. She didn't understand how she was so sure that he was looking at her. She didn't have any special gifts of perception or sight, but her intuition screamed that he was still looking. Elizabeth recited the Lord's Prayer in her head, but after a lifetime of reciting it, she didn't have to search hard for the words to play across her mind and it did little to bring her attention back to the service. Try as she might, her mind refused to do anything but command her eyes to open. Once again, she was staring into the riveting eyes of Edward Bruce. He brazenly smiled at her. Elizabeth's eyes widened and her nose flared. She allowed her head to move this time as she looked at the various members of the congregation. No one there seemed to be looking at either Elizabeth or Edward, but when she looked at the priest, his scowl was aimed directly at her. Instead of bowing her head as she should, she shot her own scowl at the impudent man who continued to distract her. The queen would undoubtedly learn of her impudence from the priest, which meant Elizabeth would be making up for lost time, forced to spend the afternoon in prayer on the prie-dieu in the queen's salon. The difference would be that the other ladies-in-waiting would watch her in her shame.

Edward, who had seen the priest watching Elizabeth from the corner of his eye, couldn't hide his smirk when the beautiful young woman scowled at him. His jaded sense of humor made him smile, while his last shreds of decency caused a moment of contrition. Edward realized what Elizabeth obviously did: she'd be spending time repenting before his sister-by-marriage, the queen. He considered whether speaking on behalf of Elizabeth would do more harm than good. He looked back at her once again; he couldn't keep himself from doing so. He was sure he'd seen her before when he'd been to court. Edward had seen all the queen's ladies-in-waiting, since they were always in attendance. But there was something different, yet so familiar, about this woman

3

with the mysterious green eyes. His intuition hammered that he might have met her before. A memory niggled, fighting its way into his consciousness. Edward had bedded a number of ladies-in-waiting over the years, but he was sure she wasn't one of them. He was quite certain he'd remember such an encounter, and as his eyes feasted on her figure, he was also certain he wouldn't have let her go. His mind flashed to his mistress, Sinead, who lived in Ireland. His stomach soured as he remembered his last night with her. As far as he was concerned, she was now his former mistress, but he wasn't convinced the fiery-haired, fiery-tempered woman would agree with her new status. Edward pulled his mind to the present, since looking at the chestnut haired, green-eyed beauty was more enjoyable than thinking of the explosive argument that ended his arrangement with Sinead.

Edward continued to stare at Elizabeth until the memory finally surged forward. It was his turn to have his eyes widen and his nose flare. It was also the same moment the young woman looked at him. His flash of recognition earned him a reciprocated smirk. She clearly remembered who he was and had more easily remembered their first and only encounter. Elizabeth Fraser. That was her name, and he remembered how she'd felt for the brief moment she'd been in his embrace. His fingers tingled and his palms itched. He now recalled in detail how they met. The young woman spread an intriguing rumor that she was his newest lover. When he overheard the whispers during the evening meal, he sought out the woman who was willing to demolish her reputation by linking herself, voluntarily, to him. He learned she had a sharp mind and was loyal to a fault. She jeopardized her position at court to create a diversion for her friend Ceit Comyn and her then betrothed, now

4

husband Tavish Sinclair. When they met on a terrace in the dark, he couldn't resist the temptation to taunt and, hopefully, tempt her. That was when Edward realized her reserved demeanor was a façade. Elizabeth matched words with him, then slipped away. He followed her into the ballroom, but she entrenched herself with the other ladies-in-waiting, making it impossible for him to claim a dance.

Edward was determined to rectify that situation. If only it weren't Advent, the second-most solemn season at court. He was thankful he'd come home now, rather than during Lent. At least he had the Christmas festivities to look forward to. That, and a woman to woo.

Elizabeth worked her way through the mass of people leaving the chapel. She tried to be unobtrusive since she had no interest in lingering. She wove around one group, then another, as people stopped to greet each other. She never understood why people liked to mingle when Mass ended, as if they wouldn't see each other during the next three meals of the day. Elizabeth intended to make her way to the queen's salon, anticipating not only Her Majesty's arrival but her own inevitable punishment. If she readied the chamber and had everything as the queen preferred, then her attempt at contrition might lessen the time she'd be ordered to spend in

5

prayer. She had no remorse, but her knees rebelled at the idea of another three hours spent bearing her weight.

Elizabeth stepped through the chapel doors and took a sharp right directly into a broad, muscled chest. Her nose landed in the small dip in the man's sternum. Strong but gentle hands cupped her shoulders and helped her to take a step back. The look of shock on the man's face surely matched hers, except when his morphed into a smile, hers turned to horror. She jerked away and turned in a complete circle as she tried to determine if anyone had seen them.

"No one has looked this way," the deep baritone murmured, wrapping around her like a fur cloak. "If I'd known I'd meet you so quickly, I might have paid more attention to where I waited."

The humor in his voice rang in Elizabeth's ears, but she failed to find anything funny about the situation.

"Excuse me, Lord Badenoch. I should have looked where I was going." Elizabeth dipped a curtsy and tried to escape.

Edward watched the woman he spent his morning fantasizing about attempt to retreat.

"Don't scamper away quite yet." He kept his voice low so only she could hear. He was sure someone was bound to see them standing together, so the least he could do was keep his voice down while he tried to seduce her.

Elizabeth's brows lowered and lines formed around her down-turned lips. "I'm not a squirrel, a chipmunk, or any other rodent. I don't scamper," Elizabeth hissed.

She spun on her heel. Edward was prepared to follow her when his name was called by the only person who could force him to stay. He stifled his sigh.

"Brother," King Robert slapped his hand on Edward's shoulder as only a brother could do. "I'm glad to see you again. We didn't have enough time to speak last night. Your arrival came as a surprise and late."

"I had no desire to sleep on the ground again."

"Just what did you sleep on last night?"

Edward ground his teeth. His brother's comment might have been accurate several years ago, but these days he rarely dallied with any woman at court. It wasn't worth the hysteria it caused when he returned to Ireland and Sinead. The woman had more eyes and ears at court than any foreign spy. Each time he wondered why he returned to her, he remembered her skills. Skills that brought him hours of pleasure when he could escape the mud and rain of the battlefield. She was also a brilliant strategist. Her advice had served him well over the past two years while fighting the British in Ireland.

"I slept on the bed in my chamber. It was nice to have the quiet and the space to myself." Edward looked at the man he called brother. Their only resemblance was in the coincidental color of their hair. Even there, the king's was closer to carrot while Edward's hair, which had darkened with age, was more russet. When they were children, their shock of red hair made many people wonder if Edward was the king's illegitimate brother rather than his adopted distant cousin. It was only the reputation of his mother that kept people from voicing their suspicions. When Edward's father died, his mother retired to a convent, where she died only a year later. Left an orphan if not in name then by status, the Bruce family took him in. Life in the Scotland was hard enough without being a child with no family. The two men were close even though Robert was several years his senior. Edward was closer in age and relationship to Robert's younger brother by blood. Both men were named Edward and had been inseparable since childhood. When Robert sent his blood brother to Ireland, his adopted brother followed.

"Sinead still got you by the bollocks." It was a statement not a question.

"No longer. She may have been the best mistress I ever had, in and out of bed, but I can no longer stomach the temper tantrums that accompany her talents. It's no longer worth the trouble."

"How did she accept that decision? Or did you slip away in the night and pray she'll forget aboot you by the time you return?"

Edward rubbed his hand across the back of his neck. He didn't intend to have this conversation with Robert in the passageway outside the chapel where people still lurked.

"Neither," Edward jerked his head in the direction of an alcove.

The two men walked to the nook in silence.

"What have you to say?" The king's face was set in stone.

"I'm done in Ireland. I'm not returning, Robert. There's no reason for me to. Edward has made inroads there and has enough men fighting for him. The local people support him as well. But you must realize the British won't back down. My presence there won't be what determines the outcome. I was but one more warrior Edward can easily replace with a local mon."

"That isn't true, and we both know it. You have a tactical mind that is invaluable."

"You must admit that is a half-truth. Sinead had as much to do with that as I did, and Edward is already enjoying her help."

The king's eyebrows shot up, but Edward shook his head.

8

"I arranged it. It softened the blow. Slightly. For both of them."

"Why do you really want to return? The fighting continues here."

"This is home."

"You have never considered this castle, or any castle, home."

"Scotland. The Highlands. They are home."

"The hills are calling you home?"

"They are," Edward admitted.

"You mean to tell me that you're ready to settle down on some farm with a wife and start breeding?"

"Perhaps not a farm and perhaps not a wife, and certainly no breeding. But I'm ready to be home."

"You say no wife, but perhaps another mistress," Robert challenged.

Edward perceived the king's suspicious look as much as he saw it.

"I watched you speaking to Elizabeth Fraser. I have also been informed by the queen, who was told by the priest, that the two of you were inappropriately staring at one another."

"That priest moves quickly for someone the size of a sow," Edward muttered.

"Then you admit it."

"I didn't admit to aught. It just didn't take you long to find me, so for you to have been enlightened by Elizabeth, your wife that is, aboot what the priest told her means he must have been in quite the rush."

"He wouldn't have been in a rush if there was naught to say."

"She intrigues me. I remember her from the last time I was here. But fear not, I have no intention of making her my mistress. I have no interest in having one."

Edward realized he was speaking the truth, even if his intention only minutes ago had been to seduce

9

Elizabeth Fraser. The notion of bedding her and moving on didn't seem as palatable as it had while he pictured them together instead of praying. He did speak the truth that he had no intention of taking another mistress. They were more trouble than they were worth. He could easily find a lonely widow or bored wife. That had been his plan before seeing Elizabeth. That plan changed when he watched her during the Mass, changing once more as he spoke to Robert. He wanted to stay in Scotland, and that was the reason for his return. But the idea of taking a wife suddenly held an appeal it never had before. An image of Elizabeth's face as she told him she wasn't a rodent made him want to smile, but he squelched the impulse as his brother stared at him.

"She won't have you." Robert's sharp words broke through Edward's thoughts and caused him to flinch and sent a stabbing spark of pain in his chest.

"She's a lady-in-waiting. Of course, she won't have a dalliance."

Robert snorted. "Being a lady-in-waiting is little deterrent to many young women. Rather, Elizabeth's father won't have you."

Edward's face became a storm cloud. "Because he assumes I'm illegitimate."

"He might, but that wouldn't matter to him. He won't have you because you'd gain him naught. You're already close to me. We have a bond that no one can influence or manipulate. You aren't advantageous enough to him because you're uncontrollable."

"You'd imagine having the ear of the king's brother would be just the advantage any courtier would want."

"You would." Robert conceded. "But everyone knows your loyalty is to the Highlands and to me, not to any one clan."

"Fraser hasn't thought like a Highlander in

nearly twenty odd years," Edward scoffed. "He's more interested in the money he can accumulate and the titles he can earn, but his clan barely benefits from it."

"He'd have you believe that, but that's because the Frasers are prosperous without much effort. He has expanded their holds and brought them more influence, so don't underestimate his loyalty to his clan. But he still won't have you. The poor lass has had four broken betrothals. The queen is sure Elizabeth is convinced she'll end up a spinster serving the queen until the end."

"That's preposterous. There is no way she'll go unwed."

"The way her father uses her as a puppet makes it very likely. She's twenty-one and has been here since she was eleven. Some are beginning to whisper she's too old. She has a pristine reputation and would make any mon a fine wife, but between those who want a younger bride and those who have no desire to tangle with Fraser, she's losing potential husbands with every year."

All the better for me. Far less competition. She might welcome my attention if no one else wants her.

"I recognize that look, Edward. She won't have you. I warn you away, for your own good and hers. Don't compromise her. Fraser won't agree to a marriage, and she'll end up as a soiled dove that my wife will have to remove from her court. Then what will she have?"

CHAPTER TWO

The king's final words echoed in Edward's head as he watched Elizabeth from the dais. His position at the king's right hand afforded him a vantage point few had. She sat chattering with the other ladies-in-waiting, but she wasn't as animated as the others. His gaze swept across those gathered on the benches. Several women sent him lusty smiles, and a few pulled at the front of their gowns to flash their cleavage. For the first time in his life, not a single one tempted him. Except the modestly attired brunette who filled every crevice of his mind.

As the meal finished, Edward again rued the season of Advent. There'd be little chance to catch her in a dance. He refused to miss an opportunity to talk to the beguiling woman. He'd have to be resourceful.

If only I'd come back a week earlier. I could be dancing with her right now. Four weeks. Four bluidy weeks before I can dance with her on Christmas Eve.

Edward watched Elizabeth excuse herself from the table as she approached the dais and the queen. He hadn't even noticed she was summoned by his sister-by-marriage. While he respected the woman, there was no love lost between them.

Elizabeth stood before the dais and dipped into a low curtsy as she waited for the queen's request. She caught the impulse to rub her knees before she embarrassed herself. The queen had been particularly indignant that one of her ladies-in-waiting wasn't fully engaged in her prayer. It was made worse that a lady-in-waiting was caught looking at a man. And the worst was that it was Elizabeth staring at Edward.

The queen gestured for her to step onto the dais, and there was no way Elizabeth could refuse. She kept her eyes averted but was certain Edward watched her. Elizabeth made her way to the queen's side and listened as she was told she was making a spectacle of herself by drawing attention from Edward. She clenched her jaw to keep from retorting it was most assuredly not her intention. The queen dismissed her and insisted she retire for the evening. That was the only blessing to this conversation. She was relieved to escape the overheated Great Hall and all the people who filled it with various fragrances and odors. She curtsied once more and made a direct path for an exit. Elizabeth didn't look back to see Edward was already gone.

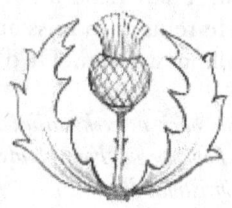

"You cannot convince me you aren't scampering now." The same baritone that caught her off-guard that morning wrapped around her. If she weren't so

14

dismayed at running into the man responsible for her three hours spent in prayer in front of the other young ladies and now responsible for her dismissal from the evening meal, she might have admitted the latter was a blessing.

"And you cannot convince me you have manners," Elizabeth snapped. She took a step back in shock at her own comment. "My lord."

She wanted to cringe, but instead proffered a shallow curtsy before trying to step around him. A deep chuckle stopped her as her lips pursed and shoulders went back before she raised her chin. Specks of blue, green, and gold danced in the candlelight as Edward's hazel eyes reflected his sense of humor.

"You're likely right. Perhaps you could teach me. And my name is Edward, not my lord."

"I could." Elizabeth sour face transformed into the practiced and seductive smile of a courtier. She swayed into him and lifted onto her toes to whisper near his ear, "But I don't want to."

Elizabeth slid past him, but Edward wasn't deterred. He followed her as she made her way down the passageway. Elizabeth could hear his soft tread, even if it was nearly silent. She wound her way through the maze of passageways with no intention of leading him to her chamber. Edward remained her shadow but never attempted to speak. After a quarter of an hour spent roaming the castle, Elizabeth led Edward toward a secluded chamber, but when he entered, she'd disappeared. Edward scanned the large music room and found it deserted. It was his turn to spin in a circle, just as he'd watched Elizabeth do that morning. There was no one there, and the only illumination was the moonlight streaming through the window.

Where the devil is she? She's no apparition, so how could

Elizabeth inhaled a deep breath as her heart continued to thud behind her ribs. She was sure Edward was confused by her disappearance, but she counted on him not knowing about the secret tunnels that ran behind most of the walls of the castle. She came to the castle a curious and bored child. With little to do at the age of eleven, she explored her new home. A few of the other young girls showed her the secret network that few were privy to. Those same young women had moved on to marriage or returned to their clans. Elizabeth was the only lady-in-waiting remaining from her childhood. A few of the newer ladies discovered the passageways as a way to arrive at assignations, but none knew their way through the miles of winding and dark tunnels the way Elizabeth did.

Elizabeth made her way to her chamber and shut the door behind her. She shared the space with two other young ladies, but she counted on there being little likelihood they'd return that night. They rarely slept in their beds, so Elizabeth breathed easier. Her maid appeared from the antechamber and helped her from her gowns. Elizabeth disliked having assistance every time she dressed, but from a practical perspective, she needed help with her court clothing and accepted that declining a maid would only draw unnecessary attention, but she disliked the fuss and the lack of privacy. Once the maid was gone, she used the water basin and scrubbed her face and neck. Elizabeth considered saying her regular evening prayers, but she decided God had already heard from her enough that day. When she laid her head on her pillow, her mind came alive, replaying the morning Mass and picturing the moment she realized Edward was watching her. It was the opposite of what she wanted. She'd hoped she was tired enough that her eyes would drop closed as soon as she laid down. Her body warmed as she recollected the interest she saw in his eyes. The deep resonance of his voice played through her ears, and her breasts hung heavy and full.

Elizabeth could see Edward watching her throughout the evening meal as though she still sat in her seat at the lower table. Her stomach had clenched, and she became lightheaded as she approached the queen. It had been the greatest challenge not to look at him as she walked up to the dais. As her mind flashed to her two encounters with him in the passageways, she pulled her chemise to her hips. Her fingers threaded through the thatch of hair above the juncture of her thighs until she found the hidden pearl to circle and press. Her other fingers slid across her seam and through the dew that already pooled at the entrance of her sheath. Her breath caught as she admitted how strong her desire was for a man she could never have. She'd imagined him like this since the night they met a few months ago.

Her fingers dipped within and spread the moisture over her bud. Elizabeth rubbed in slow circles as she pictured Edward naked. She was sure she wouldn't be disappointed. His build suggested a man

17

who was a hardened warrior. His tunic stretched across the broad chest and large crossed arms she saw when they met after the evening meal. Her mouth had gone dry, just as it did now. She kneaded her breast and her finger continued to work as the dueling sensations of pleasure and achiness began. Her thumb flicked her puckered nipple, and she began to rub faster and harder as she then pinched her nipple nearly to the point of pain. Her back arched as her hips rocked. Pleasure shot through her core and out to her limbs as she threw her head back and shut her eyes. She bit her lip to keep from crying out Edward's name.

As the physical pleasure waned, her heart felt pinched, and tears prickled behind her eyes. She rolled onto her side and tucked herself into a tight ball. A tear escaped from her eye and slid down her cheek to be absorbed by her pillow.

This is the most I shall ever have. With Edward or any other mon. It's all I've ever had. I shall die a virgin all for my father's gain. He'd leave me a spinster and lonely for the chance to advance himself. He claims he does it for our clan, but any of the alliances he arranged then broke would've been advantageous. I could be wed with a family of my own, rather than alone with only my hand to pleasure me. I'd give Edward what he wants, what I want, if I could be sure my father'd never find out. God forbid I give in and my father finally does wed me. That would be my luck.

As her tears leaked into her pillow and chemise, Elizabeth finally drifted off to sleep.

CHAPTER THREE

E dward was restless. After losing track of Elizabeth, he went to stand before the large windows and watched the stars twinkle between clouds.

What is wrong with me? I've seen the woman all of three times, and I can't stop imagining what it'd be like to strip her bare and sink into her over and over. To taste every inch of her. To see pleasure blossom across her face. Blossom. What the bluidy hell? I've never used that word in my life. I want more than that though. I want to see that spark of fire flash across her face as her eyes shoot lightning bolts at me. I'm curious aboot what she'll say next. Can I make her smile as easily as I spur her temper? What would it be like to walk through these gardens with her hand in mine, to walk into the Hall with her on my arm? How many times did I slip from Sinead's bed to avoid her clinging to me in her sleep? How many times did I run from having to wake next to her, as much as morning coupling would have been enjoyable? I never wanted her to become too comfortable in her position. But Elizabeth: I'd fall asleep and wake up every day next to her. How can I even be sure of this? What is it aboot her? I feel it in my bones that I can trust her as my wife in the daylight and my partner in ecstasy in the dark.

Edward cupped his rod as it swelled in his breeks.

He needed to make it back to his chamber before he burst. He'd take himself in hand as he pictured Elizabeth riding his cock. As he turned toward the door, the sound of the handle twisting echoed through the empty space. A shadowy figure slipped in, and the scent of roses wafted toward him. He recognized the woman and wanted to cringe.

"There you are. You slipped out of the Hall as though your arse was on fire, Lord Badenoch."

"Lady MacAdams." Edward couldn't bring to mind anything else to say to a woman he bedded on more than one occasion, but it had been a couple of years.

She glided across the room before dipping a low curtsy that afforded him a view of her sizable bosom. What once made him salivate now did nothing. As the woman before him rose, she angled herself to skim his body. Her eyes widened as his hard length brushed across her.

"It is a pleasure, my lord. I'm glad you're happy to see me," she purred. She trailed a hand over his belly before rubbing her palm over his aching cock.

Edward stifled a groan. He didn't want to encourage her, but the temptation to let her ease his raging lust was nearly too much. He remembered what she could do with her mouth and what it was like to thrust into her. He'd enjoyed their trysts, but now that the initial shock wore off, his mind screamed that it was wrong. He grasped her wrist and pushed her hand away.

"This isn't for you," he groaned.

"But it could be. Just like it was."

Her other hand moved to lift his tunic. Her hand was at his waistband before he could anticipate it. Once again temptation bit at him, and he considered letting her ease his swelling cock. It had a mind of its own as it continued to harden from the attention.

Edward released her wrist and allowed her to loosen his breeks. She sank to her knees, and Edward watched her lick her lips as she drew him from his trousers. But before her tongue struck out, he stepped back. He couldn't do it. His heart was sure it was wrong. Even if Elizabeth never learned of this, he couldn't let himself couple with another woman. He couldn't even allow another woman to pleasure him.

"Thank you, but I must decline."

Edward adjusted his breeks and fastened them.

"Decline? You've never declined me. No one will interrupt us. No one knows we're here."

"It's not that. As I said before, this isn't for you."

"And you believe it's for little Elizabeth Fraser. That simpering nitwit wouldn't know what to do with it. You'd rather get hard for a cunny you'll never have. She might be why you're hard, but she won't be the one to give you what we both know you want. You remember I can bring you to a climax that makes you cross your eyes. And that's just with my mouth."

"That was quite some time ago. Things change. People change."

"You never will. You'll always be insatiable, and once this infatuation wears off, which it will because you'll never have her, you'll regret turning me down. You'll never settle for one woman, which is fine with me. I have no intention of settling for one mon. But you'll tire of chasing a skirt that'll never rise for you. Then what? You'll be back for me to ease the ache. You had better hope I'm still available."

"I'll keep that in mind. Good night, Lady MacAdams."

Edward practically sprinted away, then made his way to his chamber and barred the door. He stripped and went to stand before his window. He looked out at the stars, just as he had been when his cock first came to life. He stroked slowly as he imagined losing himself with Elizabeth in the topiary maze his chamber overlooked. He spotted a nook he'd pull her into as he kissed a path along her neck to her breasts. He'd loosen her gown until it sagged low enough to free them. He'd snake his hands under her skirts as he feasted on the mounds. He'd bring her to the brink of release before lifting her to sink in with one thrust.

His hand sped up as his strokes became shorter and harder until his bollocks tightened. He released his seed into the linen he'd brought with him. His head fell back as he panted. His heart raced like it always did, but this time his chest tightened. He rubbed his fist over his sternum, but the tension wouldn't ease. While taking himself in hand was never as good as being with a woman, it was usually satisfying. This time, it left him hollow and lonely.

Edward climbed into his bed and looked at the empty space beside him. He could see the heart-shaped face with the emerald eyes looking back at him, but when he reached out, his hand only grasped air. Edward fell asleep to a sense of disappointment.

CHAPTER FOUR

Edward spent the remainder of the week creating accidental encounters with Elizabeth. At least he attempted to make them look accidental. As the week drew to an end, he was almost convinced she was orchestrating their run-ins as much as he was. He wavered between hoping her interest was growing and worrying that it was only a coincidence. He found her in the music room as she practiced the harp and stood in the shadows until she was done. She yelped when he clapped softly. She allowed him to escort her to the Great Hall, and he seized the opportunity to ask her about music, her preferences, and how long she'd been playing. He learned of her dislike of talking about herself and her modesty when it came to her talents. Another day, he caught her coming out of the library with several scrolls tucked under her arm and a large book clasped against her chest. She flushed prettily when she explained that her cousin Deirdre was a natural scholar, and she taught Elizabeth to read in three languages. Now Elizabeth borrowed from the monastic scholars whenever she had a chance. While she appreciated the poetry the ladies read in the queen's salon, she preferred studying history and geography. He walked her through the passageways, taking the longest route to the queen's chambers, so he could discuss her latest discovery. He found her intelligent and articulate, and Elizabeth would only admit to herself that she enjoyed being able to speak to someone as knowledgeable as she was. She was often lonely now that Deirdre had moved home with her husband. None of the other ladies-in-waiting shared her interests, and none of the men at court considered her capable of such conversation. Elizabeth found herself seeking out opportunities to see Edward, even though she was convinced she was setting herself up for heartache when, inevitably, nothing came of their burgeoning relationship.

When the Sunday Mass began, Edward found himself in the same place as the week before, but this time he forced himself not to look at Elizabeth. He discovered he had more decency than he realized because his contrition nearly strangled him. He'd learned that Elizabeth spent three additional hours in prayer for his transgressions the week before.

Elizabeth kept her eyes shut for the entire service. She wouldn't have anyone doubt her commitment to prayer, and she wouldn't allow herself to give into temptation. She was certain that Edward purposely created situations throughout the week where they'd be near each other. He orchestrated sitting near one another when he and the king joined the queen's salon in the afternoons. The men suffered through one poem and ballad after another because the queen requested her husband's company, and Elizabeth suffered through the ladies-in-waiting fawning over Edward. She couldn't stifle the raging jealousy that sprang up the first time he walked through the door. He appeared in the gardens when the queen insisted the ladies walk with her despite the biting cold. Elizabeth discovered he wasn't as arrogant as he led others to believe, and he was both insightful and patient enough to listen. By the end of the week, Elizabeth caught herself trying to angle closer to him when mingling in the Great Hall. His charm was like a magnet, and she had to admit the more she saw and learned, the more her interest grew.

The Mass ended, and the ladies-in-waiting followed the queen from the chapel. As the queen entered her chamber, the Mistress of the Bedchamber blocked the way.

"The queen is retiring for the rest of the day. She is called to spend the afternoon and evening in prayer. You shall retire to the salon and sew or read."

Elizabeth seized an opportunity she used sparingly.

"My lady," Elizabeth stepped toward the older woman. "Might I be excused? My courses are causing me great discomfort and inconvenience."

Elizabeth crossed her fingers within the folds of her skirt. She disliked lying, but she disliked being trapped in the chamber with the other young ladies even more. The woman waved her hand in dismissal, so Elizabeth didn't look back. She went directly to her chamber where she changed into a pair of breeches and a tunic she kept hidden in a box below the floorboards under her bed. She tucked her hair beneath a stable boy's cap and wrapped a plain woolen cloak around her shoulders. It looked ordinary enough, but Elizabeth had sewn black seal skin inside to insulate it.

She moved aside the tapestry by her bed and pressed a brick until a small door clicked open. She stooped to lean in and grab the torch she kept just inside the entrance. She lit it from the fire and eased into the hidden tunnel, then pushed the door closed until the latch clicked. She wound her way through the castle hidden behind the walls and in the dark.

She could navigate without the torch after half a score of years, but the light made it easier. She left the tunnels through an equally small hatch just behind the stables.

Elizabeth slipped into the stables knowing equal parts freedom and trepidation. She counted on there being few people nearby since it was the Sabbath, but she understood the gravity of being discovered. She crept along the stalls until she came to the large black stallion the stable boys kept hidden for her. Few people were privy to the animal that lived in the tucked-away stall where ill horses would have been kept until they healed. She grabbed an apple from the barrel outside the stall door.

"Hello, my boy. I've missed you. I'm sorry it's been close to a fortnight since I've been able to slip away. I wouldn't have stayed away if it could have been helped. Can you forgive me? Are you ready? Come now, we don't have much time," Elizabeth crooned as she hurried to saddle him. She led her horse from the stables and mounted just outside the door. She pulled her hood low over her face and spurred him forward.

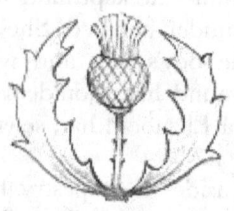

Edward smiled as he listened to a woman greet her lover. The couple wouldn't be the first to tryst in a stable. He'd done it enough times. As he listened, something seemed familiar about the voice. As the woman spoke more, he recognized Elizabeth's lilting tones. She'd spent almost half her life at court, but there were tiny hints of her Highland past. Rage unlike any he'd ever experienced off the battlefield pulsated through him.

Who the bluidy hell is she meeting?

Edward charged around the corner in time to see a small figure cloaked in all black slip out of the stables with one of the largest stallions he'd ever seen. Edward retreated to his own horse who he'd just finished saddling. Once the animal was free of the stall, he mounted and bent low to race out of the stables and after the troublesome minx who was always on his mind.

Elizabeth clattered across the courtyard to a gate few people used. The guard nodded when he recognized the pair and opened it for her. Edward was close on their heels as he marveled at how the guard had no reservations in letting them pass. He emerged through the portal just as he watched the horse and rider clear a wall few people would dare to attempt. Fortunately, his steed was a seasoned warhorse that responded to all his owner's commands without hesitation. He cleared the wall as the lone figure entered a copse of trees. Edward kept them in sight as the pair drew farther ahead of his own charger. His horse was one of the fastest he'd ever encountered, but the black beast in front of them was unlike anything he'd ever seen. Rider and horse looked to blend into one. Edward attempted to distinguish between the two as the gap widened. He leaned low over his horse's withers as the animal hurtled forward, sensing the race.

It wasn't until Elizabeth exited the trees into an open meadow that she was sure she was being followed. She lifted her elbow again to peer under her arm, but her billowing cloak kept obscuring her view.

27

She saw the rider gaining on her, but it was impossible to tell if he was friend or foe. She thanked the heavens she was positive her horse could outrun any other, but she was becoming uncomfortable as the gap shrank. Elizabeth tugged sharply on the left rein and steered them toward a fast-moving stream. In spring it would swell into a river, but in the winter, it was a freezing stream. Her horse entered the water with no reservation, having taken this route countless times over the years. They forded the stream as the water rose to the soles of Elizabeth's boots. The cold water splashed over the horse's stomach, and while she was sure it refreshed her mount, it was like shards of glass pricking through her breeches. But the wind against her face was the freedom she needed, so the momentary discomfort was a small price. She kept her body parallel to the horse's withers as they barreled downhill. An expansive wood greeted them at the base. She led them into the trees to the right in the hopes it would buy her the chance to see who followed if the rider didn't change direction.

Elizabeth stroked her horse between the ears and murmured to him to keep him from snorting and shaking his head. Despite the gallop, rider and horse were silent as their pursuer crested the hill and began his descent. The man seemed to be looking directly in front of him, so Elizabeth's heart lurched into her throat when they turned to face her hiding spot.

"Don't hide from me, Elizabeth. I'm already angrier than a shaken hive. Come out now." Edward scanned the trees to make out a shadowy form. He'd nearly fallen from his horse in panic when Elizabeth disappeared over the crest of the hill. He was familiar with how steep the decline was, and he imagined her being thrown and trampled as her horse faltered.

Elizabeth didn't move. She held her breath and

prayed her horse would do the same. He shifted slightly, sensing her tension, and she was sure Edward saw them. When he nudged his horse into the trees, she didn't know if she should remain still or try to flee. His words reached her, but it was his tone that made her nervous.

"Very well. You refuse to heed my directions, then I shall come to you. Don't believe you're well hidden. I can see you and that monster clearly."

Elizabeth's hackles went up with a need to defend her horse. He was only an animal, but he was her pet and her best friend. He intuited her every innermost thought and emotion since she received him as a colt. She also was irritated at Edward's high handedness. He had no say over what she did or where she went. It was only the knowledge that he'd report her to the queen that kept her quiet. She didn't need to add insult to injury by being rude.

Edward pulled alongside her, and before she said a word in her defense, he plucked her from the saddle. His mouth crashed down onto hers as she landed in his lap. He yanked her hood down and whipped off her cap before lacing his fingers through her hair. His kiss was punishing, and Elizabeth tasted the fear. His other hand roamed over her, but it wasn't a lover's caress. It seemed more like he was checking her for injury. It only softened when he was reassured she was hale. His tongue darted against the seam of her lips until she opened to him. Her moan of surprise and want had him lifting her to straddle him and his horse. When her mound came in contact with his stiff cock, it was his turn to groan. He cupped her backside as she shifted to get closer.

Elizabeth clung to his tunic as her head would surely float away. His tongue inside her mouth was strange at first, but curiosity replaced shock. Her tongue tangled with his, and some instinct told her to suck. Edward's response was immediate. His fingers dug into her backside painfully, but she found the touch of pain exciting. The tighter she pinched her nipples when she touched herself, the faster she climaxed. The heat radiating from Edward's chest warmed her cold fingers, and when they found their way to the laces of his collar, she slid them beneath to find scorching smooth skin. She mewled in protest when she was unable to touch more of him, so she caressed his neck and shoulders until she grazed her nails over his scalp and tangled her fingers in his hair. His responding growl vibrated through her channel deep into her core.

Edward wanted to know what secrets hid inside that soft, unyielding flesh. He wanted to strip her bare and claim her. He wanted to vow he'd protect her from anyone and everyone, including herself. He wanted to revel in how she amazed him with her fearlessness and now passion. He wanted to worship her until she couldn't take another moment of pleasure. It was only when the horses shifted that they both drew apart. They sat looking at one another, and neither was sure what to say. Edward stroked the downy skin of her cheek and tucked hairs that came loose behind her ears. The longer he sat holding her in his lap, the more his previous anger resurged. His heart hadn't slowed, and he recalled why he pulled her from her saddle and kissed her senseless.

"I should turn you over my knee."

Elizabeth drew back, her passion-glazed eyes blinking to focus. She shook her head, but Edward wasn't sure if it was in disagreement or to clear her mind.

"Elizabeth, I'm serious. My hand is itching to smack your lovely arse. You scared the shite out of me."

Elizabeth's jaw clenched as she listened to him,

but when he finished with a whisper, she understood his anger. It was her turn to stroke his cheek. She leaned forward and kissed the opposite one.

"I'm sorry, Edward," she breathed against his jaw, testing his given name for the first time. She turned her face into the crook of his neck and kissed him. "I didn't mean to frighten you."

She sat back and took in a look that matched a thundercloud.

"I ride out here all the time. I've been riding like that since I was a young girl but knowing someone was following me kept me from slowing down. I wasn't sure who you were until I saw you coming down the hill."

"What do you mean you ride out here? Unchaperoned? What the hell is your father thinking? Your mother allows it?" Edward peppered her with questions.

Elizabeth tried to scramble from his lap, but his hands cinched around her waist and pinned her in place.

"If you don't want that spanking, you will stay right where you are and answer my questions."

"I owe you no answers, and you have no right to demand them." Elizabeth clenched her teeth and hissed. "Let me go."

"I will not. You're in no position to try to get away either." Edward growled in a tone that matched hers. Coming from a man nearly twice her size, it had the opposite effect than he intended.

Elizabeth swung her fist into his jaw, and Edward's neck snapped back. The first punch was followed immediately by another to his opposite cheek. Taking advantage of him being stunned, Elizabeth pulled herself free and swung into her own saddle. Both horses were trained to remain still despite their riders' movements, so neither had taken a step apart.

She swung her horse around and took off once again.

Edward was in shock. No woman had ever struck him. Despite his surprise, he registered the look of fear and panic his last comment created. She swung before he had a chance to retract them or at least clarify. He understood she felt threatened, and he was impressed with her strength along with her wherewithal, but now he was on the chase again. Navigating through the trees was difficult, but his horse was slightly leaner than Elizabeth's. He was able to catch up and grasp her horse's bridle.

"Wait. Elizabeth, stop. It's my turn to apologize. I'm sorry for scaring you. I realize how my words sound, but I'd never force you. I'd never force myself on you."

She swung an accusing glare at him, and his heart lurched when he saw tears streaming down her cheeks.

"Why did you have to ruin everything?" she choked out.

Edward's brow furrowed.

"That was my first kiss. More than likely to be my only kiss. And you had to ruin it. You said I scared the shite out of you. What do you imagine that was like for me?"

Edward covered her hand with his and with care peeled her fingers free before bringing it to his mouth. His hands chafed her wind-chapped skin, and he breathed warm air onto her knuckles. He held his arms open to her. She paused for so long, Edward was sure she'd run again. Instead, she nodded once. He pulled her into his lap with more grace than the last time. He wrapped his cloak around them both and kissed her cheek beside her ear.

"I don't ever want you to fear me. I'd never ever

trap you. I'm sorry my words scared you," he whispered. His breath tickled her ear and when she tilted her head away he nipped, then licked, a trail along her neck to her collarbone and back up. "You didn't seem scared, or even shocked, by my threat to punish you. Didn't that frighten you?"

Elizabeth shook her head before looking at him and swallowing. Edward watched and realization dawned.

"Would you want me to do that?"

Elizabeth didn't move. She didn't move her head, not even a muscle in her face, nor did she say anything. Edward was sure she even held her breath. His hand stroked her ribs as his thumb rubbed beneath her breast.

"Beth, are you ashamed to admit that intrigues you?" Edward kept his voice hushed as though he were speaking to a skittish animal. "Is the notion of punishment what intrigues you, or is it the idea of me touching you?"

"Both." It was like she breathed the word rather than spoke it.

Edward's hand stopped rubbing her ribs, and he nudged her chin, so she looked at him. It was his turn to sit motionless. He waited for her to explain, but he wouldn't prod her if she wasn't ready.

Elizabeth's eyes roved over Edward's handsome face. She took in his cleft chin and the deep dimples that appeared when he smiled. She saw hints of them when he spoke. She pondered trailing her finger over them, but kept her hands tucked in her lap. She leaned into Edward and brushed her lips against his as the tip of her tongue darted out and swept across the seam of his mouth. When he didn't pull away, she pressed her lips firmly to his. He opened without hesitation, and their kiss built to another conflagration. This time the kiss was slow.

33

They explored one another's mouths finding each nook and cranny. Edward pulled her hand over his chest to rest her palm on his heart. He took her other hand and slid it over his chest and abdomen and onto his ribs, then up to his shoulders. When he released it, she continued to roam at her own pace. Edward found his hands were determined to find her backside again. He cupped her luscious bottom, and when she wiggled in frustration, his grasp tightened. He felt as much as heard her sigh when his fingers bit into her flesh. It had to be painful, but he was learning she liked it. One hand retreated to her breast. Rather than gently cup it as he intended, her hand moved from his heart to press his against the mound that spilled out of his large palm. Once he kneaded it with a firm hold, her hand went back over his heart. His hands gripped her with little finesse, but he was certain he'd spill himself with the excitement her need created.

They only separated when both were unable to go any longer without drawing air into their lungs. Edward continued to massage her as her head fell back. Eventually, she leaned forward and tucked her head into the crook of his neck again.

"What are you doing to me? It was never like this when I imagined--"

Elizabeth cut herself off as she realized what she was about to admit.

"Never like what, Beth? What did you imagine?"

"I never imagined it was possible for my body to ache like it does right now. I didn't realize a mon could make me feel like-- I have no way to describe it. It's not like when--"

Once again, Elizabeth snapped her mouth shut.

"Like when? Who, Beth? Who is he?" Edward was sure he'd be ill. The image of some faceless man touching her made him want to vomit.

34

"Who what? I don't understand."

"Who's touched you? You said it never felt like this. Who is it?" Edward's ears were ringing.

"No one's touched me." Elizabeth took in Edward's expression but wasn't sure what it meant. He was pale and looked shaken. "Edward, I told you, you were the first mon ever to kiss me. How could anyone else have touched me?"

"But you said--"

Elizabeth ducked her head back against his shoulder.

"I meant when I, well, when I do it. To myself."

Her tremble reverberated through him for the first time. She admitted a secret that might very well have her placed in the stocks. He was sure she never told another person what she divulged to him. He understood her trepidation and he was honored she trusted him with such a secret, even if he considered nothing wrong with it. He'd been palming himself more than once a day since he saw her again.

"Beth, there's naught wrong with that. No matter what the church says. It's natural. If God hadn't wanted us to experience pleasure, he wouldn't have made it possible."

Elizabeth sat up and looked at Edward's earnest face until he smiled. The kindness and understanding were her undoing.

"But I'm a virgin. I'm not supposed to have knowledge of such things. It'd be one thing if I was one of your bored wives or lonely widows." She shook her head. "I'm not immoral."

Edward nearly swallowed his tongue.

"I believe you're a virgin. You never came across as aught but, even when we began kissing. Your uncertainty told me. I'd slay anyone foolish enough to claim you're immoral, so I don't want to hear that from you either. As to my alleged women, Beth, there

35

is no one else. Not since I arrived and saw you again."

"Everyone knows you have that mistress in Ireland. Maybe there isn't anyone here, but there is someone."

"And you'd kiss me knowing that?"

"What mon doesn't have a mistress?"

"And if I told you this mon doesn't have a mistress? Nor do I want one."

"I don't understand. Everyone at court knows of your red-headed mistress, and if not her, then it'll be someone else soon enough." Elizabeth's suddenly tried to get back onto her own horse. "It won't be me. It can't be me."

Edward wrapped his arm around her middle.

"Sit still, Beth. I'll embarrass us both if you keep rubbing my cock." Elizabeth froze. "I ended things with Sinead before I returned to court. I won't take another mistress. Not if I can help it. I'll be taking a wife."

"Oh, God. Are you betrothed? Am I your other woman? Oh, God. I cannot be the reason you're unfaithful. Let me go."

"Stop. Stop wriggling and listen, or I'll spank you." Edward saw the lust flair before she extinguished it just as quickly. "I'm not betrothed. Not yet, but I hope to be very soon. Can you not guess who I want to marry?"

"I have no idea what political match you plan to make, but I can't be here with you."

"Beth."

"Why do you call me that?" she cut in.

"Does anyone else call you that?"

"Rarely. Some close family."

"Do you not understand yet, that I'd like to be part of that close family?"

36

Elizabeth looked back over her shoulder as her hands gripped her reins and the saddle horn.

"What are you saying?"

"Sit back down, and I'll tell you." Once again, Edward opened his arms and gave her the choice. Once Elizabeth was still, he continued. "Don't you realize I've been trailing after you like a lovesick puppy begging for any attention? Don't you realize I've been trying to get to know you and have you get to know me? Don't you realize you're the one I want to marry, Beth?"

Elizabeth shook her head as her tears once again poured forth.

"Don't say that. Don't. I can't bear to hear this. Why would you say that?"

This time when she tried to pull herself loose, Edward let her go. With a sob, she spurred her horse back toward the castle. Edward watched her go, following at a distance that left her alone but where he could, and would, still protect her if needed. Edward wondered if it might be his turn to sob.

CHAPTER FIVE

E lizabeth spent the next two days in seclusion. She used her courses as an ongoing excuse. Her maid wouldn't tell anyone the truth, and she counted on the Mistress of the Bedchamber being too modest to talk about her cycles to anyone. The other ladies-in-waiting would pretend sympathy. Elizabeth simply couldn't bring herself to appear in public when there was a chance, a very good one, that she'd encounter Edward. She was embarrassed by her wanton behavior, and she was heartbroken that he'd toy with her. It was common knowledge among everyone at court that it was pointless to ask for her hand. After four broken betrothals, the last nearly two years ago, she accepted no man was serious when they made an offer for her. She understood it was a ploy to bed her, and she wanted no part in that fall from grace. She wanted to believe better of Edward, had begun to think better of him, but he'd toyed with her when she was most vulnerable. She resented him and loathed her own weakness.

When the third day dawned, she had no choice but to escape her self-imposed prison. She had commitments that she dared not shirk any longer. She reached under her bed and once more pulled the secret box from the floorboards. Even her maid wasn't aware of its existence, since she laundered her own secret stash of clothing. This time, she pulled free a plain deep blue kirtle and gray tunic. She preferred this type of clothing since it required no assistance. She slipped into the gown and pulled on her boots, threw her cloak around her shoulders and entered the tunnels. This time she exited near the stables but turned toward the postern gate on foot. She wouldn't need to ride within Stirling, and there was no way she might leave through that gate on horseback without drawing attention. She pulled her hood low over her eyes and huddled into it as much to protect herself from the wind as to disguise herself. She slipped past the guards with barely a nod. She was familiar with which guards wouldn't ask questions and would turn a blind eye when she rode or walked into the surrounding town. While it took willpower not to check behind her, Elizabeth wouldn't risk a glance back since she'd look suspicious. This day, especially, she sensed someone watching her. She wondered if her father set a new man to trail her. He did this from time to time when he suspected she might not be where she claimed, but she was yet to be caught.

Edward watched her slip through the gate. He'd been on edge since he followed her into the bailey three days earlier. He wanted to pound down her door and demand that she return to the land of the living. He wanted to apologize, then promise that all his words were said in truth. Now he wanted to rail against her for taking unnecessary risks when she left the castle alone. He pushed off the wall he'd logged too many hours against in the past three days as he prayed she'd slip out for another ride. Years of hiding and watching the enemy taught him to be invisible and patient. Finally, today he was rewarded. He pulled his own hood low over his head and passed through the postern gate. He shot a quelling look at the guard, and the man averted his gaze knowing not to naysay the king's brother.

Edward trailed after Elizabeth, keeping her in his sights but allowing as much as four blocks to separate them. He wondered where she was headed as she passed the main street of shops and wound her way into an open expanse that separated the town center from several small cottages. She picked up her pace until she reached the fourth cottage, where she knocked on the door. Edward slipped along until he was only two doors down. He watched a young man open the door and welcome Elizabeth into his embrace. The hug was too long to be perfunctory. It was one of true affection, and Edward wanted to plow his fist into the man's face. From his hiding place the man looked too young for Elizabeth, but he was too far away to be sure. The door shut behind Elizabeth as she dropped her hood. Edward witnessed a warmth to her smile he never saw at court. His heart was pinched with jealousy. He wanted to be on the receiving end of such a glowing welcome.

Edward circled around the cottages as he took in the condition of the structures and the land surrounding them. The one Elizabeth entered was the best by far. There was a cow in an enclosure behind the cottage with a vegetable patch growing along the sunny side. There was a lean-to shed with three walls where a horse was securely tied. It was an older mare, but the animal bore a resemblance to the mount Elizabeth rode. The windows had fur hangings to cover them, and white smoke puffed from the opening in the thatch. Edward found shadows between two of the cottages where he waited without being noticed. The longer he waited, the more his temper rose from a low simmer to a rolling boil.

What the devil is she doing in there? Why is a lady-in-waiting wandering on her own both on horseback and on foot? Who was that man, and why is she in his home?

Edward waited nearly two hours before the door opened and Elizabeth's voice carried to him.

"I'll see you tomorrow, Thomas. I'll try to come earlier so I can stay longer. Take care of the girls. I love you all."

Edward's world tilted as he listened to Elizabeth. He watched her cross the field toward the town center then peered around to see if the door to the cottage remained open. He saw the young man watching Elizabeth. He watched until she disappeared from sight. The door clicked shut and then he dashed across the green. He moved quickly and spotted Elizabeth as she passed through the postern gate. He followed her through and was about to call to her when he saw her lean against the castle wall. He rushed forward, worried something was wrong, but she disappeared through the small hatch. When he reached the wall, he ran his hand over the stones, but he found nothing to open the door. There wasn't even a crevice where the door would meet the wall. After five minutes of searching, fear of drawing too much attention to himself and the castle wall forced him to give up.

Elizabeth rushed to her chamber and called for

42

her maid as she stripped down to her chemise and stored the clothes for the next day. As she soaked in the tub, she reflected on her day, spent with her half-brother, Thomas, and their half-sisters, Sarah and Amy. Elizabeth loved the time spent with her siblings, but she always left with a hollow in her heart that inevitably filled with anger. Her father sired Thomas not long after she was born but refused to acknowledge his son. Elizabeth met him when she arrived at court because she rounded a corner in the town market and came face to face with a younger version of her father. After speaking to him, she learned he was her brother, and he was well-informed about both who she was and who their father was. He also recognized that their father refused to admit to siring him, even though he paid for the cottage in which he and his mother lived. Elizabeth was further disillusioned five years ago when Thomas informed her that two babes were brought to his cottage by the village midwife. One was a year old and the other a newborn; their mother had died birthing the younger one. They resembled Thomas and Elizabeth's father too strongly to ever have their parentage questioned. Thomas's mother took them in and had been raising them as her own ever since.

Elizabeth's mood soured as she remembered how her mother turned a blind eye to her husband's philandering. It was during times like this that Elizabeth counted her spinsterhood as a blessing. Edward flashed into her mind. She sank below the water, but when she emerged, her mind was still locked on thoughts of Edward. She hadn't seen him in three days, and she dreaded seeing him that night, but there was no way to hide any longer. He occupied too many of her waking moments and flooded her dreams as well. She alternated between listlessness and restlessness as she remembered how her body reacted to his touch. She brought herself to release several times as she pictured them together in the woods, but as the spasms subsided, she remembered his words of marriage and her ecstasy fizzled.

Once dressed, Elizabeth made her way to the Great Hall and her place at the table just below the dais. She kept her eyes averted and head bowed throughout the meal. As soon as the ladies-in-waiting were free to retire, she slipped out with two other women and went to her chamber, where she cried herself to sleep for yet another night.

Morning dawned as a fresh start, and Elizabeth looked forward to seeing her brother and sisters again.

Edward tried to gain Elizabeth's attention the night before, but she refused to look anywhere but at her trencher. Edward worried that something had happened to upset her. Upset her beyond their encounter in the woods earlier in the week. He suspected her reclusiveness had been in response to their unexpected tryst. If his brother hadn't insisted upon his attendance, he would've liked to hide too. Now he wanted to know what happened in the cottage and since her return to the castle. She seemed in high spirits when she left the young man, but the young woman who sat before him that night looked anything but happy. Edward found himself waiting near the stables yet again, and his patience was rewarded. The small portal popped open just as it did the day before, and a small feminine figure emerged. Just as she did the day before, Elizabeth slipped past the postern guard and into the town. She didn't waste time, heading straight to the cottage. She didn't look around and knocked only once before opening the door. She slipped inside, and Edward was left in the shadows again.

Edward's legs cramped as he alternated between standing and squatting in the alley between the cottages. Elizabeth remained in the cottage throughout the day. She stayed inside until the sun began to set, and Edward worried she'd miss her chance to reenter the castle grounds before the gates were shut for the night. He'd just decided to seek her out when the door opened.

"I wish I spent more time with you and the girls. I miss them, and they are growing up barely knowing me."

"Lizzie, they do. They love you just as I do."

Edward ground his teeth as he listened to another man say he loved his woman. That was how he'd come to consider her. She was his, and he wasn't going to give up that easily.

"Take care of yourself and them, Thomas. Watch over your mother. She seems tired these days. She shouldn't have to do so much on her own. Our father is failing us all."

"That may be, but none of us are going to change Laird Fraser."

The tension slipped away as he pieced together that Elizabeth was visiting her siblings, not a lover but her family. Then the man's words sunk in. Fraser was neglecting all his children. Elizabeth might see him the most, but he neglected her by not arranging for her future.

45

"You're right, Thomas. I hate it, but you're right. I'm not sure if I'll be able to come again until next week. I'm sure Father has someone watching me. I'm pretty sure someone was watching me yesterday and today. Maybe even following me."

"Elizabeth. Be careful. If not Laird Fraser, then your mother will have a fit if they find out you're visiting us."

"Let them. Father should be ashamed, and Mother turns a blind eye. It's unchristian of them, for all of Mother's piety."

"Lizzie." Exasperation filled Thomas's voice.

"I know. Don't fret. I won't make it worse. I'll bring what I can for the lasses and your mother. Are you sure I can't bring aught for you? Why won't you tell me what you need?"

"Because there's naught we need that I can't provide."

"Tom, that wasn't what I meant."

"I know, Lizzie. You must go before you're locked out of the gates."

The brother and sister embraced quickly, and Elizabeth hurried through the waning sunlight.

CHAPTER SIX

Edward tried to find Elizabeth when they returned to the castle. He followed her once more at a safe distance and was glad that he did. Two men tried to step in her path just before she got to the castle gate. Edward was shocked to see Elizabeth brandish a knife, and even more shocked when he crept closer and recognized she knew how to hold it. It didn't take the two men long to realize the same thing. She was trained and willing to fight back. They edged aside and let her past. Edward wasn't so forgiving. He stepped from the shadows and launched his attack before either was prepared. He threw his fist into one man's nose and heard the satisfying crunch before swinging his fist toward the other man's jaw. The crack he heard was just as gratifying. He warned both men to stay away from women who weren't theirs. Once he was inside the castle, he searched for Elizabeth. She appeared for the evening meal, but she sat quietly for most of it. She spoke when spoken to, but she did little to engage. Edward worried the incident with the two men had shaken her. He wanted to ask her if she was all right. She seemed to be retreating further into her shell each night.

His opportunity came as the meal ended and the women rose to retire with the queen. The king decided to join his wife, so Edward was expected to follow. He angled himself to walk into the queen's salon alongside Elizabeth.

"You seem reserved tonight," he murmured. "You barely smiled and didn't seem to eat much. What is worrying you?"

Elizabeth's eyes widened both by his nearness and his frank assessment.

"Naught," she replied. "I didn't sleep well."

"Dreaming of me again?" Edward tried to infuse humor into his question to lighten the mood, but her look of shock, then embarrassment, made him wonder if his playful suggestion might have been close to the truth.

He brushed his hand against hers within the folds of her skirts.

"You've been hiding, Beth. What's wrong? Am I the reason?"

"Yes."

Edward wasn't prepared for such a blunt response. Before he said more, Elizabeth slipped away.

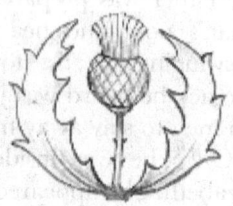

The third week of Advent was spent in a prolonged game of cat and mouse, beginning with them once more in the chapel celebrating Mass. The priest lit the pink Advent candle, and Edward breathed a sigh of relief that they were one week closer to Christmas, and one week closer to the merriment that would justify his desire to dance and celebrate with Elizabeth. Edward watched Elizabeth throughout the service, but he was more careful after the first incident that forced Elizabeth into additional hours of prayer for his indiscretion. The days that followed became a new routine for him as he tracked Elizabeth to the cottage. Her visits were shorter because she had no more excuses to avoid her duties. She slipped out when the queen retired for an afternoon nap, which meant Elizabeth only had an hour or so of freedom. Edward followed at the same distance, but was thankful Elizabeth faced no more threats along her route.

When he was at the castle, he made some circumspect inquiries about Laird Fraser and his family. It didn't take long for him to discover Laird Fraser was a known philanderer, and his wife wasn't much better. Most of the courtiers were aware of the couple's many affairs. Edward pieced together that Laird Fraser's mistresses were for his pleasure, while Lady Fraser's lovers were for politics. Not many people were aware of his bastards, but a few greased palms told Edward that the courtier sired more than the three Elizabeth seemed aware of. Edward's heart hurt and his head throbbed when he imagined how Elizabeth would react if she learned she had more siblings than she had already met. The more he learned about her parents, the deeper his desire grew to whisk her away.

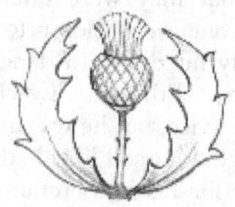

Edward waited before he moved toward the path in front of the cottages. He took one step before his path was blocked by a young man who was much larger than he appeared when Edward caught glimpses of him within the doorframe. He planned to confront Elizabeth that afternoon, but it would seem he had another confrontation first.

"Why do you keep following my sister?" Thomas crossed his arms as he blocked Edward's way.

Neither man was fooled that Thomas might keep Edward from barreling through him, but they both recognized Thomas would do some damage, nonetheless.

"Your sister?"

"You already know who I am. You know we have two younger sisters too. You know we live here with my mother. You know all of this because you've been skulking around for the past week. You've also been asking a lot of questions." Thomas's statements sounded more like accusations.

"If she's your sister, then why do you let her take such risks as going aboot town without a guard or chaperone?"

Thomas snorted as he burst into laughter.

"You don't know her well."

"I know her well enough." Edward stepped forward, so their booted toes almost brushed together.

"Just how well do you know my sister?" Edward

couldn't miss the steel creep into the young man's words. He was glad to hear the protective tone, but he wasn't in the mood to pick a fight.

"I know I want to marry her. I know I admire her. I know she frustrates me with her recklessness. And I know she's willing to put herself at risk for those she loves."

"I suppose that sums her up, but that doesn't explain why you're following her."

"But it does. She's reckless and fearless, which will get her hurt one of these days because she's also naïve."

"That she is. If you do care, I'd hurry and catch her now."

Edward scowled as he pushed past the younger man. Edward didn't bother trying to be inconspicuous as he sprinted across the field and then ran through the streets. He caught up to Elizabeth just as she slipped through the castle door. He caught the door before it closed and followed her through. He heard her gasp, and the air shifted as she struck out. He moved aside in time to only have her fist clip his shoulder. He caught her wrist and tugged her against him.

"Beth, it's me. It's Edward. Stop fighting me."

Elizabeth stilled and panted as Edward's arms wrapped around her.

"It's been you. You're the one who's been following me."

"Yes. You scare me with your disregard for your own safety. How can you consider traipsing around town is safe without any type of guard? Even if you're going to visit your brother and sisters."

"You found out," she breathed.

"You said yourself that I've been following you."

"Why? Why does it matter what I do?"

"If you weren't hiding from me, I'd have made

51

my proposal once again. I don't think you believed I was in earnest."

Elizabeth jerked away from Edward, and this time he let her go. She fumbled in the dark to light a torch.

"We can't talk in here. The sound carries out just as it does in. Follow me."

Elizabeth led them in silence as they wound through the castle until she stopped before what looked like a solid wall. She stepped aside and lifted the torch to illuminate the hidden door.

"There is a small indentation where your waist is. Press your fingers into that, and you will find a release. The door will swing in, and you'll have to move the tapestry."

Edward stepped forward and found the release Elizabeth described. He pushed into the chamber, but in the moment it took him to realize she'd led them to his chamber and not hers, she ground out the flame and jerked the door close. Edward searched for the catch to reopen the door, and when he found it, he also found darkness awaiting him.

"Elizabeth!"

Elizabeth had memorized the number of steps to travel when she walked and when she ran. Nearly half a score of years moving through the back passageways taught her to navigate with care. She heard Edward calling to her, but there was no sound of feet behind her. She made her way back to her chamber where she quickly stripped off her clothes. She rang for her maid and told her to make excuses for her. The maid was to tell her parents she had a headache or some other malady. Elizabeth had no intention of leaving her chamber only to encounter Edward in the Great Hall.

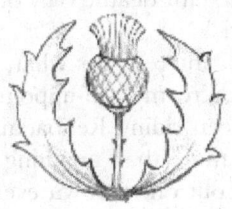

Edward was in the stables before the sun rose the next morning. He needed a long, hard ride to ease the frustration that had taken root inside his mind since he met Elizabeth. His frustration was as much emotional as it was physical. He longed for another tryst like the one in the woods. His body ached to have her pressed against his, and he wanted time to watch Elizabeth as passion bloomed into pleasure. Passion and pleasure he created. His mind swirled with everything he learned over the past week about her family, and he wanted to bellow at her for repeatedly taking so many risks.

Edward entered the silent stable to a voice he'd recognize anywhere. It came from the same back corner as it had the last time he heard it in the stable.

He finished saddling his horse and brought him out of the stall before walking around the corner.

"Still haven't learned your lesson?"

Elizabeth yelped in surprise, and her horse stomped before whinnying.

"Shh, Reubadair. You'll wake the lads."

"You named your horse Reaper? That doesn't make me feel reassured at all."

"No one asked you to feel aught."

"Beth."

"Edward."

"You're still riding without a guard and on a

53

horse that's named for death. Why do you insist upon courting disaster?"

"You take an interest, for what, three sennights, and suddenly you're my self-appointed guardian? I think not. I've been riding Reubadair since he was a colt. I trust him more than anything or anyone. And I've been riding out on my own ever since I arrived here, and that was ten years ago."

"Bluidy hell. You've been riding alone since you were eleven? What is your father thinking, leaving you unattended like this?"

"He's thinking he has better things to do. Now move your beast before mine nips at him. Reubadair isn't as patient as I am."

"I'm coming with you."

"Only if you can keep up."

Elizabeth swung into the saddle and ducked low to leave the stable. She was off before Edward had mounted his own horse. He chased after her as she charged out of the gate, with the guardsman looking askance to see Edward following her. She took the small wall without a care and galloped across the field. Instead of turning left like the last time Edward pursued her, she kept going straight. She and the horse looked like one being as they cleared fallen tree limbs and trunks. She took him around trees and through the outlying village scattering chickens in their wake. Elizabeth steered Reubadair up a steep hill and along a ridge before bringing him to a stop beside the same creek they forded the week earlier. They were further upstream where the current was swifter. Elizabeth waited until Edward nearly caught up. His horse held its own and had gained on them easily. Before the rider and mount came even with them, Elizabeth spurred her horse again as they splashed into the water. The water came over Elizabeth's boots, but her horse was sure-footed and didn't flinch at the freezing water.

"Elizabeth!" Edward called a warning, but she disregarded him. She was familiar with her horse's abilities, and she accepted his limits.

They barreled on once they cleared the opposite bank. She leaned low and was nearly flat against her mount's withers. The sound of splashes carried as Edward continued to pursue her. When they crested another hill, Edward and his horse were on their heels. Elizabeth reined in, and Edward pulled his horse to a stop beside her. In front of them stretched a valley that would be filled with wildflowers in spring and summer but was now covered in a dusting of snow. At the far end of the meadow, rugged dark smudges transformed into awe-inspiring mountains wrapped in low clouds. It was a breathtaking view.

Edward watched Elizabeth as she took in the panorama that surrounded them. Her cheeks were a deep pink from exertion and the wind. Her chestnut hair abandoned its braid long before they even reached the first ridge. She looked wild and at ease. He envisioned her passing for a woodland nymph as he saw the gleam of happiness as she took in the vista beside him. He dismounted and came around to her side. He wrapped his hands around her waist and lifted her down. She laid her hands on his shoulder and leaned in, so her body skimmed down Edward's until she reached the ground. He wouldn't wait a moment longer to taste her. His mouth sought hers, and their kiss was filled with need as they pulled each other into a tight embrace.

Elizabeth's whimper of frustration and longing brought every ounce of desire and protectiveness to the forefront for Edward. He caressed her cheek and cupped her skull as he eased the pressure from his kiss, and it transformed into a gentle communication of love and devotion. Edward poured every ounce of tender emotion into this kiss, and Elizabeth responded in equal parts. Her hands roamed over his chest when she found the opening to his cloak then skimmed his neck until she cupped his jaw. Edward took a scorching trail as he kissed along her cheekbone until he reached her ear.

"Beth," his whisper filled with reverence.

Her only response was a moan.

"You're so incredibly beautiful. You leave me breathless. I've never seen aught like you riding upon that great stallion of yours. You were one with him, and you seem a wild part of nature. You terrify me and impress me all at once. I can't decide if I should punish you or worship you. I only wish you'd allow me to do the latter."

"And if I wanted the former?"

"Were you testing me?"

"Yes."

Elizabeth's simple response was more than Edward expected. His hands found the supple flesh of her backside that was encased in tight breeks. His cock pulsed as he gripped her and pulled her tighter against him. She rocked her mound against his length as she panted and he growled. He pulled her cloak aside and brought his hand down with an echoing spank. Elizabeth moaned her pleasure and her pain. He brought his hand down four more times as Elizabeth sought his mouth again. She was insatiable as she flicked her tongue to invite his to follow her. She drew on it with the pace of his slaps. Edward finished the fifth spank and lifted her to wrap her legs around his waist. He stroked the punished bottom, and Elizabeth sank into his hold. She burrowed her head into his shoulder and sighed.

Edward sank to the ground with Elizabeth straddling him. It was his new favorite position, and he rocked slowly as their breathing returned to normal.

"I don't like you taking risks like that just to goad me. But worse, I wouldn't be surprised if you ride like that no matter whether you're alone or I'm chasing you. You truly frighten me with your disregard for your own safety."

"I'm sorry. I'm sorry I provoked you, but something stirred inside me and I suddenly needed this. But I'm also used to being left to my own devices. No one has ever cared enough to stop me."

"Oh, Beth. That makes my heart ache for you, but when will you realize, or rather accept, that I care that much?"

"I think I understand now, but it won't do any good. Edward, my father will never agree. And I can't keep doing this. I can't keep touching you and letting you touch me knowing it isn't going anywhere. It's too painful. The disappointment is crushing me."

"I'm going to find a way. I'm not letting you go. If you want this as much as I do, I won't give up. Can you have faith in me? Will you trust me?"

"I do trust you, but my faith isn't blind. I'm aware of my limitations when it comes to hope. Fate simply isn't that kind. It has a way of punishing you when you try to get too far ahead."

Edward was unsure how to respond to this melancholy admission. He held her and stroked her hair until she grew too cold for them to remain. They rode back to the castle together at a more sedate pace, but Edward acquiesced when Elizabeth silently challenged him to gallop.

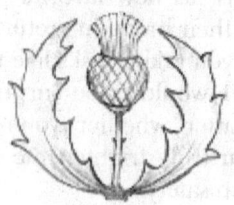

Edward paced inside his chamber until there was no putting off the inevitable. He had to join his brother and the rest of the court for the evening meal. He dragged himself from his chamber knowing Elizabeth wouldn't be there. She seemed adept at finding ways to avoid joining the court for meals.

The evening meal was interminable for Edward as the older ladies continued to flaunt themselves, and a few tried to strike up their former liaisons. He counted Elizabeth's absence as a blessing while he made it clear he was neither interested nor available. It was only Lady MacAdams who wouldn't cease her pursuit.

"I see your little dove is missing yet again. Have you scared her off already?"

"Lady MacAdams, I made myself clear several days ago."

"And I warned you that you'd make no progress with Lady Elizabeth. She seems to be hiding ever since you arrived at court. I can't picture her knowing how to handle you like a more experienced woman does."

She brushed her skirts against him as she reached out to cup his cock. This time she found nothing that suggested Edward was interested. She frowned but rubbed her hand over him. When nothing stirred, she looked up to his smirk, and his hand was a manacle as it clamped around her wrist to pull her hand from him.

"There is your proof. I'm not interested."

"Or perhaps that is the problem. You can't get it up for anyone but yourself. No wonder she doesn't want you."

"Say what you want, Lady MacAdams. We are through."

Edward walked back to the dais and grabbed a pitcher of mead along the way. He spent the rest of the night nursing his mug of mead, never refilling it.

"Are you going to sulk until Christmas? Your brooding is becoming tiresome."

Edward looked to Robert who joined him at the dais after the queen retired.

"I might."

"I warned you away from her. Now she keeps hiding. What did you do?"

"I asked her to marry me."

"After two sennights? Are you daft? Don't you remember what I told you? Why would you put her in that position?"

"Enough with the questions. You sound like a nag."

"I sound like your brother."

"Is that what you are right now? Or will you be my king again in a moment and order me away from her?"

"I might order you back to Ireland."

The men stared at each other until they both relented and took a swig from their mugs.

"Edward, it's an infatuation. Take one of the women up on their offers. Scratch your itch with Lady MacAdams. She's chasing you with as much energy as you are Lady Elizabeth."

"Robert, it's not an itch. I can't explain it, but this isn't infatuation. It's not just physical. Yes, I'm attracted to her. More so than any other woman, but I want to be in her company even if I can't touch her. I want to see her smile and learn aboot what interests her. She has a sharp mind and a caring heart. One that puts her in danger. I'd be there to protect her."

"Danger? What do you mean?"

"Were you ever informed Laird Fraser has sired at least three bastards? At least those are the ones Elizabeth knows of. They live in a cottage just outside the town. Two are full sisters to each other but only half-sisters to Elizabeth and her half-brother, who's nearly as old as her. She sneaks out to see them, and I suspect if she hadn't sensed me following her, she would've stopped in the market to bring them food."

"I'm familiar with the boy, Thomas, but I wasn't aware of any daughters. Where is their mother if they are only Thomas's half-sisters?"

"She died giving birth to the younger one. The midwife brought the babe and toddler to Thomas's mother, who took them in."

"Does he provide for them?"

"What do you think? If he did, would Elizabeth be slipping out of the postern gate and making her way through the town alone?"

Robert looked at his distressed brother and saw concern etched between his brows. There was worry in his eyes for someone other than their family.

"You genuinely care." It was a statement not a question.

"Why do you doubt me? Is it that you believe I'm incapable of caring for someone other than myself, or is it you assumed I want to tup her and move on?"

"Perhaps both," Robert stroked his chin as he watched his brother's frown deepen. "I might order her to marry you. Her father would have no choice but to accept."

60

"No. Absolutely not." Edward shook his head. "I don't want her, or any bride, forced down the aisle by your decree. I want Elizabeth to come willingly. If I can't make her see my feelings are true, then I'll leave her alone. I won't be the reason she feels trapped. More so than she already does."

"You consider she feels trapped here?"

Edward rubbed the back of his neck and debated how much to tell his brother.

"I would imagine so. She's been here ten summers and has no prospects of marriage. Other than me. You told me yourself the queen thinks Elizabeth is sure she'll die a spinster." Edward rubbed his neck again. "She's said as much to me."

"Really? And when would that be? She's barely shown her face since you arrived."

"I was going for a ride last week, and I heard someone talking. I assumed it was lovers, but it was Elizabeth crooning to her horse," Edward smiled as he pictured the scene in the stable. It was Robert clearing his throat that brought him back to the present. "I watched her take off on a black stallion. She tore across the field and took a jump only the most experienced rider should dare. She looked like she was born atop a horse. She rode faster than anyone else I've ever seen. I struggled to keep up, and you know my mount is better than most. She forded the stream to the south and charged down the hill that drops off on the other side. I feared she'd fall and be trampled. Instead, she was safely hidden in the woods waiting to see if I was friend or foe. She had the wherewithal to realize she was being followed, even if she was too naïve to accept she should bring a guard. Robert, she rides alone to escape being trapped in the castle. That speaks of desperation to me."

"And what happened when you found her in the woods?"

Edward avoided looking at Robert.

"That isn't something I will share. Just know that she left in the same condition she entered."

"Still a virgin?"

Edward growled. "Of course."

Robert held up his hands. "Just making sure."

"Robert, I haven't a clue what to do. You know the mon. Is any ground to be made if I speak to her father?"

"You can try. Tell him you already have my blessing."

Edward nodded as he drained the last of his mead. He stared into space and barely noticed Robert leave the dais once again.

CHAPTER SEVEN

"**B**luidy bleeding hell!" Edward slammed the door behind him. He'd spent the last three days trying to gain an audience with Laird Fraser while following Elizabeth to her siblings' cottage and on a nerve-jarring ride. She was aware that he followed her, but she never acknowledged him, and he didn't approach her. He kept his distance, but he refused to allow her to continue to traipse about without a guard. She resumed taking her meals with the others, but she put more distance between them now. He maneuvered his way into being in the gardens when the queen and her ladies were there. A few attempted to flirt with him, but he showed no interest. He managed to squeeze in a word or two with Elizabeth, but while she didn't ignore him, she didn't encourage him either.

Now Edward had been dismissed by both father and daughter. When the final Sunday Mass of Advent ended, Edward approached Elizabeth's father outside the king's council chamber. Laird Fraser had the audacity to laugh when Edward approached him with his offer of marriage. Edward held his temper as long as possible before it exploded. He accused her father of neglect and manipulation. He pointed out that a father who cared for his family and clan would see the benefits in securing an alliance of some sort rather than risking the next generation's security. He pointed out that he was the king's brother, which only garnered a sneer. He was ready to drive his fist into the man's face just as Elizabeth had done to him in the woods. Edward argued that no other man was willing to risk a conversation like this, and the fact that he was should speak to his sincerity and dedication. But Laird Fraser refused to budge.

"Bluidy bleeding hell!"

A pounding at the door brought his attention back to the present. He stormed over and yanked it open.

"What?" Edward bellowed, but was contrite when the page standing before him jumped. The boy appeared only to be eight or nine summers. "My apologies, lad. What is it?"

"The king has sent a message." The boy handed over the folded parchment and turned tail, nearly running back down the passageway.

Edward went to stand near the window as he unfolded the missive.

I don't know what you did, but he's sending her away.

One line and Edward's world crumbled around him. He didn't have to guess what his brother meant. He just wondered how Fraser moved so quickly. Edward had only just returned to his chamber and news of her departure had already reached the king. He recollected his meeting, and he remembered a brief moment when Laird Fraser spoke to one of his guards. Edward realized that must have been the moment he issued the order for her departure. They had argued for nearly another hour.

Edward scrambled to gather clothes and stuffed

them into a satchel before racing down to the stables. He ran past his horse to the stall where Elizabeth's mount stood chewing on hay.

A carriage. Thank God. I can catch up to a carriage.

Edward yelled for his horse to be saddled as he sprinted back into the castle. He wove his way to the kitchens where he filled another satchel with supplies. He was just about to step out into the bailey when he heard his name. Once again, it was the only voice that held the authority to make him stop.

"Going after her?"

"Did you doubt me?"

"No. I suppose I didn't. I also suppose things deteriorated rapidly with Fraser."

"That's putting it mildly. He refused to listen to me, and then we argued."

"Well, that certainly sounds like the perfect way to convince a mon to marry off his only daughter."

"Robert, I need to go."

"I presumed you might like to know where she's going."

Edward paused before he nodded.

"Castle Dunbeath."

"The Sinclairs? Bluidy hell, that's the opposite end of Scotland. You can't get further north before you drop into the sea. Why there?"

"Her cousin Deirdre is married to the youngest Sinclair brother. That was a royal debacle, and I do not exaggerate. The women were very close before Deirdre left. He's sending her there for the rest of Advent and all the way through Epiphany."

"It'll take that long just to get there. Is the mon daft, or is he so selfish that he'd send his daughter into the Highlands in the middle of winter? Is he trying to kill her?"

"I wondered the same."

"I'm leaving, Robert."

"Godspeed."

The two men embraced before Edward ran back to the stables and tore out of the bailey.

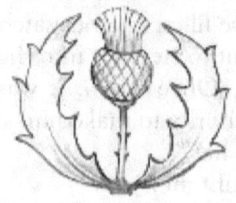

Elizabeth sat and shivered in the carriage. The heated brick she'd been given by her maid had gone cold hours ago. The furs tucked around her were insufficient to block the cold air that crept in around the hides hung at the carriage windows. She gave up looking out the windows when she realized the driver was taking the least direct route to her home—or to anywhere, really. She was sure he was trying to make her lose her sense of direction. That would've been at her father's command. He recognized that she had a mind for maps after she once led him through the catacombs behind the walls of the castle. She rued sharing that information.

Another hour passed before Elizabeth looked out the window again. She judged she should be approaching her family's keep soon. Why her father possessed the need to trick her, she didn't understand. It seemed inevitable that she'd be going to Castle Dounie.

Elizabeth scanned the surrounding area, and then swung around to look out the other window. None of the landscape was familiar. There were large hills rising in the distance that gave way to mountains. The snow that was only a dusting in Stirling was thick and crunching below the wheels. Somehow, she hadn't noticed the sound until now. Elizabeth stuck her head out and called to the driver. He didn't acknowledge her. Elizabeth wasn't sure if the wind carried her words away or if he was ignoring her.

Where the hell is Father sending me? This carriage will never make it through the mountains. Why is he sending me to the Highlands?

The answer came to Elizabeth with equal parts excitement and dread.

Deirdre. He's sending me to her. I have missed her these last months, but I can't travel into the Highlands this time of year. Why would Father put me in such danger?

Elizabeth's stomach sank as she guessed what had angered her father enough to send her away. And not only away but to put her at risk.

Edward must have asked for me. That's the only reason he'd send me so far away. He worries Edward might follow me to our keep. And he might. There is no way he can know I'm not headed there. Oh, Edward. What have you done?

The carriage hit a large ditch, then seemed to roll over a huge rock. It listed precariously before a large crack rent the air and the carriage toppled onto its side. Unprepared, Elizabeth was thrown about as the carriage slid down an embankment before crashing to a stop against a tree.

It took her a long moment before she was able to orient herself, and her head stopped spinning. Something warm oozed on her forehead, and she saw blood after she swiped her gloved hand across it. Elizabeth took a deep breath before pushing herself onto one of the squabs. She inched her way until she was within reach of the door handle on the side that stuck into the air. She twisted it, but nothing happened. She looked closer and saw the door was dented at the hinges. Grasping the fabric that lined the walls, she held on as she pulled herself into a crouch. She pushed the window hanging out of the way and pulled herself free. She cursed the long skirts that wrapped around her legs, making it hard to scramble out. Once she made it through the window, she sat on the carriage and looked around.

The rear axle on the side in the air was clearly broken. There was no longer a wheel attached. She looked to see where the driver and coachman were, but neither were to be seen. The horses were no longer attached to the carriage because the shaft had split. She shimmied down the side and landed hard into the packed snow. Her trunk was halfway up the hill but still closed. She trudged through the snow until she reached the chest and flung it open. She pulled out two pairs of wool leggings, an extra tunic and kirtle, and three shawls. She snapped the lid shut and sat down to pull off her boots. She fought, but eventually succeeded in pulling one pair of leggings over the other. She hurried to put her boots back on. She stood and unclasped her cloak before putting the spare tunic on and wrapped the shawls over her head and then replaced the cloak. She folded the spare kirtle several times before tucking it into her belt. She opened the chest again and found a scarf and an extra pair of gloves.

Once Elizabeth had on as many layers as she could manage and still be able to walk, she used her hands to help her climb to the top of the hill. She looked around and found the coachman laying in a puddle of blood. His head had a long gash that began on the man's forehead and ran to the back of his skull. The driver was nowhere to be seen, and neither were the horses. Elizabeth scanned the area and looked for any sign of highwaymen. There was nothing but an open expanse of white that merged into the mountains in front of her and the open trail behind her. She walked back the way they came and noticed a solid form that lay to the side of the road. She realized that she'd found the driver, and checked to see if he still lived. The angle of his neck told her there was no chance he survived the fall.

As she approached, she noticed fresh hoofprints. There was only one set. Once again, she looked around to see if she might find one of the horses. She whistled thrice before a whinny answered her. She continued to whistle as she followed the sound of the animal. She understood she might be going in the wrong direction if the sound echoed, but she took her chances until she saw another set of hoofprints. She approached the animal slowly with her palms outstretched before her. The animal stomped in place but let her approach. When she got close enough to grab the bridle, she ran her hand over one front leg, then the other. She ran her hand along the animal's flank and checked his hind leg before walking in front of the horse and around to the other side. The horse seemed to be uninjured but still spooked. She walked the gelding back to the road and looked around. She had no idea where she was. She hadn't seen any hints of villages or towns nearby. They hadn't passed any, but that didn't mean none were to be found.

I'm better off going back the way I came. At least I'm sure that leads to somewhere. I have no idea what is up ahead.

Elizabeth struggled to mount even when she found a stump. Her extra layers of clothing were awkward and unwieldy. Once on the horse, she thanked the heavens for small mercies. She'd learned to ride bareback as a child, and even though she hadn't done it in years, she was able to control the animal easily. That was in large part because the

69

mount did little more than plod through the deepening snow.

Elizabeth had to wipe her eyes repeatedly as snow coated her eyelashes. She had her scarf pulled up over her nose and mouth and her cloak pulled as tightly closed as it would go. Even with the extra layers on, she was freezing. The cold was sapping her energy, and she grew sleepy. She understood what that meant for her, so she fought her body's urge to close her eyes.

Elizabeth was sure her name floated on the wind, but she was unable to see anything beyond a few feet in front of her. She tucked her chin again and huddled over the horse's withers as she tried to block the shifting wind.

She heard her name again and looked to see a figure moving toward her at a gallop. She strained to catch the voice again. It floated on the wind.

"Edward! I'm here!" She tried to yell, but her voice cracked.

"Edward!" she pulled down her scarf and mustered the deepest breath before calling out again.

"Beth, I'm coming!"

Elizabeth squeezed her horse's flanks and nudged it into a trot. She gripped the reins to keep from slipping until the figure riding toward her became clear. She'd recognize the figure anywhere. Their horses pulled alongside one another, and just as the last time they met on horseback, he pulled her from the saddle to sit in his lap.

"Oh, Beth," he murmured, his hushed words filled with agony.

Elizabeth's gloved hands cupped his jaw as she pulled him to meet her. Their lips collided and teeth gnashed against one another as they kissed with a hunger born of fear and anguish. Edward pulled his cloak around them both as he held her in his arms, and their kiss continued.

When they both needed to breathe, they rested their foreheads against one another, but a moment later, Edward drew back as he touched his head. His gloved fingertips were red. He gently peeled the shawls back from Elizabeth's forehead to reveal the gash that still bled.

"It's not that bad. Head wounds always gush for ages. My head hurts, but naught more is wrong."

"Naught more? You're nearly frozen through wandering in the middle of a blizzard," Edward growled.

"I meant naught more was wrong with my head," Elizabeth giggled.

"You'd laugh at a time like this?"

"I'd rather do that than cry. My eyes might freeze shut."

Edward pulled her in for another long kiss.

"What am I to do with you?"

"Hopefully, get me somewhere warm."

She nestled against his chest as he gathered her horse's reins and turned his mount in the direction they came from.

"What happened? Why are you injured and alone?"

"I'm not sure exactly. I was looking out the window for a while when I realized we should have been nearing my clan's keep, but naught looked familiar. I deduced my father was sending me to the Sinclairs, to Deirdre, but why would he risk sending me into the Highlands in the middle of winter? I was trying to puzzle through that when the carriage hit a ditch, then a boulder. It tumbled over the embankment and down the hill. I'm uncertain if the axle broke causing the carriage to pitch sideways or if that happened during the fall. Either way, I pulled myself out and put on extra clothes, then climbed my way up the hill. I found the coachman dead with a gash on his head. The driver wasn't far away and had a broken neck. The horses were nowhere to be seen. I started back this way and whistled until one of the horses answered. I'd been riding half an hour maybe before I heard you calling me. How'd you guess?"

Edward ran his hand over her back as much to console himself as to warm and comfort her.

"Robert told me you were gone, and he told me you were headed to Castle Dunbeath. I set off immediately, but you weren't easy to track. Your father must have anticipated I'd follow you, so your driver took a very scenic tour of the area around Stirling before taking this road north. Once I was clear of the town and surrounding villages, I found the only set of carriage tracks and prayed they were yours. I didn't pass anyone else on the road, but I did pass a village aboot an hour ago. I'll take us there. Hopefully, there's an inn or at least someone willing to take us in."

"Eddie, I'm tired. Can I sleep, please?"

Edward looked down at the hunched figure leaning against him. No one had called him Eddie since he was a child. He'd have been insulted by anyone else who used the diminutive, but it was music coming from Elizabeth. He had his own pet name for her, and he liked that she found one for him.

"No, my love. You can't sleep. If you do, I might not be able to wake you. You're tired and the cold is sapping your strength, but I need you to stay with me a little longer. I promise you a hot meal and a bath if I can arrange it."

"My love? I rather like that." Edward would have rejoiced if her tone weren't so groggy.

72

"Beth, stay awake. You must stay awake." He pinched her ribs, but the layers of fabric made it impossible to grip any flesh. "Beth, kiss me."

"What? I mean I will, but why?"

"If it'll keep you awake, then kiss me."

"Gladly. Why did I waste so much time when we might have been doing this every day?"

Before Edward answered, Elizabeth pressed her lips to his and licked the seam. His surprise had him opening his mouth. Her tongue darted in and swirled around his. It explored all it reached and flicked at his, tempting him to thrust his into her mouth. She welcomed him with a moan as she sucked. She shifted restlessly, and Edward groaned as his cock rubbed against his tight breeches and the horn of his saddle.

"That didn't sound like a happy groan."

"It wasn't, sweetheart. You make me so hard every time I'm near you. Hell, any time you come to mind. And touching you makes me leak as I picture filling you with my cock and my seed. Right now, my cock is screaming, and it's not in joy."

Elizabeth swallowed before pulling her skirts to her knees as a surge of freezing air collided against her swollen nether lips. She jostled about but managed to turn to face Edward while straddling his cock rather than the leather beneath them. She arranged her skirts to cover her legs again.

"I'd make my confession now." Elizabeth looked into hazel eyes that smoldered with unspent lust, but something tender flickered there too. "You're the most handsome mon I have ever seen. I'm dripping right now. I'm like that every time you're near. You're on my mind every night as I bathe, then again when I climb into bed. I picture you when I wake. Each time, I bring myself to release daydreaming aboot you. I ache right now to learn what it would feel like to join with you. I want to know."

Edward stared into mossy-colored eyes that were honest if not wary.

"Beth, I won't take you as my mistress. I won't dishonor you by compromising you. I want to make love to you. And that's something I've never done before. I've coupled, I've tupped, I've fucked, but I've never made love. You're the only one I want. But I won't do any of that unless you're my wife. I'll bring you pleasure with my hand and my mouth, but I won't take what isn't mine."

"What aboot if I offer you what is mine to give?"

Edward shook his head.

"That's not enough, Beth."

"And once I give in and marry you, you scratch your itch and move on while I'm bound to a mon who no longer wants me. I'd rather discover pleasure with you while we both want the same thing than bind ourselves only for you to regret it."

Edward sat stunned as he looked at the woman he was proposing to a second time. She assumed he'd be unfaithful. She didn't want to marry him. But she was willing to couple with him.

"Is there someone else you'd rather move onto? Someone you can have without guilt once you're no longer a virgin? Am I just an itch for you to scratch before you can feel free to bed whoever you want with no maidenhead to protect?" Edward bit out between clenched teeth.

"No. There is no one else. There never has been. My father would never allow it, so what was the point of breaking my own heart?"

"Then you assume I'll leave our bed for someone else's. You already decided I'll be unfaithful. Is that the type of cad I've proven to be, or are you going off my reputation?" Edward rued the

74

choices of his previous life, the one before Elizabeth.

"I hadn't really pondered that. But yes, you do have a reputation. And what aboot when you leave me behind to return to Ireland? You want me to believe you won't find Sinead again?"

"What do you mean you hadn't thought of that? What were you thinking? And I'm not going back to Ireland. Never again if I can help it. And if I must, you're coming with me. I'm not going anywhere else without my wife."

"I never agreed to marry you. And isn't it obvious why I assume you'll keep a mistress?"

"Apparently, it is completely murky to me as to why you're convinced of that."

"What mon at court doesn't keep one? Even your brother does. More than one."

Edward reared back and pulled the horses to a stop.

"I'm not my brother. I'm neither Robert nor Edward. I'm not your bluidy father either. In case you, and everyone else in the blasted court, has forgotten, I'm a Highlander. My word is my honor and my pledge. I don't give it unless I mean to carry it out. I'm not interested in another woman. I have no idea what the future holds for either of us, and I can't foresee if you'll ever love me as I do you, but regardless of whether we fall in or out of love, I'd never shame you or any wife by being unfaithful."

Elizabeth was shaken by all that Edward poured forth. She tried to take it all in.

"But you bed married women. The bonds of matrimony cannot be that sacred to you."

"I admit I have. Those women were married in name only. Their husbands had their mistresses and carried on their own lives. It was acceptable to both parties that they take lovers once the wife bred an

75

heir. They may as well have been unwed or widows for the value they placed on their marriages."

"And that made it all right?"

"It makes it a far sight different from what I want with you. I won't have a marriage in name only with any woman. I'd remain a bachelor instead, but I don't want to remain one. I want to be your husband. I want to get as far from court as we can and make an ordinary life together."

"As if lairds don't keep a leman."

"Elizabeth," he growled, "I'll turn you over my knee. You're picking an argument and testing me when there is no need. I'm willing to pledge to you and God that I'll have no other woman. Are you questioning my faith too? I'm ready to lay my palm against your arse for being so disagreeable for the sake of being disagreeable."

"You're that angry with me?" Elizabeth shrank back.

"I'm not angry. Frustrated. But not angry. I'd never spank you out of anger. I don't hit women. But I would paddle your backside for trying to cause a rift between us."

Elizabeth studied Edward as she looked into hazel eyes that were windows to an iron will. He didn't flinch or look away. Her gaze swept over his body taking in the broad shoulders willing to take on her problems, to share her burden. The strong arms that held her in place and steadied her whenever her world spun, especially when she was near him. She rested her hands on the powerful thighs that carried him as he followed her for her protection. Her hands skimmed up his abdomen and traced the etched muscle as it flexed beneath her palms. She rested her hands over his heart that pounded a steady but rapid pace.

"I believe you. It scares me that you'll disappoint

76

me. More than disappoint me. Break my heart. Edward, it would crush me if you betrayed me. I want to give my whole self over to you, but if you toss that aside, I can't imagine how I'd recover."

"Beth, I'll never do that. But you don't give yourself enough credit either. It might seem as though the world would end, but you're indefatigable. You will always survive. Your will is just as steely as mine, and I foresee some epic battles between us, but be reassured no matter what, I won't leave you." He brushed his lips against hers and murmured, "Call me Eddie. No one else does. It will be yours alone."

"I'd like to have something that no one else has. Something that is just mine. And no one really calls me Beth anymore now that Deirdre's left court. Some of my family calls me Lizzie or Liz, but you're the only one who calls me Beth."

"Then that shall be mine."

"Just as I'm yours." Elizabeth held her breath to see if he understood.

Edward sucked in a breath.

"Are you saying yes?"

Elizabeth nodded.

"Say it. I need to hear it," he beseeched.

"Yes. I'm yours as long as you are mine."

"I've only ever been yours. No one else has ever held my heart. I love you, Beth. I don't understand how I'm certain so soon, but I am."

"Perhaps it's God's will. Perhaps it's the fae. But try as I might to refuse it, I love you too."

Edward nudged his horse forward as they came together for a languid kiss. It wasn't passionless, but rather overflowing with love.

"I promised you a hot meal and a bath. But I'd promise you more. I'd handfast right now. I don't want to enter that inn without being married. I want you to have the protection of my name. I fear we'll be separated because we're unwed or worse, turned away. I wish to tend you tonight and take care of you. I also don't want to spend another moment knowing we're not wed."

Elizabeth shifted restlessly.

"I want to marry you too. I'd handfast as well." She bit her lip and looked down until he lifted her chin. "I'd like you to be my husband before we are shown a chamber. I want--"

Even with her chin raised, she was unable to look Edward in the eyes.

"Don't keep secrets from me. What is it? Are you suddenly shy to admit that you want us to make love?"

"Oh, no. I'm not shy to tell you I want you inside me. I want to learn what it's like to have you thrust into me until I can't help but scream out your name."

Edward growled and pounced. His hand cupped the back of her skull as he drove his tongue into her mouth mimicking the motion he intended to use all through the night. When he pulled back, her lips were swollen, and her chin abraded by his stubble. He peppered her chin and jaw with light kisses to take the sting away.

"I'm all right, Eddie. I meant I wanted something else. I just— I can't admit it."

"You can tell me aught. Are you embarrassed?"

She nodded her head, and he raised an eyebrow.

"Could I whisper it?"

"Yes." A shiver shot up his spine as he couldn't imagine what his bonny little bride might say next. Her comments from a moment ago nearly had his cock explode, and he was tempted to pull her from the horse and take her against a tree. The weather was the only thing that stayed him.

"I want that spanking," Elizabeth whispered beside his ear. Her warm breath sent another shiver through him, and he trembled when her tongue traced the shell of his ear before flicking and sucking his lobe. "I want your palm against my arse. I'm tired of fighting you. This. I want to give in."

Elizabeth shrank back and tucked her chin.

"Look at me, Beth." There was a commanding tone that he'd never used with her before.

She looked up immediately.

"I'll gladly give you what you want. If this is the only time because you don't enjoy it after all, that is fine with me. But if you do enjoy it, and you want more, then I'll happily oblige both for punishment and pleasure."

"Is this something you have always liked?" Elizabeth's voice was tiny as she pictured him spanking other women.

"Stop, Beth. Stop imagining me with someone else. I've never spanked another woman. I've never cared enough aboot one to want to protect her from outside dangers or herself. I haven't spanked one for pleasure either. There is just something aboot your arse in my hands that makes me want to touch it in every way I can imagine."

"Every way?" Elizabeth purred.

Edward looked into her eyes and saw curiosity.

"What knowledge do you have of that?"

"You remember I use the hidden passageways, don't you? What do you imagine I have heard and observed over the years?"

"You've watched people couple?" Edward's heart sped up.

Elizabeth nodded.

"I learned a great deal aboot what can happen between a mon and a woman, or multiple people." She scrunched her nose at the end.

"Good, because I'll never share you."

She smiled before continuing, "I'll gouge out a

79

woman's eyes before letting another touch you. Anyway, that's how I learned that touching myself brought pleasure."

"Did you do that while you watched others?"

Elizabeth nodded sheepishly.

"Is that something you plan to continue doing?"

She shook her head. "Not since I met you again. I— I don't need to. I just picture you. I don't want to anymore."

"Good, because I won't have you looking at any naked mon but me."

"And I shall be the only naked woman you look at?"

"Obviously."

"You're not repulsed by my immoral behavior?"

"I'm in no position to pass judgement. And I must admit that having a bride who knows what will happen but has never experienced the joys of coupling excites me. We can try aught you've seen and wondered aboot, or we can make up our own ways to pleasure one another."

"I never considered I'd admit such things to anyone else. I've never even confessed them."

"You don't need to share those things with anyone. Not even me, if you don't want to."

"I do want to. Only with you."

They looked at each other for a long moment before they beamed at one another.

"I can't bind our hands, but you can place my plaid over them," Edward suggested.

Edward regretted not being able to offer Elizabeth one of the most revered parts of the hand-fasting tradition. If they waited until they arrived at the inn, it might be too late. Without a ribbon or chord to wrap around their wrists, Elizabeth nodded and pulled the corner of Edward's plaid to cover the hand he laid upon her lap.

Elizabeth looked into Edward's eyes and saw tenderness that took away the chill, if only for a moment. Edward inhaled before squeezing her hand and beginning his vows.

"I vow to give you the first cut of my meat, the first sip of my wine, from this day it shall only your name I cry out in the night and into your eyes that I smile each morning; I shall be a shield for you back as you are for mine, nor shall a grievous word be spoken aboot us, for our marriage is sacred between us and no stranger shall hear my grievance. Above and beyond this, I will cherish and honor you through this life and into the next. I plight thee my troth."

Edward swore a vow of fealty to Robert when he was a young man. Until that moment, it was the most sacred pledge he'd ever made. As he gazed into Elizabeth's eyes, he understood the significance of his commitment to his bride. He'd place her before all others and above all things.

Elizabeth's heart felt like it tripled in size as she listened to the reverence in Edward's voice. She prayed her voice would convey the depth of her emotions. She entwined their fingers as best she could before placing her other hand over his heart.

"You cannot possess me for I belong to myself, but while we both wish it, I give you that which is mine to give. You cannot command me, for I am a free person. But I shall serve you in those ways you require, and the honeycomb will taste sweeter coming from my hand. I plight thee my troth."

Together, they intoned the last verse of their vows.

"Ye are Blood of my Blood, and Bone of my Bone. I give ye my Body, that we Two might be One. I give ye my Spirit, 'til our Life shall be Done."

Neither moved as they gazed at one another, absorbing the devotion that passed between them. When the moment passed, Elizabeth raised her chin as Edward slipped his hand from hers and cupped her jaw. He leaned in and brushed his lips against hers before she parted them. Their lips fused together in a kiss unlike any they had shared before. It was an achingly tender exchange that expressed the love they had just professed.

CHAPTER EIGHT

They arrived at a small inn as the sun began to set. Edward helped her dismount and a stable boy took their mounts. Edward led her inside and tucked her arm through his. He scanned the room's occupants and was mildly reassured that it wasn't full. The weather wasn't fit for man nor beast. There were a couple of drunken men in one corner, but they hadn't noticed Elizabeth yet. They approached the bar, and Edward arranged for a chamber.

"Please have someone bring the food up along with a tub and as much hot water as you can manage. My wife was traveling in our carriage when it overturned. It's by the grace of God that she survived, but she was badly jostled. I'd have her soak in a tub."

"Aye, ma laird."

Edward and Elizabeth followed the innkeeper up the stairs to the last room on the left. The man opened the door, and the couple was greeted by a surprisingly well-appointed room. The bed was large enough to accommodate them, and a fire already burned in the grate. It was clean, and the linens looked fresh.

"The bath and meal will be up shortly," the man said as he backed out of the chamber.

Edward came to stand behind Elizabeth and placed his hands on her shoulders. She reached up and drew them around her waist. He intended to give her time to get accustomed to the idea of them sharing a chamber. He'd seen her eying the bed.

"Will you help me undress, Eddie?" her hushed tones were almost too soft for him to be sure, but when she looked over her shoulder, he was certain he hadn't misheard.

Edward was once again surprised by his young bride's fearlessness. He also recognized her practicality. She had so many layers on that it was hard for her to reach.

"Gladly, wife."

Her smile dazzled him, and he almost forgot what he was supposed to do. He gave her a peck, but she caught him and wrapped her hand around his neck to hold him for a longer kiss.

"If they don't hurry with that water, they will be kept waiting in the passageway." She murmured as Edward straightened.

He helped her take off every layer until they reached her chemise. He peeled the last pair of leggings from her as he kneeled before the chair in which she now sat. He ran his hand along the inside of her thighs as his rod twitched when she squirmed. She tried to move her sheath closer to his hand, and he obliged her by swiping his thumb along her seam. As he ran his fingers over her heated skin and slid between her folds, he pushed her chemise up to her hips. Elizabeth's knees fell wide, and Edward received his first view of his wife's treasure. He nipped his way along the inside of her thigh until he reached her juncture. He swiped his tongue along her sheath then kissed a trail back down the other thigh. Eliza-

84

beth's hips jerked as his tongue made contact with her sensitive skin. He tested her with one finger, and her hot channel drew him in as her muscles clenched.

"More. I can take more."

Edward stretched to kiss her lips as he slipped two more fingers in. She was unbelievably tight. He fisted his cock through his breeks and rubbed as his fingers worked in time. He leaned forward and flicked her bud with his tongue before sucking it into his mouth. He grazed his teeth along it as Elizabeth moaned and gripped the arms of the chair. She pressed her heels into the floor and lifted her hips in offering. Edward sunk his fingers into her hips and pulled her toward him. His tongue lapped at her as his fingers sped up.

"Eddie, I'm close. Oh, Lord. It's never been like this before. Oh, I'm so close. Please don't stop."

Edward had no intention of stopping until she screamed his name and he tasted her release. Neither had long to wait.

"Edward!"

Elizabeth's cry was one of pleasure and capitulation. Edward sank back onto his haunches, and Elizabeth slid from the chair to straddle his knees. She pulled at the waistband of his breeches.

"Now," she growled. Edward tried to stay her hands, but she slapped them away. She unlaced his breeches and pulled the flap wide as his cock sprung free. She gasped when she saw its length and thickness. It surpassed anything she'd ever spied. She licked her lips as a knock came at the door.

"Five minutes," she bellowed, and Edward chuckled.

Elizabeth examined his cock, and Edward wondered if something was wrong.

"Beth?"

"I'm trying to decide if I want to suck it first or ride it."

Edward spluttered.

"What have I unleashed?"

Edward lifted her hips and lined her sheath up with his sword but paused until she nodded. She sank down onto him as he surged up. Her nails dug into his shoulders as she whimpered.

"Beth, I'm sorry. It will stop hurting in just a moment. I promise this is the only time it will hurt."

"Be quiet. I'm fine."

She held his jaw as she swooped in for a kiss. She began to rock her hips, and Edward cupped her bottom as he guided her. She picked up a rhythm they both wanted.

"Beth, I'm close, but I'm not coming without you."

Elizabeth offered him her breast, and he latched on as he pinched the other nipple. She shattered around him, yelling his name once again.

Edward followed her over the cliff.

A knock came at the door once again, and this time the couple gave in because if they turned the servants away a second time, they'd go without a meal and their bath. Elizabeth stood on shaky legs as she made her way to stand behind the screen, and Edward pulled his breeches back into place. He let the servants in but paid no attention when the three young women tried to flirt with him. He went to stand by the screen to talk quietly to Elizabeth.

"Are you all right? That wasn't how I pictured making love to you for the first time," he whispered.

"I'm fine. More than fine actually. That was indescribable."

"I agree. I had no idea how--" Edward snapped

his mouth shut, but Elizabeth's direct look prompted him to finish. "I had no idea how different it'd be with someone I care aboot. Someone I love. It was unlike aught I've ever done before."

Once more, Elizabeth's beaming smile nearly blinded him. Edward didn't care that the servants were still filling the tub. He stepped behind the screen and pulled Elizabeth into his arms. She rested her head against his chest, and he kissed the top of her head.

"You're my wife now, to have and to hold forever more. Beth, I love you."

"You're my husband now, to love and honor forever more."

Edward smiled as he nipped at her nose.

"I'm the Highlander. I thought I was the one who staked my pledge on honor."

"I can think of something you staked."

"Shh. Lass, you're horrible. I never would've imagined you had such a randy sense of humor," Edward laughed. "I rather like it."

"I had no idea I did either. I never had anyone to share it with before."

"Not even Deirdre?"

"No, not even her. She might have a similar mind, but we never dared talk aboot it. Being separated from Magnus was a tender topic for her, so I tried not to bring up a discussion of men. And what women do to them, or I suppose with them." She winked at him.

She received a pinch to her backside as he plucked the ribbons at her shoulders, and her chemise pooled around her ankles. It was the first time Edward saw his bride completely bare. His cock surged back to life once again. He seemed to be in a permanent state of semi-arousal that flared to life whenever she was near. As he looked at her broad hips and rounded backside that he enjoyed grasping, he unfastened his breeches and let his cock spring free. He sighed as the pain of having it trapped within his breeches eased. He stroked himself as he watched her look at his cock again. She made a soft mewling sound as she pushed her breasts together and kneaded them. She stepped forward and tugged on his tunic, trying to lift it over his head, but she was far too short. She sank to her knees and unlaced his boots. She pushed his breeches to the ground as he shucked off his shoes. Slowly, she reached out to take Edward's rod into her hand. Her tongue darted out and lapped up the shiny liquid that dripped from his tip. She savored it a moment before running her tongue the length of his cock. She whirled her tongue around the tip before sliding her mouth onto him. She took as much as she could and forced herself to relax when she worried she might gag. She'd seen women do this before when she spied on other couples. She recognized the motions, but she never imagined the sensations. When her initial panic subsided, and she settled into a rhythm with her mouth and hand, she found she enjoyed it. Edward scooped her hair away from her face and listened to his own groans, but she kept her eyes closed as she concentrated.

"Beth, stop." Edward pressed on her shoulder, but she batted him away and sucked harder. "Dear Christ on the cross. Beth, I'm not coming in your mouth. Let go, or you will get that spanking you so richly deserve and so badly want."

Elizabeth wasn't deterred and picked up her pace until Edward lifted her under the arms and she was off the ground. He pulled her legs around his waist and impaled her. His hand came down with a hard swat to her bottom. She moaned as she pressed against him and took him deeper. He repeated the spanking as he alternated sides. He walked them toward the wall and braced her back against it.

"You asked for it, little one." Edward drove into her over and over as her moans grew louder. Neither was aware of whether the servants were still there or had left. The more Elizabeth moaned, the more aroused Edward grew until he realized he must be hurting her. He slowed his pace only to have her yank his hair in protest.

"Why are you stopping? What did I do wrong?"

"I'm not stopping, and you did naught wrong. I'm moving us."

Edward held her nestled against his chest as though she were something precious and fragile. He only believed the former, not the latter. He peered around the screen and found they were the only occupants in the chamber. He walked to the tub and stepped in while Elizabeth clung to him. Water sloshed over the sides onto the towels placed around the tub. He lowered them into the water, and the mood transformed from urgent to erotic as they soaked in the warm water. Joined, they bathed each other and washed one another's hair. It was only when they were finished with their ablutions that they began to move again. The motions slow and drawn out as they both inched toward their peak. They shattered together as they held onto one another.

Bone weary but finally warm and well fed, the couple climbed into bed to doze, waking throughout the night to make love before falling back to sleep in one another's arms.

CHAPTER NINE

I t was early the next morning when they set off again. This time Elizabeth rode her own mount. Edward bought a saddle from the innkeeper after he helped Elizabeth dress in her many layers. She worried about how he'd stay warm with so few clothes, and he attempted to soothe her worries by reminding her that he suffered far worse on more battlefields than he could count. When she looked ready to burst into tears, he realized telling his brand-new bride how many times he nearly died wasn't the best way to calm her fears.

Once they were underway, both agreed it was much easier on the horses and safer for them both with separate mounts. The weather held and no new snow fell, but it was already deep which made the journey arduous on man and beast.

They rode for most of the morning, but the blowing snow and wind made the horses stumble often. Ice formed around the horses' noses, and Edward kept watch over Elizabeth to make sure she was awake. He feared she'd give in to sleep like she wanted to the day before. They made little progress, and by midday, Edward accepted it was too dangerous to continue on. He needed to find them shelter as the temperature kept falling. It was nearly impossible to make out anything more than an arm's length in front of them, but Edward took the reins to Elizabeth's horse and kept them moving. Elizabeth knew better than to argue, even if she was as good a rider as, if not better than, Edward. She understood he wanted to keep the horses from drifting apart.

Edward shielded his eyes when he thought he saw a dark mass off to the left. It was unclear what it was, but it looked more like a building than a hill or trees.

"Elizabeth, over there," he called over the howling wind. He nudged his horse off the road into even thicker snow. He dismounted, but insisted Elizabeth remain on her horse. He led the two animals through the snow drifts until they approached what looked like a deserted cottage.

"Don't get off your horse yet. If I call to you, be prepared to ride. If I tell you to go, don't look back."

"I'm not leaving you."

"Yes, you will. Beth, I can't be sure what may be inside. I can't protect you if you insist on disobeying me. I'll send you away if it's the only way to keep you safe." Elizabeth opened her mouth but snapped it shut when Edward continued. "I won't be gainsaid on this. Your safety is far too important to me to give in to you."

Elizabeth nodded as she pulled her cloak and hood around her. Even with the extra layers of clothes, the wind bit through and chilled her to the bone.

Edward drew his sword and moved toward the cottage. He circled it twice before testing the door. It opened with a shove, but he was able to get inside. There was no one there, and he didn't see any animals that posed a threat. Edward didn't see any snow or wetness accumulating anywhere inside, so he was reassured the roof was in good condition. There was wood stacked near the fireplace, but little else was there. One table and a stool stood in the middle of the room, and a straw tick mattress lay in the corner, but it had seen far better days. Once he poked around to make sure no critters would dart out, he went back for Elizabeth. He lifted her from the saddle and carried her into the tiny dwelling. Once on her feet, she busied herself making a fire while Edward found a bucket and collected snow. He unsaddled the horses and brought them inside. There was no place else for them, and they couldn't risk the animals freezing to death. It didn't take Elizabeth long to get the fire roaring, and the chill began to ease from the room.

"This isn't quite the honeymoon I would've liked to offer you." Edward pulled Elizabeth into his arms as he found a small, uncovered patch of skin by her temple to kiss.

"I'm with you, and we're safe. I don't need aught else."

"You're an unusual woman for one who has spent so many years at court. I'm not acquainted with another lady-in-waiting, or any courtier, who'd be so accepting of this lot."

"Would it do me any good to turn my nose up at a shelter that may be what keeps us alive? Would it do me any good to curse and rail at you for something you cannot control? Would it do me any good to be ungrateful to the mon who risks his life to find me and then professes his love to me? I don't think it would." Elizabeth tilted her head back and looked into his eyes. "I'm not thrilled aboot the weather or the reason for us being stuck here, but I won't deny I like having this time with you. No one is here to stop us. I don't have to watch Lady MacAdams or any other score of women fawn over you, and I don't

93

have to hold my breath waiting for my father to yank me away from you."

Elizabeth felt Edward stiffen when she mentioned her father. She raised a brow, and he shook his head before sighing.

"Beth, I don't want you assuming I hid this from you or that I tried to trick you. I honestly didn't consider your father until you mentioned him." Edward watched as the look of uncertainty transformed into suspicion. "He refused me. He wouldn't even entertain the idea of us making a match."

Elizabeth pulled away and stalked over to the fire. She threw sticks into it, and Edward wasn't sure if he should approach or give her space. He took a few tentative steps toward her, and when she didn't ward him away, he pulled her back against his chest.

"I don't care what he says. I'm past the age of majority. If he didn't want me to marry you, then he should've married me to someone else sooner. I'm tired of being ignored until I'm considered useful, then put back on the shelf when I'm not."

"You don't want to end the handfast?"

"The only way this handfast is ending is when a priest says amen."

Edward wrapped his arms around her middle and squeezed.

"I'm sorry, but I really didn't remember him until now."

"I believe you. I wasn't thinking aboot him either. I wish I hadn't. He's not as ambitious as Deirdre's father and mother were, but he's just as manipulative and neglectful. This is his comeuppance for failing me as my father and protector."

"Beth, if you change your mind between now and when we return, you need only tell me, and I'll release you."

"Don't expect me to be so gracious."

Edward kissed her neck and along her throat as she tilted her head to give him access.

"Are you refusing to let me go?"

"That's right. And you had better not be willing to let me go. In the most practical of terms, I might already be carrying your babe. I don't picture either of us would want a child born with the stigma of bastardry."

"I wouldn't accept that."

Elizabeth turned in his arms and pulled her gloves off. She grazed the pads of her fingers over the bristly hair on his jaw. She tucked his russet hair behind his ears and rubbed his lobes when she realized they were nearly frozen.

"You said you aren't going back to Ireland. Were you planning to stay at court?"

"No. I told Robert I wanted to go back to the Highlands. That's what called me home."

"And now? Are you still going back to the Highlands?"

"'You?' Why aren't you saying 'we'?"

Elizabeth shrugged one shoulder but continued to gaze at him.

"I'm not leaving you at court. My home is where you are. If you want to remain at court, then that is where we will stay."

"How soon can we leave? I mean once we return and the king sanctions our marriage. How soon after that can we go?"

"I'd say the same day, but you see the weather. It wouldn't be safe to attempt to travel that far north until after the spring thaw."

Elizabeth swallowed the sob that wanted to escape. She looked at the fire, but Edward cupped her cheek, and she leaned into it.

"Do you dread going back that much?" She nodded. "Then we will retire to Culcreuch Castle. No one is occupying it but servants and some tenant farmers. If you don't mind a quiet place without much pomp and frills, then it might be a nice distance from court. We return when summoned but otherwise keep to ourselves. Are you sure you wouldn't get bored or tired of me?"

"Hardly. Your novelty hasn't worn off yet, and if what you taught me last night is any marker, you will hold my interest in this life and the next."

"Cheeky minx."

"Only for you," Elizabeth winked before growing serious. "I don't want to stay there any longer than I have to. I have no reason to remain. The queen has been kind and generous, but she isn't an easy woman to serve. I don't hold any ties to my parents. The only people I'd miss are Thomas and the girls."

"Then we invite them to come with us."

"You make it sound simple."

"It can be. Your mother will be glad to have them away from Stirling. Your father won't stop us from moving them. The only objection will be our marriage and you leaving with me."

"Eddie, do you wonder if the crash was really an accident?"

Edward's heart seized at her hushed words. He'd been dreading that question. She kept it to herself for as long as she could.

"I have no way to be sure, my love."

"Don't try to protect me from this. The axle was broken cleanly. It could have broken then the carriage tumbled or the other way around, but either way I remember a loud crack before the coach began to fall."

The bile rose in Edward's throat as he considered the possibility that Elizabeth might have been purposely endangered.

"Eddie?"

"Now I don't want to return you to court until I ascertain who'd harm you."

Elizabeth pulled away and walked to the door. She struggled but pulled it open. The snow accumulation was above her knees when she turned to look back at Edward.

"We may not have a choice. We aren't going anywhere soon."

Elizabeth and Edward spent three days trapped within the cottage. Edward collected fresh snow that Elizabeth melted for them and the animals, and foraged leaves and grass for their mounts. The innkeeper filled Edward's satchels, so they had more than the bannocks and dried beef Edward took from the castle's kitchen, but it wasn't much and ran down quickly since it was only meant to last them a day. They spent their time talking about their childhoods and experiences at court. Edward was six years her senior, so she was too young for him to have noticed before he left for Ireland, and his tastes hadn't run toward the virginal during his brief visits. It was too cold for them to take off any clothes, and they were both fatigued from the lack of food. They spent most of their time cocooned together as they talked. Edward realized his intuition or God's wisdom granted him a rare treasure when Elizabeth came into his life. In turn, Elizabeth never felt more cherished or appreciated than she did when she was with Edward. It might not have been a romantic setting, but the time spent together was savored. By the morning of the fourth day, Edward sensed Elizabeth's restlessness and nervous energy.

"What is it?" he asked softly as she shifted positions once more.

"It's almost Christmas."

"I know, sweetheart. That's been plaguing my mind too."

"Will we be able to leave before then?"

"I'm hoping we will be able to leave before midmorning. The snow is melting, and the temperature has been climbing the past two days."

"I wish to celebrate our first Christmas together with something a bit more festive than dried beef and stale bannocks."

"I'll find you the largest roast duck the kitchens can prepare, and I'll carry mistletoe in my pocket. I'll kiss you under it every chance I have. I haven't aught to give you, but I'll make our Christmas special whether we are in the wilds or at court."

Elizabeth snickered.

"Aren't they one and the same? Though I may have been dismissed from the queen's employ. If I haven't been, but I don't attend Christmas Eve Mass, I will be. She won't forgive me for missing the service."

"Even if nature decided otherwise?"

"If she doesn't have faith it was God's will, then it may as well have never happened."

"That does sound like my gracious sister-by-marriage."

"I don't want to return. The idea of Culcreuch Castle sounds better each day, but I accept that we must. We must have the king's blessing, or my father may try to overturn our marriage. He might have the archbishop or Pope annul it."

"We shall cross those bridges when we come to them."

Elizabeth nodded but said no more. They left before midday and made steady progress throughout the afternoon and early evening. The sun was setting when they rode into the bailey at Stirling Castle.

CHAPTER TEN

E dward and Elizabeth entered the castle with the intention of Elizabeth going to her chamber to remove her five layers of clothing and to make herself more presentable while Edward sought his brother, the king. They weren't given that opportunity. Two guards stepped before them and issued a command that they appear before the king. They looked at one another but followed the guards. They entered the king's Privy Council chamber to see most of the council assembled. Seated near the king was Laird Fraser.

"Lizzie," the courtier caught himself. "Elizabeth, what are you doing here? You're supposed to be halfway to Castle Dunbeath by now."

Edward tucked Elizabeth behind him and threw his shoulders back. When he stood to his full height and showed the expanse of his broad chest, he was far larger than most realized.

"Aboot that. You risked your daughter's life to keep her away from me. What sort of mon sends his daughter to the northernmost Highlands in the middle of December? What sort of mon sends his daughter with a clearly inexperienced team that can't drive in snow?"

Edward's accusation drew gasps, and the king stood. He looked between his adopted brother and the man in question. He raised one eyebrow at Fraser.

"I did arrange for her to leave here, but my driver is experienced and has driven my family since he was a young mon. He's known Elizabeth since she was in swaddling clothes."

Elizabeth peeked around Edward. "Father, Duncan wasn't my driver. I didn't recognize him or the coachman."

"What's this? Elizabeth, are you sure? I spoke with Duncan the morning you departed."

"It wasn't him."

"Who the hell was driving your carriage?" The king roared.

"I'd like to understand that too." Edward interjected. "My wife nearly died when it overturned."

He stood with his hands on his hips awaiting the inevitable fallout from his declaration.

"Wife? Wife?" Fraser spluttered. "Not in this lifetime."

Elizabeth stepped beside Edward, and when he wrapped his arm around her shoulders, she wrapped her arm around his waist and leaned against him.

"There's little you can do. The deed is done. I'm past the age of majority, so I can make my own decisions, and I did since you refused to. There is naught that can be done to undo what has transpired. Many times."

Elizabeth's glare challenged her father, and the man stood shaken by his mild-tempered daughter's transformation.

"Your Grace, your brother has manipulated and defiled my daughter. I demand this union be annulled and recompense paid."

"Fraser, silence. I gave Edward my blessing be-

102

fore he set off chasing your daughter. I sanction this union. And if I were you, and I learned my daughter was nearly killed, I'd be more concerned aboot finding my missing driver."

"Your Grace?" Elizabeth spoke up.

"Yes, my lady?"

"Your Grace, may I be excused? I'm not at my best."

Edward pulled her close and spoke before Robert did.

"We're going to our chamber. Beth hasn't eaten properly in days, and she needs to get warm and sleep in a proper bed."

"Where have you been keeping my daughter?"

"Father, stop bellowing. You haven't thanked Edward for saving my life. He found me and protected me. He made sure we found an inn the first night because the weather was so foul. He found a cottage when the weather kept us from traveling. He did what was needed to find us food while we were stranded for days. He made sure we made it back here alive. He did all of this in a tunic and cloak. I have seven layers on, and I'm sure I may never be warm again. Father, he might have died trying to care for me."

"If you were at an inn and then a cottage, you were never at a kirk. You aren't legally wed. I don't have to acknowledge whatever agreement you pretend you've made."

"We handfasted. I'm a Highlander. We're married." Edward's words were an edict.

"Fraser, I've already told you that I sanctioned this union. It's time to accept the decision has been made. It was made before Edward left, and quite frankly before you sent Lady Elizabeth away. What is needed now is a ceremony before a priest."

Once again Elizabeth was convinced she had to be the voice of reason.

"Your Grace, tomorrow is Christmas Eve. We can't be wed until after the Mass. That means Christmas is the soonest any priest would marry us."

"Then you and your groom have a day to prepare."

Elizabeth and Edward retreated to her chamber, but Robert decreed they weren't to share it until after their wedding. It was the concession he made to Laird Fraser. Edward bit his tongue and agreed, but he wasn't pleased.

Edward checked her chamber before allowing her to enter. He wanted reassurance the carriage accident was just that, an accident, but until then he wouldn't take any chances. Once Elizabeth was inside, Edward pulled her into his embrace, and they stood together reveling in their moment of quiet after the confrontation with Elizabeth's father.

"I'll come to you tonight," Elizabeth murmured.

"Beth, I detest the idea of you roaming aboot the castle. What if something happened to you? You fell or banged your head? If something went amiss, no one would be any the wiser where you are."

"You worry like an old woman."

"Because I have something more precious than all the jewels and gold in the world."

"I love you, too."

"Tell me how to get from my chamber to here?"

"It's far too complicated. If anyone is likely to end up lost and never found again, it'd be you muddling your way here."

"What do you propose?"

Elizabeth bit her lip and shrugged. "I suppose two nights won't kill us. You kept me waiting before, I suppose I'll survive." Elizabeth laughed and swatted his backside before shimmying away.

"Cheeky. I'll remind you of that."

"I shall hold you to it."

A knock at the door interrupted their banter. A team of servants arrived with a tub and steaming hot water, along with a tray piled with various scrumptious offerings. There was enough food for two, so Edward waited while a maid assisted Elizabeth with her bath behind a screen. They shot each other looks of disgust but accepted the situation. Once Elizabeth was dressed in a fresh chemise and a warm robe, they sat together before the fire. The meal ended as another knock sounded at the door. Another team of servants cleared away the tub and dishes. A guard stood at the door and stared at Edward until Edward relented, kissing Elizabeth goodnight.

The next day was Christmas Eve, and the court transformed into a magical and enchanted playground for courtiers. Servants lit candles in all the chandeliers and wall sconces. Boughs of evergreen were hung throughout the passageways and the Great Hall. The ladies replaced the subdued gowns worn during Advent with brightly colored gowns for the Christmas season. The day sped by in preparation for the midnight Mass that would welcome in Christmastide, and Elizabeth spent it in the queen's salon with the other ladies-in-waiting. They sewed stockings and garments to be distributed to the poor the day after Christmas. Elizabeth was welcomed by the queen with more warmth than she anticipated. She read aloud from the queen's favorite book of poetry. As the hour grew late, the ladies followed the queen to the chapel. The queen looked over her shoulder and caught Elizabeth's eye before tilting her head toward Edward. Elizabeth attempted to hide her shock, but she curtsied and took her place beside Edward. He entwined their fingers within the folds of her gown.

The next two hours were spent in prayer and song as the court welcomed the birth of Christ. Elizabeth reflected how her journey to this day began in this chapel when she sensed someone watched her. She peeked at Edward as he kneeled beside her, and she found him looking at her just as he had four weeks earlier. His eyes crinkled at the corner, and his dimples appeared as he smiled. Their hands were folded in prayer, so he pressed his elbow against hers. She returned his smile before bowing her head again.

The congregation left the nave and moved to the Great Hall to begin the festivities. Elizabeth found a new place set for her on the dais. She looked around the hall and marveled at how it transformed from the somber gathering place that lacked decoration during Advent to a fairyland that twinkled and shone. The celebrations stretched into the early hours of the morning, until most of the revelers barely kept their eyes open. Edward and Elizabeth shared a secret glance as they both considered slipping away together, but the queen and ladies-in-waiting had other plans. Elizabeth was whisked away to her chamber where the two other ladies-in-waiting fell into their beds alongside hers. It was the first time in months that either slept in their beds, but Elizabeth was too tired to consider that the queen had sent them as chaperones. When they rose midmorning, they made their way to the queen's salon. The ladies sequestered her where they spent the remainder of the morning and into the afternoon leisurely reading and talking. Elizabeth's eyes drifted closed more than once until the queen gave her permission to sleep on a chaise. She was exhausted from the ordeal of being stranded in a blizzard, so she was grateful to catch a few hours of sleep before she was roused by a giddy group of young ladies who helped her ready for her wedding.

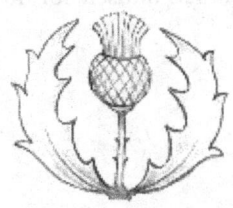

Edward had grumbled as he watched Elizabeth leave with the other ladies-in-waiting swarming about her. He sat on the dais next to Robert and observed the last of the revelers trickle out as some sought their beds and some sought someone else's bed. He appreciated Robert's calming presence. Even though he considered himself already married to Elizabeth, a nervous excitement coursed through him at making it official before friends, family, and everyone in between.

"To consider only four weeks ago, you swore you weren't interested in a wife and a farm. Now you've asked to retire to Culreuch Castle with your bride."

"I wasn't acquainted with Beth then, but I find the notion of being a gentleman farmer rather appealing."

Robert chortled.

"I don't quite believe that. But until the weather thaws, you can remain at Culreuch. After that, we will decide which keep you will become laird of, and you can return to the Highlands."

Edward breathed easier as he pictured the life he and Elizabeth would create together.

"Little brother, I suggest you get some sleep before the ceremony. I suspect your bonny wee bride will be keeping you up tonight." Robert laughed as he stepped down from the dais.

Edward made his way to his chamber where he slept and then readied himself for the service.

CHAPTER ELEVEN

E dward stood before the altar and priest as he waited for the rear doors of the chapel to open. He glanced at the priest, who returned his look with a scowl. The same man who informed the queen of his inappropriate attention to Elizabeth was the man who'd now marry them. Edward grinned with a sense of vindication, but it didn't last long when the trumpets blared, and he caught his first glance of Elizabeth. His breath whooshed from him as he beheld a vision far more exquisite than he ever dreamed. Her father stood beside her, and Edward swallowed as his bride walked toward him. She wore an ice-blue gown that sparkled with silver thread inlaid around the collar and the hems of her sleeves and skirt. The neckline plunged low enough to reveal her creamy pale skin; the skirt was cinched tightly at the waist. Edward once again felt his palms itch to wrap his hands around her and pull her against him. Her chestnut hair had intricate braids looping around her crown, but much of it hung free in waves and curls. If her smile weren't so warm, she might have appeared as a perfect ice queen. She shimmered like an icicle as diamonds in her ears and around her throat cast prisms of light as she moved toward her groom. She didn't take her eyes off him as she approached. Edward stepped down to greet her, ignoring the gasps as he broke tradition. He took Elizabeth's hand and tucked it around his arm.

They stepped up to the altar, and the wedding Mass proceeded. They held hands throughout the ceremony, even when it was expected that they would fold their hands in prayer. As the ceremony drew to an end, Edward helped Elizabeth to her feet and drew her in for a kiss. They ignored the clearing of throats and the tsks of disapproval as they took their time and savored the blessing of their union. They drew apart and Edward swung Elizabeth into his arms. He carried her past the crowds and into the Great Hall until they reached the dais. He placed her on her feet and chuckled when he looked up to see someone had placed mistletoe above their seats. He pointed up and nipped at Elizabeth's neck as she took in the small garland. She pulled Edward in for a kiss as people filed in and took their seats. The rest of the evening was spent gleefully giving in to people's demand that they kiss.

The feast presented to them was beyond anything short of when the king married. The combination of welcoming Christmastide and a wedding meant they were favored with every possible course. Edward and Elizabeth fed one another as the musicians strummed carols in the background. The festive nature of the holiday along with the hope that goes along with a new marriage filled the Great Hall with cheer.

When the meal was cleared away, Edward escorted Elizabeth to the floor and twirled her around in the dance he spent the last month dreaming about. They danced and laughed until neither had the energy to keep going. Well-fed and merry, they had eyes only for one another. The revelers and merrymakers continued to celebrate even when Elizabeth and Edward shared a look that communicated their need to escape. They retired to their newly shared chamber where they undressed one another and fell into bed.

Edward pulled a small box from beneath his pillow and grinned at Elizabeth.

"Wife, I have something for you to mark the occasion."

"Is this a wedding gift or a Christmas gift?"

"Open it and see."

Elizabeth opened the box to find a sparkling emerald set in a gold band. Edward lifted the ring from the satin upon which it rested and revealed a pair of crimson-red ruby earrings. He slid the ring onto her finger and kissed each fingertip.

"Eddie, they are breathtaking."

"They shine only because they are held by you. The ring is for our wedding and the earbobs are for Christmas."

Elizabeth leaned in for a kiss as she reached behind her and under her own pillow. When they broke apart, and Edward opened his eyes, he found a long narrow box resting between them.

"Go on. Open it!" Edward chuckled at Elizabeth's giddiness.

He lifted the lid and found a beautiful sgian dubh that held a jewel-encrusted handle. The agate shone with hues of blue and green that nearly matched his hazel eyes.

"We seem to like one another's eyes, husband," Elizabeth chirped.

Edward couldn't take his eyes from the dagger. It was the first gift he'd been given since he was a boy and received the sword he still carried.

"Beth, you have no idea how special this is to me."

"I noticed you carry a couple of daggers, but a sgian dubh comes in handy."

"That's not what I meant. No one has given me a present since I was a lad."

Elizabeth was sure she saw his eyes glisten, but she would never point it out.

"Then this is a merry Christmas after all."

They were left to their own devices until they emerged four days later, blissful and even more in love.

"Robert, I'd like to retire to Culcreuch by the end of the week. As you're aware, Sir Arthur Galbraith is here at court with his wife, so they are not in residence at the keep. It's close to Stirling, but far enough away to keep Elizabeth away from this intrigue." Edward gave his brother a hard stare, daring Robert to challenge him. Few people would be so demanding, yet Robert's brothers were among those few. "I don't want to keep Elizabeth here any longer. You and I both realize it isn't safe for her. Not until we resolve the carriage mystery."

Robert looked long and hard at his brother, trying to remind Edward who the decision maker was even though Robert had already arranged for the staff at Culcreuch to prepare the keep for the arrival of his brother and sister-by marriage.

"You may depart as soon as you are ready. I have

no love lost for any of the Frasers. I think the sooner you are away, the sooner we will both have peace of mind. Galbraith will not object to having you as a guest provided you don't eat him out of house and home. Besides, my Elizabeth will have my bollocks if aught else happens to your Elizabeth, and that's before the Sinclairs weigh in. I'm certain your Elizabeth has written to her cousin, and there is little chance Deirdre won't have shared the events with at least Magnus, if not Liam, too."

"That is not such a bad thing. I actually wouldn't mind having at least two of the brothers help to investigate the accident. None of them love being at court, so I'm certain they will be honest. They have naught to gain since the Sinclairs have been in your favor since the beginning. Hell, all five Sinclairs are your godchildren."

"You have a point. Tavish and Magnus are both familiar with court, and both of their wives were ladies-in-waiting who are familiar with how to navigate life here. Both brothers are tenacious and not easily intimidated. And Ceit, Tavish's wife, was one of the best spies I've ever had. Deirdre is certainly one of the most intelligent people I've ever met; her reasoning is faster and more astute than most."

"Do you think they'd come?"

"There's no question aboot their willingness to come. They'll understand it isn't a choice. The question will be whether either of the brothers will be willing to leave their wives if the investigation takes them away from court."

"Protective, are they?"

Robert shot Edward a rueful glance before chuckling. "They are no worse than you are."

"Good Lord, then they will be angrier that bears with burrs in their paws if you try to send them away."

"And what will you do if you must leave Elizabeth here to direct the investigation?"

Edward had already thought of this possibility, and there was no possibility or permeation that he found acceptable. He detested leaving Elizabeth at court when the reason for leaving was a so-called "accident" that might have killed her. He was aware Elizabeth was close to her cousin, Deirdre, and she had developed a friendship with Ceit; however, without those women's husbands at court, he was unconvinced that there would be adequate protection for his bride.

"I will have little choice but to entrust her to your care." Edward's tone lacked humor or sarcasm. His stare was hard and determined as he issued a silent challenge to his brother. Although Robert was the king, there was much that happened at court that he couldn't prevent. That someone may have plotted against Elizabeth or her family was proof of that.

"I will ensure that guards are posted at your chamber doors every night, and Elizabeth will have an escort throughout the castle and anytime she might leave the grounds. I would recommend your bonny bride not go gallivanting on her horse as she usually does."

"Aye, well, she hasn't done that since we married. The accident scared her enough that she's refused to leave the castle grounds without me. I do trust you enough to keep her here rather than alone at Culcreuch."

"Your faith in me is inspiring, little brother." Robert's voice was just as dry.

"She might already be carrying your niece or nephew."

"Do you think so?"

"It's too soon to know, but you know we've been, er--"

114

"Blind to the rest of the world. Disinterested in anyone other than each other. Pawing at one another."

"Yes, I suppose you could say that." Edward was embarrassed neither by how much he loved his wife, nor how enchanted he was.

Robert clapped a hand on Edward's shoulder before offering a true smile. It was a smile that Edward recognized, one that wasn't kingly, but brotherly. "I won't let any harm come to her. I care for her as my sister, and I understand how important she is to you. She is under my personal protection. She may chafe at how overprotective I am, but I will remind her that you expect no less."

Edward grinned at his brother as he nodded his acceptance. "If you are as overprotective as I am, then you may see a testy side to my bride."

"I'll keep that in mind."

Edward left Robert's antechamber as his brother moved into the Privy Council chamber. He went in search of Elizabeth, searching first in the queen's solar. A guard knocked on the door and opened it to a chamber filled with young women, including his sister-by-marriage. The queen sat upon her chair working on her embroidery. Edward was aware of the other women who were sewing or reading, but his eyes immediately found Elizabeth seated in the window seat, her sewing in her lap. As though someone whispered in her ear, her head snapped toward the door as Edward stepped inside. She stood, dropping her needle and lace to the floor. Bending, Elizabeth scooped up her sewing and took a step forward before remembering the queen hadn't granted her permission to acknowledge or go to Edward. She glanced toward the queen, who gave her a nearly imperceptible nod, allowing her to glide across the room to where Edward held out his hand. Laying her hand in his palm, a charge of electricity shot up her forearm straight to her heart. Despite spending four days tucked away in their love nest, Edward's touch still excited her just as much as the first time he kissed her. She made her back rigid to keep a shiver from passing through her. Beyond guiding her through the door, neither looked at the other, nor did they speak. They were aware that plenty of attention followed them because of their courtship and brief seclusion. While neither was uncomfortable with the entire court knowing they were blissfully in love, they didn't trust anyone who might overhear their conversations.

When they arrived at their chamber, Edward held the door open as Elizabeth stepped through the doorway, then froze. Her choked gasp had Edward pulling her back and behind him. He drew his sword as his gaze swept the room. He saw no immediate threat or even anything out of place. Elizabeth tugged on his arm and pushed past him, rushing to her armoire where she discovered someone had broken the lock. Edward once more pulled her behind him as he eased the doors open. Several gowns were on the floor of the closet, many ripped and in disarray.

Elizabeth swung around and rushed to her chest, which sat at the foot of their bed. That lock was also destroyed, with material peeking out from under the lid from when someone hastily shoved it back in. She waited for Edward to lift the lid before staring down at the tangled mess of undergarments and parchments she'd stored beneath the clothes. She lifted the fabric out and kneeled to go through the correspondence she stored in the chest for safekeeping. Among the missives were letters exchanged with Deirdre over the years, both from before she joined the court and since her marriage. There were also letters from her mother from when her parents traveled back to Fraser territory on extended visits home. Elizabeth had been at court for so long, she craved any description of her childhood home.

"Why would anyone do this? What do they think I have? What could I have that anyone else wants?" Elizabeth spoke around the lump in her throat. She sorted through the parchments trying to put them back into order, noting that at least three letters from her parents and two from Deirdre were missing. Nothing important came to mind from those letters.

"I don't have answers to those questions, my love, but I will find them." Edward eased Elizabeth to her feet and led her to the chair before the fire. He sat down and pulled her into his lap. "What is missing?"

"I'm not sure that there is aught missing from the bureau since I only keep my gowns there, but there are missives from my mother and Deirdre that aren't among the others. Why would anyone care aboot those?"

"What were they aboot?"

"The ones from my mother described clan members that I remember from my childhood. She mentions things aboot the keep that she wants updated or how some fields flooded or are too dry. She talks aboot what she bought from the market, trinkets she'd bring back for me. Deirdre wrote aboot Magnus in the early letters. They were still

117

courting, and she'd tell me some things they wrote aboot or what it was like to see him at the infrequent clan gatherings. More recently, she told me what it was like to join a clan that cared for its people and cared aboot *her* rather than what she could gain them. She wrote of how strong the bond is between Magnus and his brothers and sister. She marveled at how protective they are of one another. And she spoke of how happy she was to live with Magnus after all the years her parents kept them apart. I thought none of it would interest anyone other than me."

"Beth, did any of the letters from your mother or even Deirdre describe the condition of the Fraser keep? Did they talk aboot any walls in disrepair, or any changes in the number of guards or illnesses that weakened the clan? Aught like that at all?"

"A few over the years, but you know my mother and father are at court right now. She hasn't been back on Fraser land in months, not since they celebrated the beginning of spring with Beltane. That was eight months ago. There's been no reason for her to send me a missive when she sees me here every day."

"Has your father been back since then?"

"Yes. He returned a few months ago for Samhain. He wanted to meet with my uncle aboot the harvest and some matters here at court, but I have no idea what those were."

"Did he ever write to you?"

Elizabeth inwardly scoffed at the idea before shooting Edward a wry glance.

"Eddie, I don't think my father has ever written to me. It would require more words than he has to spare for me. Besides, why would he do it when he could tell my mother what to say to me?"

"Did your mother and Deirdre date the letters?

Someone reopened these but was in a hurry to refold them."

"Yes. Both of them always dated their letters. Sometimes a messenger would deliver more than one at a time, so it helped to figure out in what order to read them." Elizabeth looked through the letters once again to remember when the missing letters were written. "From your questions, I gather someone wants to learn of any weaknesses to the Fraser keep. They hoped that either my mother or Deirdre included something that would help them plan an attack or information to hold against my father or uncle."

"That is my guess. Do you have any idea who it might be?"

Elizabeth's laugh held no mirth as her mouth turned down. "It could be any number of people. The Hays are still ill-tempered aboot Deirdre's marriage to Magnus being upheld and the dowry they lost, not to mention Archibald Hays's death. The Keiths were displeased that the Hays were gaining more territory from Deidre's impending marriage. The Hays sandwich them and they would rightfully feel threatened if the Hays' holdings were to expand. The Gordons weren't happy for the same reason, but I bet the Ogilvies were grinning from ear to ear that Fraser lands would shrink when Deirdre's dowry lands passed to the Hays. They would assume the loss might weaken us. However, the Gordons have been our allies, and they surround the Ogilvies on all sides except for the north, which borders the sea. I'm not sure the Leslies would care that much aboot land changing hands since their land doesn't border ours, but it borders the Hays further from the Frasers. You understand how complicated clan borders can be. But land exchanges hands all the time, since that's the reason people make alliances and marriages. It's rarely the woman but the land she brings with her that interests potential suitors."

Edward pulled Elizabeth closer and kissed her temple.

"You know that I never cared aboot your dowry, don't you? That had naught to do with why I married you."

"I do. I know you even turned down some monies that would have come with me and insisted the land be my dower lands in case something was to happen to you. But you are the king's brother. Only you and Edward don't need to gain a woman's dowry. The king could abscond with any land you or your brother might want." Elizabeth spoke the words without rancor; they were simply the truth. It made her grateful that the man she married chose her because he loved her, not because he wanted to gain something, though many said she pursued Edward for the prestige of being part of the royal family. At times like this, Elizabeth would have rather Edward been a pauper, or at least a lesser noble with no ties to court.

"Robert said we can remove to Culcreuch before the end of the week, but I'll make certain we're ready to leave at first light." Edward looked about the chamber and wondered whether his decision was the right one. Should they leave to get Elizabeth away from whoever thought her useful in their nefarious plan? Or should they remain and resolve this issue before leaving? His need to protect his wife was so great that he wanted to pack and leave that very moment. However, there was a greater danger in traveling at night than in spending one more night in Stirling. Beyond that, he would have to inform Robert of the break in. "We can go to our new keep and get familiar with the land and the people before we return here. We can stay there until Magnus and Tavish arrive with their wives."

"Deirdre and Ceit are coming?" Elizabeth couldn't hide her excitement at the thought of seeing her friends once more.

"That's Robert's plan. He wants Magnus and Tavish to assist with the investigation of your accident. He trusts them and says that I can trust their wives to support you. Beth, tracking who did this may take me away from court. I don't want you alone at Culcreuch with the laird and lady of the keep here at court, and I don't like the idea of you being here without me, but Robert assures me you will be well guarded."

"I expected as much. I mean, the Sinclairs coming is unexpected, but I accepted you might have to go sooner rather than later. I feel better knowing Deirdre and Ceit will be here. They know their way around court life, and I enjoy their company."

"Robert said as much. He's sending a messenger to extend his invitation." Elizabeth and Edward both recognized it wasn't an invitation but an order that no one, not even the Sinclairs, could ignore. "They should be here in just over a fortnight if there aren't any late winter storms."

"Then we should expect that there will be storms. Highland weather loves to taunt anyone who thinks to tame it or take it for granted. What shall we do in the meantime?" Elizabeth grinned as she wriggled in Edward's lap. She felt the hard press of his iron length against her hip, and she wanted to forget that someone had been rifling through her belongings. She wanted to feel safe in her husband's arms and enjoy every minute she had with him before he might have to leave. Edward was on his feet and carrying her to the bed before she finished speaking. He had her laces undone so quickly Elizabeth was unprepared for the chill air to hit her skin. When she shivered, Edward went to the fire and poked it back to life. He undressed as he approached the bed. He slid into bed next to her and pulled Elizabeth into his arms.

"No matter what happens, I will always put your safety and that of our family ahead of all else. Robert couldn't do that for his wife, but I can for mine. If need be, we will go to the Sinclairs and get as far from court as we can while still in Scotland. I won't keep you anywhere where you might be in danger."

"And I love you all the more for caring so much aboot me. Most men would consider naught beyond their lives and duties here at court. Losing Robert's ear would concern them more than protecting their wives."

"And they are lesser men for it. You and any bairns the Lord blesses us with will always be my highest priority."

They melted into one another as their hands roamed over familiar peaks and valleys. Their sounds of passion echoed throughout the room as their bodies eventually fused into one. It was well after the midday meal before they were prepared to face the world again. They left their chamber to make Robert aware of latest development. Edward was also certain he needed to find Elizabeth's father to discuss the possibility of a looming attack on the Frasers.

CHAPTER TWELVE

"**B**luidy hell, Robert! What if Elizabeth had been alone in the chamber when these bastards broke in? Would my wife of a week be dead? Would they have stolen her, too?" Edward felt the cords in his neck straining, and he wanted nothing more than to wrap his hands around his own brother's neck. Robert's nonchalance might be the death of him. It was only Elizabeth's wide-eyed shaking of her head that kept Edward from challenging his brother. Edward and Elizabeth sat in the private chambers of the king and queen, all guards and courtiers having been dismissed.

"I already promised to post guards outside your chambers at all times. I will have the more discreet members of my court ask the servants if they saw anyone skulking aboot or entering and exiting your chambers. I will make inquiries aboot any unknown animosity toward the Frasers or you. Did you consider perhaps someone is not happy aboot *you* marrying Elizabeth?"

Elizabeth knew the king referred to Sinead. She felt ill picturing her husband's former mistress. Jealousy and insecurity coursed through her, threatening to smother her while angered by the possibility that

Edward's past could endanger either of them. She clenched her jaw to keep from speaking and clenched her fists in her skirts to keep from lashing out.

"I've thought aboot that, but Sinead has moved up in her own estimation. She now has the king's real brother in her bed. I doubt she misses me." Edward was tempted to look at Elizabeth as he spoke, but he admitted to himself that he was too much of a coward.

"You are my *real* brother," Robert bit out. "And that's why I'm suspicious. You said yourself, she has more spies here than any foreign monarch, more than even Longshanks. I will send a missive to Ireland to see what is cooking there. If our brother even hints that your past is catching up to you, I'll stuff the woman's head on a pike. Her usefulness to the cause will run out."

Elizabeth continued to watch the brothers argue, nothing about their conversation making her feel any better. Her gaze darted to Queen Elizabeth to see how she responded to the heated discussion. The usual serenity was plastered on her visage, but Elizabeth saw the hard set of the queen's jaw and how her throat bobbed as she swallowed several times. Their eyes locked, and the queen's face softened, but there was a determination that Elizabeth sensed would be in her favor.

"Perhaps you two could refrain from discussing the groom's history of bedsport in front of his bride. That might be a conversation better had in private." The queen glared at Robert and turned her nose up at Edward.

Edward looked at Elizabeth at last and wished he hadn't. He realized she struggled to restrain her temper, and he read the hurt and doubt that whipped through her sharp mind. He pulled his chair closer to hers and took her hand before sitting down. He glanced at Robert and Queen Elizabeth before leaning toward his wife's ear.

"I'm so sorry, Beth. It was cruel of me to let Robert bring that up or to say aught aboot her in front of you. I took for granted that you would understand I no longer care for Sinead at all. Even when I was with her, my feelings were never aught like what I've felt for you since the first time I saw you. And I don't mean in the chapel but when we danced in the Great Hall. I will kill her myself and not lose a wink of sleep if her hand is in this. Even if it's only to pass along information."

Elizabeth nodded her head, unable bring herself to look at Edward.

"Your Majesty, my husband said we could retire to Culcreuch before the end of the sennight. Is that still the case?"

"If Edward believes you are safer there, then yes, you may retire there while Edward further investigates this issue."

"No!" Edward was on his feet as Elizabeth uttered a whimper. "Until the Sinclairs arrive, Elizabeth does not leave my side. Whether we stay here or leave, you will not separate me from my wife."

"Wouldn't you rather lead the search? Wouldn't you rather your wife be far from where the threat exists?"

"And can you be certain it won't follow her without me to protect her?"

"There is a full garrison at Culcreuch, and I can send more as her escort."

"No, Robert. I will not agree to this. Whether you're my brother or my king doesn't matter to me now that I have a wife. I swear to you, if you push me on this, I will take my wife where no one can find us. Not even you." Edward seethed, and it was now Elizabeth's firm grip on his arm that kept him from launching himself at Robert just as they had when they were young men training together in the lists. "I won't risk losing my wife for eight years."

Edward couldn't keep from throwing that final barb at Robert. He recognized he crossed a line from which he might never return. Robert and his sister-by-marriage both looked ready to do him in, but he wouldn't back down, nor did he regret the low blow. While his sister-by-marriage fumed, Edward counted on his brother's guilt still being so great that he would never put Edward in the same position.

"Very well. I believe my wife would appreciate a reprieve from your presence."

Edward and Elizabeth took that to be the signal that dismissed them. In the passageway, Elizabeth trembled so violently that Edward feared she would collapse. He lifted a torch from a wall sconce and moved them into the nearest alcove, where he put the torch into a sconce. He tried to pull Elizabeth into his embrace, wanting to comfort her and reassure her, but she pushed away.

"Don't. I don't want you to touch me." Elizabeth's voice was ragged as tears streamed down her face. "I don't know whether I'm angry or scared or just incredibly jealous, but I know I'm not pleased with you, and I'm not ready to stop being upset with you."

Edward was at a loss for what to do to soothe his wife, but he understood her feelings. It had been insensitive to discuss Sinead in front of her, and unleashing his temper was enough to scare her on its own, let alone directing it toward the king.

"I'm sorry we brought up my past in front of you, and I'm sorry that I frightened you with my temper, but I'm not sorry that I will defy aught Robert says if it might put you in greater danger.

And whoever is threatening you has a short life ahead of them. Woman or mon."

"Is she as beautiful as the rumors say?" Elizabeth whispered.

Edward ran his hand through his hair. He could lie to make her feel better, but she'd know. He could tell her the truth, but it would do nothing to ease her insecurity.

"She is a very attractive woman, and her fiery temper draws men who wish to tame it. She also has the support of the local people and has a network of spies that support Robert's cause. All of that makes her an alluring woman."

Elizabeth nodded, but she was unable to force any words out. The tears fell faster and harder as her mind refused to release the image of Edward in bed with the faceless redhead. She turned, but didn't step away when Edward laid his hand gently on her shoulder.

"Beth, it rains there just as much as here. It's bluidy cold and disgusting mucking aboot battlefields. It was lonely, too. Sinead served a purpose. She eased that loneliness, and she brought support to aid our forces there. I'm certain this isn't the first time you've wondered aboot her. Have you ever wondered why I've never brought her to court even though plenty of men keep mistresses here? Have you ever wondered why I was able to leave without looking back?"

"You didn't bring her because there were distractions here, or as I've heard it, her temper made it more trouble than it was worth to bed women at court. She didn't need to travel to keep her talons in you. She had a purpose, as you said, so you didn't take her away from her spy network. You haven't looked back because I'm now that distraction." Elizabeth's tone was hard, no trace of her sobs from only moments ago.

"Don't." It was Edward's turn to refute her. "Don't ever say such a wretched thing again. You are not a distraction. You are the only person I love at the moment. And the only person I have. I can't trust Robert will put us ahead of what he believes is best for the nation or the fight. I can't blame him for it, but I will never forgive him for it if you suffer. I never brought Sinead because I didn't care what she did, or who she did, while I was away. She certainly wasn't faithful to me. I was able to walk away because I didn't love her. By the end, I barely cared what happened to her. I suggested my brother Edward bed her so I could leave without looking back over my shoulder. Before you, I planned to go my entire life without marrying. I have no need to. Robert has his heirs, and I was never in line to inherit anyway. When I returned to court, I wanted to retire to an estate in the Highlands where I'd be content. I married because I love you, and the possibility of not having you at my side every day until the Lord takes one of us is unbearable. I married you because I have never felt like a better mon than when I am with you."

Elizabeth turned and melted into Edward's chest as sobs wracked her entire body. She shook as she clung to Edward's tunic.

"I feel so plain when I hear her described, and you were with her so long that you must have some feelings for her. It's not that I fear you would ever be unfaithful. I just worry that you will run out of things to love aboot me. That you will walk away as easily from me as you did her."

"Oh Beth, *mo chridhe*, I can't foresee what the future holds for us, but I am old enough with enough experience to recognize I've never felt this way before, that what is between us is not something simple. There is no one else who has ever held my heart."

Elizabeth nodded but still clung to him. "Why would you bait Robert like that? He is still king. He could toss you in the dungeon of some remote keep that I could never find. He could put your head on a pike or have you dangling from the gallows."

"But he never will. He knows our brother and I will always be his staunchest supporters. And as long as I don't challenge him in public, he will never keep me from voicing my opinion. Edward and I keep him humble."

"Just as long as he keeps you alive." Elizabeth kept trying to burrow closer, but her tremors slowed.

"How are you feeling now?"

"A little less jealous, quite a lot less scared, and maybe not so angry."

"We will take a tray in our chamber and leave at first light. I want us away from here until your relatives arrive."

"I suppose the Sinclairs are my relatives now, even if it's rather indirect. Will Robert send for you when they arrive?"

"I'm sure he will. We can spend the next few sennights in peace as we get to know the land."

"As much peace as we can have when I'm certain you won't let me go anywhere without at least four guards."

"Only four? You underestimate me, my love. At least ten."

Elizabeth offered him a watery smile before they made their way back to their chamber.

CHAPTER THIRTEEN

T he horses snorted and stomped as steam from their nostrils puffed into clouds around their bouncing heads. The bailey was filled with guards in the royal livery as well as those who wore Edward's insignia. Elizabeth quietly said goodbye to her parents while Edward finalized plans with the heads of the guards. Reubadair kept looking in her direction, both hearing and smelling his owner. When Elizabeth noticed Edward walking toward her, she crossed the bailey and took the hand he offered. She was prepared to mount Reubadair on her own, but two large hands wrapped around her waist before hoisting her into the saddle.

"If you rode a slower or weaker horse, you would be riding with me. But I trust this beast to carry you through Hell and back if need be. He's almost as loyal and devoted as I am."

"Aye, and you can be a wee beastie at times, too." Elizabeth winked.

"I shall remind you of just how wild I am." Edward waggled his eyebrows, and Elizabeth's laughter lightened his mood. He'd silently simmered the night before, pushing his temper aside to reassure Elizabeth. His tension was nearly palpable as the party prepared to ride out, but Elizabeth's jest lifted much of the weight from his shoulders.

Moments after Edward mounted, the party that consisted of Edward, Elizabeth, a half-dozen of Robert's royal guards, and a score of warriors who would remain at Culcreuch during their stay clattered out of the bailey and onto the road leading north away from Stirling.

Edward's head was on a swivel as they left the castle, then the town of Stirling. He had a sense of foreboding that settled into his mind as they left the city gates. The guards encircled Elizabeth, and while he knew he should ride in the lead, he was uncomfortable leaving her side. He appointed the head of his own guard to lead while the head of Robert's contingent rode closer to the rear. He wished now that he'd made her ride with him; however, he also knew that he couldn't swing a sword effectively if he needed to defend his wife. He scanned the horizon as much as he looked off to the sides of the road. He'd instructed the guards riding in the rear to look behind them consistently. He wouldn't have anyone sneak up on them from behind.

They rode in peace for an hour, but Elizabeth could more than sense Edward's tension. It radiated from him and showed in the strained cords in his neck and the creases between his brows. She hadn't pressed conversation and was content to continue in silence since Culcreuch was a short distance from Stirling, only an hour and a half's ride as long as they kept at a canter. She, too, scanned the horizon, but tried to be more subtle as she watched the sides of the road. She knew she wouldn't be as perceptive as Edward, but she was just as unwilling to be taken by surprise. She didn't share with Edward that she still had nightmares about the carriage accident. She didn't wake screaming or sweating, but her dreams were vivid, nonetheless. She now felt fear creeping up her spine as she imagined being thrown from Reubadair's back. He was as loyal and steady as a warhorse, but that didn't mean he was completely imperturbable.

"I won't let aught happen to you, Beth, but I do appreciate that you're alert." Edward spoke as he heard the sound of water nearby. "We aren't that far from the keep now, but we'll turn off the road in that gap in the trees and let the horses drink at the burn. You can refresh yourself there, but don't wander off. If you need privacy, I'll accompany you and stand on the other side of the tree. Do *not* go anywhere alone, and don't stray far from the horses."

Elizabeth glanced at Edward and once more felt the tension that rippled through him. She nodded and followed him silently into the trees. It was only moments later that they approached a stream that flowed along a rocky embankment. It would be difficult for the horses to drink, and she didn't trust herself in her skirts to be able to keep her balance. Edward swore softly under his breath. He looked further north, searching for a better place to stop. He signaled that the party continue along the bank to a spot that looked easier to approach.

When they came to a patch of riverbank that had dirt merging into the water rather than rocks, the group dismounted. The men led their horses to water, and the animals guzzled, thirsty after riding hard over rough terrain even if only for a short time. Elizabeth tugged on Reubadair's reins, and he gladly took his place among the others. She passed the reins to one of the men and looked for Edward. He stood with his sword drawn, his back to the stream.

"We aren't far from the keep, but it'd be unwise to continue pushing the horses without a rest. I thought you might benefit from having a moment to stretch your legs." Edward glanced in Elizabeth's direction and reached out his hand. She gladly took it as he wrapped his arm around her waist. He dropped his voice for her ears only. "And I worry that after all our bedsport, you'll be sore. I don't want your skin to chafe while you ride astride."

"My love, I wore woolen leggings beneath my skirts for that reason. You know I ride often and over just as uneven land, so I'm not uncomfortable. I am eager to reach our new home."

Edward knew she left unspoken her eagerness to get off the road and not have him whittling every moment as he rode next to her. He also knew that his tension was making her nervous, but he refused to lower his guard for even a moment, lest someone make a move.

"Eddie, can you take me to a tree?"

Edward nodded, and they walked to a giant oak tree. Edward walked around with Elizabeth checking both the nearby trees and the ground. He didn't want Elizabeth stepping into nettles or poison ivy. When he was certain it was safe for her, he moved to the opposite side, giving her privacy. When she was finished, she stepped back around the tree.

"Go back to the others while I make use of the tree, too."

"I don't mind waiting."

"It's all right. I'll watch you. Just don't look back," Edward chuckled. "You haven't had a chance for a drink. Splash water on your face and neck. You'll feel much better."

Elizabeth paused for so long that Edward thought she'd refuse, but eventually, she nodded and turned back to the stream. Edward unfastened the laces to his leggings and was about to relieve himself when all hell broke loose. Men on horseback broke through the trees while archers approached on foot, firing at man and horse indiscriminately, knowing that any casualty would slow their pursuit. He watched in horror as a man bent low over the side of his horse, galloping toward Elizabeth, poised to grab her. He screamed her name, telling her to run. Instead, she stood her ground, waiting until the last minute before jerking aside and thrusting a dirk into the neck of the man prone to snatch her off her feet. The man toppled from his horse, dead before his body hit the ground. Elizabeth pulled the dirk from his neck and swung around as the rider behind the dead man approached, this time more cautious. This man seemed more intent upon running Elizabeth over with his steed than capturing her. She once again waited until the man and beast were directly in front of her. She jumped aside, reaching up to grasp handfuls of the man's tunic. She threw her weight backward and used the momentum of the horse to pull the man from the saddle. Her dirk was through his sternum before the man could catch his next breath.

Edward was sure his heart stopped during the time Elizabeth engaged with the men on horseback, then it surged into his throat as he charged toward her. Elizabeth lifted her skirts and ran toward him, but with her focus on Edward, she didn't anticipate a third man determined to capture her. She looked over just as the horse's head nearly rammed her and tried to skirt the animal. The rider grabbed the back of her kirtle and a handful of hair, yanking her off her feet. Edward approached at the same time, unable to see Elizabeth but able to understand the man was attempting to kidnap his wife. His sword entered the man's side at such an angle that Edward feared it would impale Elizabeth when it went clear through.

Elizabeth screamed as her body was suddenly flung backward as the man jerked from the sword that pierced him, her back crashing into the horse's flank. She felt herself falling, fearful she'd be trampled under the steed's hind legs. She landed hard enough to knock the wind from her as she watched the horse's hoof pass over her face close enough that she could see the nails in the horseshoe.

Edward was certain Elizabeth would be crushed under the massive animal's hoof, but somehow the horse's gait managed to miss her entirely. As his own men fought off their attackers, his archers picking off one man after another, Edward slid next to Elizabeth's curled body. He brushed the hair from her face, straining to see if her chest moved.

"Eddie," Elizabeth gasped. "Can't--catch--"

Edward scooped Elizabeth up, regretting having to move her when she whimpered, but they couldn't remain in the open while the battle was still raging. He took her down to where the horses still drank, most oblivious to the fighting going on around them since they were battle-tested warhorses. He pressed in between his horse and Elizabeth's, prepared to mount if need be but using the massive bodies to shelter them out of sight. It was clear from the three men who were determined to harm Elizabeth that this attack was intended to capture or kill her. While he longed to slay each and every man who was a part of this ambush, and he felt guilty for not leading the fight, he wouldn't risk leaving Elizabeth alone. He'd done that once, and the consequences proved to be dire.

Elizabeth squeezed her eyes shut as Edward carried her away from the nightmare. She sensed the horses moving around her and understood that her husband was hiding them while also preparing to flee with her if need be. She feared falling and her eyes snapped open as Edward crouched low with her still in his arms. She felt the solid muscles of his legs beneath her backside and could feel his pounding and racing heartbeat. Despite its rapid pace, she found it reassuring as she burrowed into his chest and hid her face against his shoulder. She forced herself to take deep breaths to calm her lungs and heart. When she was sure she'd gotten enough air to keep from passing out, she looked around. It was difficult to see much, but she glanced under the horses' legs and could see the feet of the men fighting. She watched as the dance between opponents slowed before a whistle rang through the air.

Edward had never been so grateful to hear the whistle that signaled the end of battle. He rose to his feet, feeling shaken not only from resting on his haunches while holding Elizabeth but also from the all-consuming fear. He'd ridden into enough battles to have a healthy respect for the unavoidable fear that his life might end that day, but he'd always overcome it and faced battle without reservation. This had been unlike anything he'd ever experienced. Fear overwhelmed him as he tried to protect his bride, unwilling to lose the one person who meant more to him than his own life.

Elizabeth tapped Edward's chest until he looked down at her. He saw her mouth moving, but the ringing in his ears from his pounding heart blocked out the sound. He read her lips saying he should put her down, and she even pointed to the ground, but he shook his head, refusing to release her until he saw for sure that the battle was over. He nudged his horse aside and scanned the surrounding area. He only saw his men still on their feet, the enemy all dead or on the brink. He watched his men circulate among the fallen, looking for their own men who could be saved and finishing off those enemies who had not yet met their maker. Slowly, Edward lowered Elizabeth to her feet, steadying her until he was certain her legs wouldn't give out. Elizabeth slid her arms around Edward's waist and pulled him to her with a strength that surprised him. They clung to one another, their foreheads pressed together as they both tried to calm, but it was only a moment later that their mouths crushed against each other. The kiss was desperate as they both sought to reassure themselves that the other was alive and well. Edward kissed her temple and cheekbone as she kissed his throat.

"My lord?" One of the men approached, and Elizabeth buried her face against Edward's chest, both embarrassed that they'd been caught but also because she was unready to let him go, even knowing he had duties that he could no longer ignore. "Angus, the king's captain is dead and at least ten others along with him. Most of the men have injuries, but none serious enough to keep them from riding the rest of the way and guarding our lady."

Elizabeth hadn't heard anyone call her "our lady" since she was a young child still living on Fraser land. At court, there was no one other than her immediate family that was part of the Fraser clan, at least not ones that she saw or spoke to. She knew her father had his own guards, but they rarely saw her. It warmed her to know that these men were loyal to her and considered her to be one of them. She drew in a breath and pressed her shoulders back as she turned to face the warrior.

"Show me which men are in the direst need of stitching and have someone fetch me my satchel and a bottle of whisky." When the man raised his eyebrows, she chuckled. "There is more than enough whisky to spare. I know someone has brought some. We're Scots after all."

Elizabeth turned toward Edward and warmed to

her toes with the look of pride that shone in his eyes. She squeezed his hand and kissed his cheek.

"I love you," she whispered.

"And I love you, little one. You're braver than most men I know. You'll make an excellent lady of the keep wherever we finally wind up."

They separated as the warrior led Elizabeth to where several men sat, their clothes clearly bloody. Edward spoke with his men about what they saw as the ambush began, along with making plans for the men who perished. They were forced to remain in the clearing for longer than it had taken to ride from Stirling.

CHAPTER FOURTEEN

It was nearing dusk when the much smaller entourage rode through the gates of Culcreuch Castle. Elizabeth was filthy and exhausted but grateful that Edward insisted she rode with him the remaining part of the journey. Edward was certain that another attack wouldn't come that day nor that close to the keep, so he risked not being able to wield his sword for the assurance that Elizabeth wouldn't collapse off her horse. He also needed the reassurance of her in his arms. He feared it would be sennights before he'd allow her beyond his reach. Edward swung down from his saddle before reaching for Elizabeth who toppled more than leaned into his grasp.

"You're exhausted and must be starving. Which do you want first: food or rest?" Edward murmured as an older man with thinning hair approached. The couple recognized that he must be the seneschal of the castle as he hurried to greet them.

"Neither. I want a bath or a dunk in the loch at this point," Elizabeth whispered.

"My laird, my lady. We're relieved you've arrived. We feared the worst as the day grew late." The seneschal looked beyond the couple, his eyes

141

widening as he took in the bedraggled group, the injured in particular.

"Someone attacked us aboot half an hour from here. My men need attending, and my lady wife is in need of a bath. And who are you?" Edward's clipped tone matched his expression as he surveyed the bailey then the wall walk, determining the castle's defenses before being willing to allow Elizabeth to enter the keep.

"My apologies, my laird. I am Iain, the seneschal here. Welcome to Culcreuch." The man bowed to Edward and Elizabeth. "My lady, if you'll follow me, I've arranged baths be sent to your chambers. My lord, if you care to retire to yours, I'm happy to lead the way."

Edward towered over the man, and he was sure he intimidated him. He didn't experience a moment's remorse. The day's events made him skeptical of everyone at the castle. It was impossible to be certain who arranged for the attack. While he doubted it was Galbraith, with the man's loyalty to his brother, it was impossible to be sure there weren't spies here who'd be glad to pass along information to this faceless enemy.

"Our chamber." Edward glanced down at the man as he continued to observe the guards moving about the battlements.

"My pardon?" Iain stumbled.

"Our chamber, Steward. There is no "laird's" and "lady's" chambers. There is "our" chamber."

The steward trembled at this point and flushed red, the color spreading even to his balding pate.

"As you wish, my laird. Please follow me, if you will." Iain turned away and crossed the bailey to the steps leading into the keep, looking back to check over his shoulder.

Elizabeth felt for the man, but she understood

Edward was establishing himself in charge of the keep for the foreseeable future. It wasn't so much for Iain's sake as it was the men from the garrison who came out of the barracks and milled to observe their new leader. Elizabeth looked up when Edward wrapped his arm around her shoulders and pressed her against his side.

At first, she thought he was being possessive, but when she caught his expression, she noticed the fatigue and worry etched in the lines that now creased his forehead and around his mouth. He was ensuring she made it the distance to their chamber. He was trying to take care of her. Elizabeth understood Edward suffered tremendous guilt that the attack even happened let alone when his breeches were down, and he'd just told her it was safe to walk in the clearing alone. She rested her head against his shoulder until they entered the keep, the Great Hall sprawling before them.

It was one of the largest great halls she'd seen despite going on procession with the royal court and visiting many castles. She looked about and observed banners and tapestries hanging from the walls. They needed airing out and beating with a wooden stick. Elizabeth glanced next at the large hearths that were blazing to keep the winter chill at bay. She strained to look beneath the grate in which the logs rested. She caught sight of the mountain of soot in both. She looked around, noticing small things like sconces that needed the melted wax removed. The servants already pulled out the tables and benches for the evening meal, and it relieved her to notice they were clean and almost gleaming. The rushes on the floor smelled fresh. She noted someone efficiently oversaw the day to day running of the keep but maintaining it sorely needed attention.

An older woman bustled in from what Elizabeth

assumed were the kitchens. The woman was short and round with rosy cheeks and dimples. She greeted them with a smile while Iain continued to slash glances between Edward and Elizabeth, not at all sure what they would expect of him next.

"My laird, my lady." The older woman bobbed in a surprisingly low curtsey for how old Elizabeth estimated her to be. "I'm Margaret, but everyone calls me Maggie. I'm the housekeeper here. My lady, forgive me, but you look like you need a bath, a meal, and a snug bed. All in that order. Please follow me."

Maggie reached out an arm as though she was prepared to take Edward's place while escorting Elizabeth above stairs. She'd follow the housekeeper without qualms if it meant she received those three promised comforts, but Edward wouldn't release her, instead walking with Elizabeth as they followed Maggie.

"Newlyweds, are you? That's what we heard. My laird, it is nice to see you tending to your wee wife. She looks ready to keel over. Guards announced your approach, saying many of the men looked the worse for wear. I figured you might be, too. A bath is awaiting you with the fire stoked. I've sent up a platter of food in case you aren't in the mood to return belowstairs for the evening meal. And there should be warm bricks already under the covers."

Maggie prattled on as she led the way to the third floor, explaining that the family chambers were well above the ground floor to protect the family in case of an attack. It would give the laird's family more time to hide or escape if attackers had to climb more stairs. She rubbed her knee once they reached the landing. Elizabeth peeked up at Edward worried the woman's ramblings would annoy him, but he grinned for the first time that day, and Elizabeth's belly tightened at how hand-

144

some he was. They passed through a large doorway and entered a bedchamber that must have occupied at least a third of the floor. Elizabeth's eyes widened as she caught sight of the bed pushed against the wall but tucked far into the chamber away from the door and the windows. It could fit four of Edward in it.

"Don't lose me in that," she whispered.

"I'd have to let you go to do that," he slid his hand down her back and pinched her backside.

"Keep that up, and they'll be changing the sheets because I won't be able to wait till after my bath."

"Our bath, I promise there'll be little waiting once Maggie leaves."

Maggie watched the couple with a knowing smile before she moved toward the door.

"I'll send up a maid to assist you, my lady. Everything you should need is near the tub. I'll send up your satchel and other belongings to you later. In the meantime, I'm certain Lady Galbraith wouldn't object to you borrowing one of her robes and nightgowns."

"There's no need to send anyone else. I will tend to my wife." Edward removed his sword and rested it against the chair closest to the tub.

"Well then, I shall leave you to it." Maggie opened the door but looked back at the young couple. "You remind me of my Iain. Still just as lusty as the day we wed. Aye, the seneschal is my husband," she added at the end when the couple looked surprised. Neither would have guessed that they were wed, nor that anyone would ever describe Iain as insatiable.

Once Maggie closed the door behind her, Edward and Elizabeth melted into each other, hands roaming everywhere as their mouths fused together. Edward pulled pins from Elizabeth's hair not caring where they landed. He began tugging at the laces to her gown but growled when they knotted.

"How many kirtles did you pack with you?"

"Two others but I need to hang them up to let the wrinkles drop out."

Edward spun Elizabeth around and severed the laces with his dirk. She gasped as the weight of the gown slipped off her shoulders. Elizabeth peered back at him in time to watch him return the knife to its sheath. She wiggled her arms out of the sleeves and pushed the kirtle to the floor.

"One step ahead of you now, husband. Do catch up." Elizabeth offered him what she hoped was a saucy grin, and by the way he ripped the length of plaid and his tunic over his head, she knew he was as impatient as she was. Normally, he would've unfastened the plaid first. He pushed his leggings down his trim hips as he watched Elizabeth push her own woolen stockings down before tugging to get her boots off. He hopped about as he yanked his off, earning him a giggle from Elizabeth. It was only a matter of moments before they stood naked. Edward pulled her into his embrace and lifted her, guiding her legs around his waist, impaling her with his hardened cock. He walked them to the wall next to the tub before pressing her back to it. Edward thrust over and over, reveling in Elizabeth's moans as she squeezed his rod in response to his grunts. He couldn't slow himself. The need to be a part of Elizabeth, to feel how alive and safe she was, and to claim her in a way that no one could ever take away possessed him.

"I'm so close, yet I don't want it to end. I want you harder, and yet I want it slower. I just want you, Eddie." Elizabeth scored her nails against his scalp as her fingers tangled in his hair, her other arm gripped around his shoulders. Edward's teeth grazed the pulse point in her neck over and over until finally he latched his lips around her collarbone, intending to leave a love bite. Elizabeth's clothes might hide it, but he would know that it was there, marking her as his. Elizabeth's head fell to his shoulder as she repeated his action, drawing extra hard to ensure the mark would last several days.

"Mine," they gasped together as neither withstood the need for release any longer.

As their bodies stilled, Edward's kisses were like butterfly wings brushing against the skin behind her ear. Her fingers now stroked the hair away from his face. When he was certain his legs would hold him long enough to step into the tub, he lowered them into the hot water. They both sighed as the heat and steam soaked into their sore bodies. Elizabeth rested her head against his shoulder, and in turn, Edward rested his cheek against the crown of her head. They both remained silent and motionless as they welcomed the relief that flowed through them after the terror they both experienced. It was in silent agreement that they didn't bring up the day's events. They knew the matter would be there the next day. Elizabeth ran her fingers over the deep division between the muscles in Edward's chest before brushing them up onto the ridge on the right side of his chest. Her fingers trailed along until they reached his nipple which she circled with the pad of her finger. She drew the path over and over as Edward stroked her back, his hands moving in opposite directions as they slid from her shoulders to her rounded bottom. She felt him stir within her, her weight on him having kept them joined.

"Need you," Edward whispered.

"Me, too."

This time their movements were slow, conscious about not splashing water over the side as they enjoyed the erotic feel of the water lapping around them and the smooth glide of Elizabeth's sheath over Edward's sword. As sensation drove Elizabeth to rock more, she arched her back, letting her head fall back. The position thrust her breasts forward in offering to Edward. He latched on like a starving babe, but the way his tongue swirled and flicked her nipple proved he was all man. A man who hungered for his wife as one hand gripped the breast he suckled while the other bit into the soft flesh of her buttocks. Elizabeth held his shoulders as she moved her hips. Edward didn't try to control anything about this joining, letting Elizabeth bask in all the pleasure she garnered from their lovemaking. It was only when his body no longer obeyed his best intentions that both hands gripped her hips as he thrust upwards.

"Yes. It was good before, but this is what I want."

Elizabeth's words snapped the little self-restraint Edward had, pressing her down to grind her nub against his pelvis as he surged upward over and over.

"Beth!" Edward bellowed as his seed burst forth.

Elizabeth continued to rock against him until only moments later her moans filled the chamber and she was screaming his name. She collapsed against him, her entire body trembling from the exertion and excitement. Edward wrapped his massive arms around her, a shield to the cool air and the rest of the world.

"What I wouldn't give for this water to remain hot long enough for me to nap here with you, just like this."

"Mmm," Edward kissed her hairline. "How I wish my body could remain just as we are, or at least until we are both asleep."

They remained clasped in each other's embrace until neither could ignore the need to hurry through their cleansing as the water chilled. After Edward finished pouring the clean water over Elizabeth's hair, unable to withstand the temptation not to nip at her breasts as she leaned back, he helped her to her feet. He snatched a drying linen off the stand where it hung before the fire. He wrapped Elizabeth in it and lifted her out of the tub before grabbing a linen for himself. While she huddled within hers shivering, he wrapped his around his hips and reached out to rub her shoulders and back. Elizabeth wrapped another drying linen around her hair before picking up the robe that was also warming before the fire.

"Maggie and her maids thought of everything," Elizabeth mumbled around the bite of cheese she pilfered from the platter. "As tired as I am and as much as I want to climb into bed and fall asleep against you, I'm ravenous."

They munched on a wheel of cheese, a small loaf of bread, and several different dried fruits, taking turns feeding one another. When a knock came on the door and a maid entered with her satchel, Elizabeth knew she had the excuse she needed. Still famished even after their meal, she pulled a kirtle out and snapped it, hoping to release a few creases. Now that she had clothes, she had little excuse not to return belowstairs for the meal.

"We should put in an appearance, Eddie. It seems wrong to arrive and then hide away. At least you should go down." Elizabeth knew there was no way Edward would leave her alone in this chamber so soon after their arrival, so she'd have to join him.

"There's no need to maneuver me. I know you have a healthy appetite after making love. I spent four days in a love nest with you, remember? We'll go down for the evening meal. I can't have my wee wife wasting away without sustenance. What would I do if you didn't have the energy to wake me throughout the night to satisfy your lusty needs?" Edward darted away as Elizabeth playfully reached out to smack his backside. Both appreciated their ability to jest after everything that transpired. They floated into one another's arms, grinning knowing that it was just as often Elizabeth who initiated their nocturnal couplings as it was Edward.

"Are you in need of more beauty sleep, Eddie? Should I let you rest if my needs are so taxing?"

"Not on your life." Edward tickled her, enjoying her laughter and the way her body squirmed against his. He could feel himself hardening, and Elizabeth must have too because she froze, hunger of a different kind gleaming in her eyes.

"We have enough time, don't we?" Elizabeth questioned.

"Aye."

Elizabeth turned and walked to the foot of the bed, already pulling her skirts to her waist. Edward assisted her after his leggings fell out of the way. She leaned forward as she pressed her hips backward. Their coupling was fast and hard as Edward reached around her, stimulating her bud until she was thrusting her hips against Edward just as hard as he thrust into her.

CHAPTER FIFTEEN

They arrived at the evening meal just as it was being served, their cheeks still flushed. They burned brighter from the knowing looks cast in their direction. Elizabeth smiled throughout the meal, but was glad that they placed course after course in front of her. Edward was discreet in serving the larger portion on his side of the trencher before sliding it to Elizabeth's.

"They'll still catch me guzzling away. I'll be larger than the side of the stable if I keep letting you push more food in front of me."

"You don't eat like this often."

Elizabeth tried to swallow a snort as she looked at her husband. "I eat like this after we make love, and since we do that morning, noon, and night, I eat like this at every meal. I don't get this hungry even after a long ride on Reubadair."

"Are you comparing me to your horse?" Edward teased.

"You're both fine stallions that I can ride for hours."

Edward's chuckle flowed from their seats, making many at the tables below look up at the grinning laird who only had eyes for his wife.

"I suppose I shall take that as the finest of compliments, since you hold your horse in the highest esteem." Edward shook off a droplet of sauce from the piece of goose he grasped. He raised it to Elizabeth's mouth, and she leaned forward to take it, sucking the juices from his fingers. She was quick so as not to draw attention, but a few raunchy comments floated up to them. Elizabeth shrank back into her seat.

"That's not the first impression I want to make."

"That the laird and lady love each other? That bodes better for the people here than a couple who can't stand the sight of one another. A happy laird and lady make for a happy clan, and while we reside here, it's our influence that will affect the way they live."

"I agree, but they need not watch me acting like a tavern wench at the first meal we attend."

Edward only grinned and waggled his eyebrows, earning him a hand beneath the table that cupped his rod. He choked on the bite of his food, unprepared for Elizabeth to take up his challenge.

"Do that again, and we will make a scene when I toss you over my shoulder and carry you abovestairs before they serve dessert."

"Does that mean you intend to do that after dessert?" Elizabeth offered her most innocent look of astonishment.

"Play with fire, little one, and I will singe you." Edward offered her another bite. Elizabeth angled her head to hide how she curled her tongue around his fingers before licking them.

"I am but tinder to your spark."

They grew quiet for the rest of the meal, both too eager to leave to continue teasing one another. When the music began, and the diners pushed the tables to the side for dancing, the couple attempted to make their escape, but the clan cheered for them to join the dancing. Unable to refuse without displaying poor manners, Edward swung Elizabeth into a country reel. They attempted to do their duty by being gracious with each person they partnered, but neither relished seeing the other dancing with someone else. When the reel ended, and a song began that would allow them to remain together, Edward reached for Elizabeth, but a young man slid in front of him and asked for Elizabeth's hand. She politely refused, saying she'd saved this dance for Edward. She shrank back when anger flashed in his eyes, and pain raced through her hand and arm as he squeezed her hand and wouldn't let go when she attempted to pull away. A warning growl from over the young man's shoulder forced him to release Elizabeth, lest Edward shove him out of the way. His glare was menacing as Edward looked at the younger man. It was clear the man who approached Elizabeth was a warrior, but he looked like a young boy compared to Edward's size and chiseled, battle-hewn good looks. Edward crossed his arms as he stood between Elizabeth and the interloper.

"My wife declined," Edward hissed low enough for few people to hear, but his stance was drawing attention.

"I didn't hear her," the man spoke without fear.

"Do not lie, *boy*. I saw her shake her head, and I heard her. If you are that hard of hearing, you shouldn't serve as a warrior. A field of turnips might be a better calling." Edward glared at the other man but did nothing more. "What's your name?"

"Mitchell."

"Is that your Christian name or your clan?" Edward demanded.

"Christian name," Mitchell was growing surly and refused to answer more than he had to.

Elizabeth watched as the young man dug himself

'deeper and deeper. No one at the keep was unaware of Edward's authority as the Earl of Badenoch and Lochaber and the current laird in residence. At this point, the matter was no longer about Mitchell insisting upon a dance or even grasping Elizabeth's hand for too long. It was about his outward defiance to Edward.

"You are foolish, not brave," Elizabeth muttered. She moved to return to the dais, but Mitchell spun around and blocked her path.

"And you are little more than a whore," he mouthed. Elizabeth understood what he said, as did others who stood nearby. Elizabeth's small hand gripped his throat, her fingers pressing against points that made him splutter. She didn't have the strength Edward had, but her hand was the right size to still immobilize Mitchell.

"Say it aloud if you're that brave," Elizabeth challenged him.

Edward was livid. He didn't know what Mitchell whispered to Elizabeth, but he'd never seen her react like this. Only the attack earlier had shown she was willing and able to kill to protect herself. Even the time he noticed her carry a knife in Stirling, it had been to ward off an attack, not engage in one. He grabbed a fistful of Mitchell's leine and tugged him backward, out of Elizabeth's reach but into his. He shook the younger man hard enough to make Mitchell's teeth click together.

"Repeat what you said," Edward demanded.

"I didn't say aught," Mitchell sneered.

Elizabeth stepped forward, but Iain slipped in front of her. He leaned toward Edward but out of Mitchell's reach. He lowered his voice to keep everyone in the clan from knowing what a few people saw. "He called the lady a whore."

Elizabeth was sure the young man would die that

154

night. Edward's face drew into an expression Elizabeth was sure terrified more than one man into wetting himself on the battlefield. A muscle ticked in his jaw as he clenched his teeth, and Elizabeth glimpsed a vein pulse in his neck. She didn't fear him, but feared for the brash young man who would've seen his life flash before his eyes if he wasn't so arrogant. Elizabeth prayed for the sake of the clan and their stay at Culcreuch that Edward didn't kill Mitchell.

"Who claims this whelp as their son?" Edward's voice rang out. There was silence in the crowd as they collectively held their breath. "Orphan?"

Edward looked down at Iain, who was shaking his head. The young man had parents somewhere.

"Where are they?" Edward shook him again.

"We are here, my laird." A man pushed through the crowd with a cowering woman at his side.

Edward released Mitchell with a shove toward his parents. He glared at the father before softening his gaze, only slightly, when he looked at the mother.

"Your son is no longer allowed in the keep, not even within the walls. If I lay eyes on him again before I leave Culcreuch, I will challenge him. There is no chance he will win. Thank God for his life, the little it's worth."

The older couple pulled Mitchell through the crowd, swallowed by the buzzing of whispers as the gossip began.

"Let me clear," Edward's voice boomed over the din, and the people fell quiet. "No one speaks ill of my wife without facing my wrath. Laird Galbraith is still your chieftain; I have no intention of taking over your clan. Lady Elizabeth and I are here for an extended visit, but we are not interested in usurping anyone's position. That said, if this is the behavior of your warriors, this dishonor and arrogance, then you should fear for your future. But I believe Mitchell doesn't reflect your clan. So far, Lady Elizabeth and I have only seen kindness and hospitality. We appreciate this warm welcome of a veritable feast. Let not the whisky and ale go to waste nor the musicians grow old."

Edward signaled to the musicians to play again and he reached out his hand to Elizabeth, who gladly followed his lead as they launched into the dance they were meant to have. The couple remained belowstairs far longer than they would have liked, but they wanted to ensure the clan recognized they held no ill will to them. Edward sensed the wheels turning in Elizabeth's mind, and he, too, wondered if Mitchell might have been a spy sent to test them. Or perhaps he might be a future danger if he became attached to whoever wanted to harm Elizabeth.

When Elizabeth stumbled twice while dancing and leaned more against Edward, he knew she'd reached her limits, even if she was too proud to admit it. He led her through the twirling crowd toward the stairs. Maggie and Iain met them there.

"We apologize for this evening's dust up." Iain humbled himself. "Mitchell has always been a hothead, and it will see him in Hell one of these days."

"Aye. His poor mother is beside herself with how he turned out. Neither she nor her husband are aught like the lad. They're honorable people, good parents to their other children, but the lad has always been trouble." Maggie shook her head as she looked wistfully toward the keep's main doors. "You did right to banish him from within the walls. I've never trusted him, and I doubt most people would tolerate him after the way he acted. He's safer away from those who caught what he said. More than one mon was ready to defend our lady."

"Thank you, Maggie." Elizabeth's heart was ready to burst at the warmth in the woman's eyes.

Once more, she felt welcomed when another person referred to her as "our lady." She remembered she and Edward wouldn't make their permanent home here, but it still felt wonderful.

"Please have a tray sent up for Lady Elizabeth in the morning." Edward looked down into Elizabeth's emerald eyes and smiled. "My hope is that my wife will sleep in and recuperate from today's ordeals."

"Yes, my laird. My lady, we have moved your chest to your chamber. You should have all that you need. If you leave out the kirtle you'd like to wear, I'll be sure it's brought to me when the maid delivers your tray. I'll have it ready for you when you rise." Maggie dipped into a curtsey before she and Iain shuffled away.

"What's wrong, little one?" Edward felt Elizabeth pull away as they made their way up the stairs.

"You said the tray is for me. Where will you be? I thought we were sharing a chamber." Though spoken softly, Edward still heard the strain in her voice.

"You fear I'll sleep somewhere else, with someone else." Edward commented rather than asked. "Beth, I'm spending the night exactly where I want to be, and that's tucked under the covers next to you. I simply anticipate waking before you, and I want to investigate the castle's defenses before you wander around on your own."

"Do you realize how I would have panicked if I woke alone and you hadn't forewarned me by asking for the tray? I would have feared something happened to you. That somehow someone had taken you." Elizabeth tried to keep the tremor from her voice but was certain she failed.

"You'd fear for me if you awoke alone? You wouldn't fear I abandoned you?" Edward saw the flash in his wife's eyes and knew that she'd fear for him, but she'd also fear that he abandoned her. She'd said as much when she questioned whether they were sharing a chamber. "Beth, I'll never be slipping off to meet another woman. There will never be another woman. I'm not your father or any of the other men at court. You must know that. That's why I want to return to the Highlands."

"I know, but it's hard. From what I understand, my father didn't set out to be unfaithful to my mother. From what I've learned, they were quite close when they first married, but drifted apart. Then they both took lovers." Elizabeth shrugged.

They arrived at their door, and Edward pushed it open, entering first as he swept the chamber looking for anything out of place or any intruders. Edward led Elizabeth over to the cushioned chairs and pulled her into his lap. He held her as she curled into his warmth. He understood her fears stemmed from being overwhelmed by everything that happened that day. He held his own fears that if they returned to court or if Robert sent him off to battle, Elizabeth might grow tired of waiting for him and find her own lover. Edward didn't believe she was that type of woman, but he understood what separation and politics could do to even the most loving marriage.

"What if it's you?" He muttered against her hair.

"Me what? She leaned back.

"What if you're the one to find someone else?"

Elizabeth's eyes opened into saucers as her mouth gaped. She snapped it shut, but her eyes remained wide.

"You think I'd be unfaithful to you?"

"You seem to believe it's possible for me to wander. Why shouldn't I fear the same?"

"You fear that?"

"Aye," Edward looked away, but not before Elizabeth glimpsed raw pain.

"Eddie, I will never leave you. Not for another mon, not for another home, not for aught. I'm not your mother," she whispered the last two words. "And I'm not Sinead."

Edward's head whipped back around. "What's that supposed to mean?"

"I know your mother left you behind when she retired to the convent. It's why Robert's family adopted you. And I doubted Sinead was faithful to you, and I suspected that is why you weren't faithful to her when you returned to court. You've said as much. I heard aboot her temper before you told me aboot it, but I'm also acquainted with many of the ladies you've bedded."

"Beth, you are too close to the truth. Leave off." Edward shook his head, and Elizabeth gazed into the fire after the abrupt end to their conversation.

Edward regretted snapping at her and realized they were still getting to know one another. Her past might have been a clean slate, but his was murky and sullied.

"I'm sorry, Beth. I shouldn't shut you out like that. Yes, it is still painful all these years later that my mother's life shattered so much after my father's death that she gave up on raising me. And I did consider at one time that Sinead might be a more permanent part of my life as my mistress, but I learned I was wrong by walking in on her when I returned from scouting a day early. We came to an agreement, and we abided by it for quite some time. When we were apart, we were free to do as we pleased, but when we were together, we were exclusive. Her temper and jealousy grew when I had to travel between Scotland and Ireland more often. She became possessive but refused to give up her own liaisons, claiming that they were all to help the cause and allowed her to gather more information. When I broke

159

things off for good and returned to Scotland, I intended to bed a few women and then retire to the Highlands."

Elizabeth was uncertain she wanted to learn all of this now that Edward began explaining. Hearing him speak so casually about bedding other women made her feel worse rather than better.

"I even considered seducing you when I first noticed you in the chapel, but by the time we spoke for the first time and Robert stopped me, I was certain I wanted so much more with you. Or at least I wanted the chance to discover if there could be something more. I realized that I didn't want another mistress or even a few conquests. I wanted something real and lasting. With you. I'd never imagined that before. Even with Sinead, I assumed she might remain my mistress indefinitely, but I never considered making a home with her or having bairns. Thoughts of those two things fill my head whenever I think of you. I don't want to accept it's possible that our love might fade. I'll do all that I can for the rest of my life to ensure it doesn't."

Elizabeth cupped his jaw in her hands and placed a soft kiss on his parted lips. She didn't press for anything more, and neither did Edward. The simplicity and gentleness spoke of love rather than lust.

"I admit to jealousy, knowing you've been with women I know and seeing women fawn over you. I don't like it, but I have faith that you would never betray me. It's just hard to remember that when other thoughts crowd into my head."

"I can understand that. I'm often jealous, too. I despised watching the way men at court salivated over you, following you with their eyes. More than once I feared you were already involved with another mon. When I heard you with Reubadair the first time, I was livid. When you rode off alone and went

160

traipsing through town on your own, I was irate. But Beth, I want no one but you. Naught could ever be better than what I have with you. Why would I stray when naught and no one will live up to you?"

Elizabeth took a deep breath before a long sigh seemed to cleanse her heart of her fears, at least the fears of Edward's unfaithfulness. It didn't change the fact that what she'd said earlier was also true.

"I still would have panicked. I would have feared something happened to you. I've woken next to you every morning since we wed, and even before that while we were at the inn and in the cottage. It would have been a shock to roll over to cold sheets."

"Would it be better if I always kiss you goodbye before I leave our bed?"

"I suppose. I'm not a late sleeper normally. I have developed bad habits since getting married. I have a husband who spoils me." Elizabeth gave Edward's jaw a peck. "I suspect I will rise just as early as you most mornings once we settle into a routine. I may not be the lady of the keep, but I can still help. I suppose you'll go to the lists each morning. I just don't like the fear that overwhelms me when you're in danger."

"When have you ever seen me in danger? I've had to watch you in danger time and again. Today will never leave me."

Elizabeth looked at him as though he'd lost his mind. Once more her mouth was agape; all she did for a moment was shake her head.

"Of course, I've seen you in danger. Why do you think I was trying to run back to you today? You had your breeks around your ankles while men were trying to kill us."

Edward's mouth tightened into a flat line. She insulted him even though he realized she didn't intend offense.

"I wasn't helpless. You intended to defend me with your dirks when I had a sword I've spent my life training with? And my breeks were not at my ankles. I'd barely unlaced them."

"I didn't mean to imply you can't defend yourself, but I saw you looking defenseless," Elizabeth grimaced as the word slid past her lips, knowing she was tripping over her own words. "It terrified me an attacker would creep up on you. I was positive I had to get to you."

"That's why you didn't run, even though I was shouting for you to go."

"I don't think I even heard you. My focus was on getting past those first two horsemen. I lost sight of you as the third one rode up. Before I realized what was happening, he lifted me off my feet. I watched you running with your sword raised like a lance. I jerked away to make sure you didn't spear me with your sword, and the mon flung me backwards as you buried it in him. I hit the horse's flank and was certain the animal would trample me. It was impossible for me to tell where you were or whether you lived. I just waited for the inevitable pressure of the horse's hoof, but it never came. The next thing I knew, you were kneeling over me then picking me up."

"Mo ghaisgeach beag." My wee warrior. Edward stroked the hair back from her face as he looked into her sparkling green eyes. The firelight flickered, and the reflection made it appear as though she had diamonds twinkling on a bed of emeralds. They were mesmerizing. "I love that you want to protect me, but I was certain my life was ending as I watched you take on those two men. When the third one grabbed you, I wasn't able to consider aught but him and getting to you, so he couldn't take you. I love you more than aught, little one. I can't imagine living without you."

162

"And you don't realize I'm the same way? I would sell my soul to the Devil if I was certain it would keep you safe."

"We're quite the pair, aren't we?" Edward smiled, his teeth flashing, making him look boyish. Elizabeth's breath hitched as she looked at her handsome husband. She hadn't seen him offer this smile to anyone else. It was special to realize she was the fortunate recipient of something rare.

"We are. And I wouldn't have it any other way." Elizabeth leaned forward for another soft kiss.

"As long as you don't take unnecessary risks, I won't stop you from riding like a daredevil. But if we're ever in that situation again, you must run, Beth. Just run. Trust that I will get to you, but I can't protect you if you get yourself killed."

It wasn't long before they climbed into bed, stripped to their skin, Edward sinking into Elizabeth. They went slowly, taking their time to heighten and lengthen their pleasure. When exhaustion refused to release its hold on them, they collapsed into a deep sleep.

CHAPTER SIXTEEN

E lizabeth woke as the sun peeked into the chamber, and she found herself wrapped in the embrace of muscular arms, her back pressed against the searing heat of her husband's chest.

"You're still here?" Elizabeth's voice rasped as she rolled toward Edward. Her husband's fingers skimmed over the bare skin of her back.

"Mmm. It seems fatigue claimed me, too. I didn't intend to sleep this late, but I suppose I was too comfortable to notice the sun rising." Their lips brushed against one another. "Good morning, little one."

Edward rolled Elizabeth on her back and was pressing her legs apart when a knock on the door preceded someone pushing it open. Elizabeth scrambled to pull the covers up while Edward grumbled something that sounded like *get out*. A young maid entered but stumbled when she saw Edward sitting up in bed, the sheet pulled across his chest. It was Elizabeth's turn to grumble, but Edward had a lock of her hair wrapped around his finger. He leaned in to whisper in her ear.

"She'll disappear in a moment. Then we can work up the appetite needed to clear that tray."

"My lady, Maggie said I am to gather your gown to have it brushed out and prepared for the day."

Elizabeth groaned. She'd forgotten about that. She had no intention of letting a maid rummage through her chest, but she needed to have a gown readied. Elizabeth pulled the robe from the foot of the bed and shimmied into it while trying to protect her modesty. She looked up and realized she need not have worried. The maid was too busy staring at Edward, who in turn, was watching Elizabeth. She slipped from the bed and moved about the chamber gathering a fresh chemise, tunic, and over kirtle. The keep was draughty, and she knew she needed more layers. As she moved around, gathering what she needed, she watched the maid who gawked at Edward. The young woman gave up trying to gain his attention, but she did little to hide her interest. Elizabeth handed the garments over, but didn't let go.

"Aye, we all know my husband is a handsome mon, but do more than gawk, and you will find yourself scrubbing chamber pots until we leave."

The maid's eyes widened as she bobbed a curtsy and practically ran from the chamber. Edward's laughter only got louder as Elizabeth harrumphed before climbing back into bed. He pulled Elizabeth beside him before once more rolling her onto her back. This time he didn't pause before surging into her.

"I find I rather like my wife to be possessive of me." Edward grinned.

"I'm no worse than you are." Elizabeth would have said more, but her mind blanked as the sensations coursing through her took priority.

"I had five brothers to share with growing up and never did like it. Now, I want what is mine to be mine alone."

"I didn't have any sisters to share with, so I never learned how."

Edward's groan rumbled in his chest, and Elizabeth found she no longer wanted to talk. The way they moved proved without a doubt they belonged to one another.

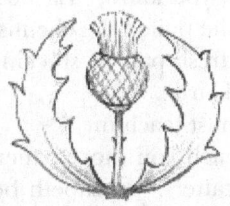

After they devoured the food and completed their morning ablutions, Edward insisted that since he'd already remained in the chamber this late into the morning, he could wait until Elizabeth was dressed and able to go belowstairs with him. Maggie returned with Elizabeth's gown, tsking about how the couple was taking years off her life with how they frightened everyone, but she beamed a wide smile, nonetheless.

"Just like me and my Iain," Maggie chortled before growing serious. "My lady, here is your gown. If there is aught you need please don't hesitate to let me know. I'll be in the kitchens with Bethea, the cook, planning the week's menu if you'd be willing to assist."

"I doubt either of you need my help," Elizabeth shook her head.

"Mayhap, but we'd like it, anyway."

"I'll be down just as soon as I'm dressed."

"And I'm supposing you're not in need of a maid again."

"That's correct," Edward cut in. "I'm the best lady's maid my wife can find."

Maggie walked to the door muttering, "It's a mite trickier getting her into the gown than getting her out." But she was gone before either Edward or Elizabeth could say anything about her comments.

"She is right, you know," Elizabeth grinned over her shoulder as she pulled the chemise over her head. She pulled on a fresh pair of stockings, then reached for her tunic and kirtle.

"Then you must teach me."

"I need to teach you more patience or all of my laces will be in tatters." Elizabeth bent to pick up a piece of ribbon from the gown she wore the day before. Edward couldn't resist tapping his wife on her backside. "Have you always been so playful? Were you the most easygoing of the six of you?"

"Not nearly. Edward was actually the one who rarely let aught faze him, and he always had some joke or off-hand comment aboot everything. Thomas was the troublemaker, but had a knack for making sure he was never in trouble. Niall and Alexander just wanted to be included. I was more observant and withdrawn, while Robert was pensive."

"Then why now? I would think after what you've seen and had to do in battle, you would be even more serious."

"I am with everyone but you."

Elizabeth's heart once more fluttered when Edward directed his boyish grin at her.

"Do you smile like that for anyone else?"

"Like what?" Edward tilted his head as he considered Elizabeth's question. The warmth of Elizabeth's presence did wonders for his soul, soothing the anguish that had taken root after so many years of fighting. He realized he was genuinely happy when he was with her. "I suppose not."

"You seem relaxed and younger when you grin."

"I have you to thank for that. No one else makes me want to smile like this, and I hardly ever consider myself feeling young. Boyhood seems like many lifetimes ago."

"I like this side of you. I like how happy you seem and that I'm the only one you gift with that smile. Remember I like a good secret; after all, I did spend years creeping through those passages."

"Don't remind me. I still can't believe you memorized your entire way around Stirling Castle without seeing the light of day. Makes my head and chest hurt."

"Now you sound like my gram." Elizabeth giggled as she dashed through the door Edward held open for her.

Elizabeth joined Maggie and Bethea in the kitchens while Edward made his way around the battlements before joining the men in the lists. He spent the entire morning there, even taking the noon meal outside while Elizabeth ate and chatted with the women of the clan. She assisted with the menu planning and received a tour of the storage rooms from Bethea.

The woman was proud of how well stocked the larder remained despite it being the middle of winter. When they were through, Maggie led Elizabeth on a tour of the keep. She explained that Lady Galbraith oversaw much of the running of the keep as chatelaine, but she also hinted that the lady of the keep wasn't well versed in some less-noticeable tasks that needed doing. Maggie implied that she tried to provide guidance, but Lady Galbraith was unwilling to consider suggestions.

"Perhaps we could offer them the gift of a freshly cleaned keep upon their return. It seems the least I can do for their gracious hospitality."

Maggie snorted at Elizabeth's comment about gracious hospitality, but nodded nonetheless.

"I think airing out the tapestries would be a nice touch. Knocking off the dust and soot would make them shine once more. Then we'll keep them looking bright by cleaning out the hearths, so there isn't soot to rise and cling to the weaving." Elizabeth offered a conspiratorial grin as Maggie nodded her head.

"Aye, my lady. It will be as you wish."

CHAPTER SEVENTEEN

The next month began as a whirlwind of tasks for both Elizabeth and Edward. Elizabeth oversaw the improvements around the keep while making suggestions for spring garden planting. She even assisted with keeping the account ledgers. The castle's defenses impressed Edward. Even though he lost a few of the men he brought to Culcreuch, the warriors of Clan Galbraith proved capable of defending their home. The men from Robert's livery left the day after they arrived, but promised the king would send them back once Robert summoned them to court.

After the first fortnight, they had taken care of the initial tasks, so there were fewer projects for either of them to occupy their time. The weather was still too cold—even snowy—for them to visit the loch or picnic. They rode most afternoons when the sun was at its warmest, but they took a score of guards with them and never ventured far afield. Edward and Elizabeth were all too aware of the threat that remained. Neither spotted Mitchell when they left the castle walls, but they heard rumblings that the young mon was trying to stir up trouble for the couple. He spread tales that Elizabeth was unchaste, coming from the royal court where the ladies gave away their favors to anyone. He insinuated that Edward was planning a siege of the castle, so he could wrestle the lairdship of the clan from their rightful leader. Most people took the rumors for what they were: bitter falsehoods. But enough of the younger adults of the clan listened to him to make Edward uncomfortable.

When a messenger delivered Robert's missive that the Sinclairs had arrived at court, it was impossible for him to be more relieved that he could plan their departure. He recognized Elizabeth's restlessness here, feeling just as trapped as she did at court. At least in Stirling she'd have her cousin and friend at her side. They made the necessary arrangements to travel, and Robert sent two score warriors to accompany them.

The large contingency of guards, along with Elizabeth and Edward, departed at daybreak. It saddened Elizabeth to leave Maggie and Bethea, and Edward had come to like and respect Iain. Elizabeth suspected they would return to Culcreuch again before they made their way north. She reassured the women this wasn't goodbye forever. The ride back to Stirling was brief and uneventful, for which Elizabeth and Edward were grateful.

"Beth!"

Elizabeth spotted her cousin Deirdre standing on the steps of the keep. Deirdre was the only other person who called Elizabeth by the pet name. Everyone else used her full name or Liz; her half-brother and half-sisters called her Lizzie. She reined in Reubadair and tossed the reins to a groom, sliding from the saddle before all the horsemen cleared the gate. She dashed to the group awaiting them. Deirdre, Ceit, and Elizabeth collided in a tight embrace as Edward shook hands with Magnus and Tavish Sinclair. He was familiar with the behemoth brothers, having met them previously at court, even fighting in skirmishes with them. He respected the family from the father down to the four brothers. He'd only briefly met their sister Mairghread when she was presented at court; she'd been far too young to capture his attention.

"Well met." Magnus's deep voice seemed a perfect match for this size.

He was the largest of the four brothers, standing only a hairsbreadth taller but his mountainous frame was broader than any of the others. Magnus's next oldest brother stood beside him. While Magnus towered over most people with arms and legs that resembled tree trunks, Tavish's barrel chest displayed his imposing strength. Their wives looked like dolls compared to their hulking husbands, but Elizabeth told Edward both wives were equal matches for the brothers and kept them both on their toes. Edward was glad to have them all on their side if they were to investigate the carriage accident. After the incident on their first journey along with a month away from court, the accident seemed long in the past; however, Edward was aware Elizabeth still dreamed about it. She muttered in her sleep, telling him how cold she was and how she searched for him. He'd do anything to allay his wife's fears, and God help whoever was responsible.

Elizabeth paused from chattering with Deirdre and Ceit when she noticed the king looming in the doorway. She hissed to Edward and tilted her head in Robert's direction. Edward grinned when he saw his brother, but that sense of relief dampened knowing that something serious must have happened for Robert to greet them but not appear in public. Edward reached out his hand to Elizabeth and led the small group of friends inside. Robert nodded, but didn't speak until they reached the antechamber that separated the Great Hall from the passageway to the Privy Council. Edward's heart sank knowing Robert wanted to speak to them here rather than where he conducted meetings. The antechamber was where Robert and his wife retired to before the evening meal or if they wanted to speak privately to someone. A secret passageway ran behind the chamber, but it was the one part of the castle Elizabeth never visited, fearing what would happen if someone caught onto her movements and accused her of spying.

"I have two pieces of news, and I suspect neither will be particularly welcomed." Robert settled into his seat before the husbands ushered their wives into chairs around the table. Magnus, Tavish, and Edward slipped into seats beside the ladies. "Isabella Dunbar has reported overhearing part of two men's conversation concerning Elizabeth's accident. She stated she recognized the voices but hasn't figured out who they belong to. We now have proof people here at court were involved, if not responsible. Isabella heard naught that indicated why they targeted Elizabeth, only that they needed to be careful not to get caught."

Elizabeth's hand turned cold as she squeezed Edward's. He sensed the fear that her father was responsible still lurked in the back of her mind even though he'd been on his best behavior after their wedding. Edward also knew but never shared with anyone other than Robert, the queen, and Elizabeth that Sinead had spies at court. It was how she knew if he even looked at another woman, let alone what Robert planned for Ireland. He held Sinead on his short list of suspects.

"My other piece of news is that a young knight

from the MacLellan clan arrived here a few days ago. He was raised by and served Longshanks." Robert paused for effect as six sets of eyebrows shot up and three manly scowls took root. "He claims he wants naught more than to earn a plot of land here in Scotland and return to his roots. Sound rather like you, Edward," Robert added. "His father had been an English knight who married into the MacLellan clan, but he and his wife were both murdered a year apart by English border raiders. He's brought news that the English intend to cease harrying the Kerrs and our eastern border in favor of our western border clans, including the MacLellans and the Dunbars. It seems he has developed a fondness for Lady Isabella. I am sending him along with the three of you to scout the border and report back on where the English have made camp."

Three male heads shook as the scowls grew deeper. At least one man growled.

"I'm nae leaving Ceit here at court. Nay. I came to help with an investigation here at court, nae to leave ma wife unprotected in this pit of vipers." Tavish stood with his feet hip-width apart and arms crossed, his brother mirroring him in what everyone at court recognized as the Sinclair stance. If the king were not godfather to all five Sinclair siblings, Tavish wouldn't have dared speak to Robert thus, but he was confident Robert wouldn't punish him.

"I willna either," Magnus barked before softening his tone. "Ye ken I bare a deep affection for ye and Queen Elizabeth, but after what has already happened to Deirdre at court, I willna leave her here without me. I already lost ma wife once; I amnae risking it again."

Elizabeth's heart seized remembering how her cousin had suffered for seven years. Deirdre's parents kept her as a virtual prisoner at court and

175

hidden from Magnus, the man she'd fallen in love with as a child and handfasted with when she became a woman. Deirdre had also faced an unwelcome betrothal that nearly cost her and Magnus their lives.

Elizabeth also knew Tavish had a right to his own fear. Ceit had been a lady-in-waiting alongside Elizabeth and Deirdre, but her father used her as the means to make amends for the branch of the Comyns no longer opposing Robert's reign. However, Robert returned the favor by making her a double agent to spy against her uncle. The man had still harbored intentions to capture the throne. They had caught Ceit between a king and power-hungry tyrant. Her uncle's men beat Tavish to the point that he almost died trying to protect Ceit.

Elizabeth could also tell that Edward seethed at the suggestion that he abandon both her and the investigation. Robert raised his hand to cease the objections before leaning back in his chair with his arms crossed. All six people sitting across from him realized that further disagreement was useless. The king's mind was made up, and even his brother was still one of Robert's subjects.

"You will depart within the next day or so for the border. Don't engage if you can avoid it. I merely want information aboot the English and this knight. I would learn whether he is on our side or is still a spy for Longshanks."

Edward couldn't believe his ears. His brother intended him to leave Elizabeth behind after two attacks and someone breaking into their chamber, so he could babysit some English knight trying to ingratiate himself into the Scottish court.

"No."

All eyes turned toward Edward, shocked that he'd continue to refuse the king. They were all family in the chamber, but even the others realized when to stop fighting.

"I'm not leaving Elizabeth. I brought her back from Culcreuch under the impression that I'd begin the investigation and she'd remain under my protection. There is a reason I didn't leave her alone at Culcreuch. Now you're sending me away for God knows how long when someone is trying to kill her. No."

Edward noticed the tremors of anger beginning in his belly, and like a spider's web, they spread into his limbs. He was furious with Robert for being so flippant about his now sister-by-marriage's future, along with his duplicity to Edward.

"This Englishman who claims to be a Scot introduced himself only a few days ago. His cousin, Laird Malcolm MacLellan, sent a sealed missive vouching for the mon's trustworthiness. It said the mon even trained the MacLellan warriors on how to fight the English more effectively. The opportunity is too great to pass up, and I trust no one more than the three of you."

Robert pulled a sheaf of parchment toward him and began flipping through the pages dismissing any further conversation. Elizabeth and the others rose, making their bows and curtsies before walking to the door.

"Go with Deirdre and Ceit. Don't go to our chamber alone or walk the passageways alone. I will find you shortly." Edward leaned close to Elizabeth's ear.

"Edward, no. Don't make this worse. The king isn't interested in any of us arguing with him. Please just come with me."

"That king is still my brother. I won't argue with him. There's no changing his mind, so I'll have to leave you behind. However, I'm not finished discussing the terms under which I'll leave you here. Go with the other ladies."

Elizabeth nodded reluctantly before following the others out. Edward spun on his heel and stalked back to the table. He refused to sit, forcing Robert to look up at him when the king acknowledged him. The dark look on Robert's face should have been enough warning to Edward, but he continued anyway.

"How could you? You know bluidy well what happens when we entrust others to protect our wives."

Robert jerked back at the reminder of how King Edward, the Hammer of the Scots, stole Robert's own wife and kept her under house arrest for eight years.

"That is uncalled for," Robert's voice rasped. "They didn't steal her from under my nose while at court. And you remember we lost our brothers in the process. There are plenty of people to ensure your wife's safety."

"'Your wife.' She's *your* sister now, or have you not recognized that yet?"

"I recognize the comfort of my family cannot come before the safety of an entire country."

"Bah. There are plenty of others you could send besides the Sinclairs and me. Plenty you have sent before. I didn't return to Scotland or here to babysit some half-bred, wayward knight."

"I wouldn't let him hear you describe him as such. He's a similar build to you, and I've seen him in the lists. You couldn't guarantee your own life."

"So, you choose him over me?"

"Don't be so petulant. You aren't a child, and you recognize you have duties to the crown, not just me. Besides, do you expect to coddle your wife the entirety of your marriage? Will you refuse to ride out with your men if, or rather when, I give you a keep?"

Edward was tempted to reach across the table and grab Robert's tunic to shake him.

"I'm not coddling her, you self-righteous prig. Someone has tried to kill her twice. You didn't see her nearly frozen to death in that blizzard, so tiny on the horse as she fought to find her way home. You didn't see her defend herself against three horsemen set to capture or kill her. You didn't have to watch her curl into a ball on the ground, waiting for a horse to trample her. How dare you? If aught happens to her while I'm gone, I will never forgive you. Brother or not, we will be through."

Robert paused before responding. Both he and Edward had short tempers that they both had learned to contain. Robert had never seen his brother this worked up before; it was unlike him to call names. After having his wife taken from him early in their marriage, Robert recognized the fear in Edward's eyes. He admitted he hadn't had to contend with such close calls to his wife's life before her capture. He wanted to sympathize with his brother, but he also was convinced Edward was the only man besides the Sinclairs that he trusted with such a mission. If he misjudged the newcomer, he could send his men into a trap that would weaken the entire border. Robert was unused to having to explain himself these days, but he accepted he owed it to his brother. He stood up and walked around the table, pulling out the chair beside Edward and gestured for him to sit down.

"As your brother," Robert began, "I want naught more than to see you and your bride settled far from aught to do with this war. I want to wish you well and visit your bairns as they grow. I want to promise that I can always keep you as safe as you wish to keep your wife. But as king, I cannot do that. You and our brothers have paid dearly for my ambition, and rather than resent me, you've all stood beside me through every skirmish, every battle, everything. I wish I could repay you by granting your wish, but as king I need the very best men I have on this mission. If I've erred in believing this mon, then I'll be sending our troops into a trap. I need you and Magnus and Tavish there to ensure that doesn't happen. I can't lose the security of the entire border, not when the purpose of you going is to ensure the English cannot gain any more of our land from our countrymen."

"I know, Robert," Edward closed his eyes as he shook his head, wishing to shut out the world and in particular the pleading he saw in Robert's eyes. "What can you do to ensure she's safe? I can't lose her."

"I would have her keep company with Deirdre and Ceit whenever she can. I'm guessing it would please Elizabeth to share a chamber with her cousin, and Ceit is now Deirdre's sister-by-marriage, so I'm certain she'd be welcome, too. I can ensure a guard posted outside their door every night along with a guard below their window if you like. My Elizabeth is already aware of the situation and has arranged for members of her own personal guard to escort the ladies wherever they wish to go. It wouldn't surprise me if Lady Isabella doesn't also join this group. She will be fearful for this young mon, Sir Dedric as they call him, as I predict he will ask for her hand soon. I will do everything in my power to keep her safe and happy."

"I will hold you to that, brother. I wasn't jesting when I said that we will be through if aught happens to her." Edward rose and embraced Robert as his older brother pulled him into his arms.

"Fear not, little brother. Just keep yourself alive to come home. I've lost enough of this family that I don't know that I could bear losing you, too." Edward heard the catch in Robert's throat and remorse choked him for not considering that these decisions might be difficult for his brother, nor considering that Robert worried about him.

"I will serve you well," Edward pounded Robert's back before pulling away. Robert clapped him on the shoulder, giving as good as he got.

Edward left feeling marginally better than when the others departed. He tracked down Elizabeth, and they retired for the evening, unwilling to share one another with anyone else. A missive came late into the evening stating that arrangements were complete for the men to ride out in the morning.

CHAPTER EIGHTEEN

Dawn came all too soon for both Elizabeth and Edward. They dressed and made their way to the bailey. While Deirdre stood with Magnus and Ceit stood with Tavish, both couples locked in tight embraces sharing searing kisses, Elizabeth clung to Edward. He was unwilling to break their contact despite the large crowd milling about. While as the king's relatives they were slightly more circumspect, Edward pressed Elizabeth's body against his, memorizing the sensation. His kiss was deep, possessive, and promising. Elizabeth met his passion with her own. They only broke apart when gasps and whispers drew their attention. Elizabeth turned to see Lady Isabella Dunbar locked in her own kiss with a man dressed like an English knight, but without the full armor. She couldn't help but grin. She hadn't been close with Isabella, even disliking her at times for following along with some meaner ladies-in-waiting, but Elizabeth noticed the young woman struggled just as much as she did to keep her composure through both being caught kissing a man who wasn't her husband—or even betrothed—as well as the anguish of saying goodbye to this man.

Edward pulled Elizabeth back against him for

one more kiss before he and the other men mounted. He looked back thrice before losing sight of Elizabeth on the other side of the gate. Elizabeth followed Deirdre's lead as they approached Isabella. The young woman sucked in a breath of surprise to see the three former ladies-in-waiting approach her. She was even more surprised when they embraced her, reassuring her that they were in the same boat. Isabella stuttered a "thank you" and an apology for her past behavior. Elizabeth was unsure how Deirdre would react since she'd been the recipient of Isabella's actions, but she should have trusted her cousin to have the grace to accept it. Deirdre, Ceit, and Elizabeth understood how powerful the group of ladies-in-waiting were, how they isolated and alienated anyone who didn't conform. They didn't blame Isabella for trying to endure her service to the queen.

The next month seemed interminable to the four ladies. Deirdre and Elizabeth resumed their habit of reading and translating ancient texts, both loving the puzzle of deciphering bygone era relics. Isabella joined them in the castle's scriptorium as she pursued her passion for Pictish history and its influence on Clan Dunbar. Ceit was the only one who hadn't been an academic while at court. She'd been too busy ferreting out information to relay to both her king and her uncle. Now that she no longer had to fear the tangled web of espionage, she enjoyed reading for pleasure. Ceit often took her place in the window seat and read the Greek philosophers' works translated into Latin. She didn't care for the books of flowery poetry since they all had to endure hours of it in the queen's solar.

At night, Elizabeth retired to a chamber she

shared with Deirdre and Ceit. It was the one she and Edward shared after they wed and the one where they spent a brief night before Edward rode out. It was the most spacious of the three chambers the couples occupied. They invited Isabella, offering a trundle bed, but most nights she refused to intrude that much on the family.

Elizabeth appreciated the company as they all tried to while away the days, but the constant presence of other people wore her down. Everywhere she looked, the posted guards watched her. She felt exposed, and it was a constant reminder that Edward wasn't there. She tried to convince herself not to keep track of how many days he'd been gone, but there was no helping it. Robert and the queen encouraged all four ladies to dine on the dais, enjoying the best of what they served and knowing it also made it impossible for any man to ask them to dance or to even approach without the king's notice. They all declined to dance regardless of where they sat.

"I don't recall how I used to survive these evening meals," Ceit mused. "The men are insufferable as they strut aboot like peacocks, and the women's vanity makes me question whether I was ever so petty."

"You weren't," Deirdre reassured. "You weren't around enough to fall into the trappings of court life."

Ceit grinned as she remembered that the longest stretch of time she spent at court was while Tavish attempted to court her. Already betrothed to him, unbeknownst to her, he'd set out on a mission to woo her and convince her that his feelings were in earnest. His reputation as a rake had proceeded him.

"You smiled and bore your time here," Elizabeth murmured to Deirdre. Deirdre had arrived unexpectedly at court and become gravely ill for several days. No one was told why she became a lady-in-waiting nor did they understand why she refused to gossip aboot the men at court, only dancing when forced. Only Elizabeth was privy to Deirdre's secret: she and Magnus were handfasted, and Deirdre refused to accept it was only for a year and a day. In her heart and mind, they were still wed despite not having heard from Magnus in years. Elizabeth and Deirdre suspected Deirdre's parents were responsible for that.

"I did, but I am glad that it is over. I'd much rather be at home at Castle Dunbeath than here. Besides, there will be no more bairns if Magnus isn't here to practice." She rubbed her rounded belly, smiling while thinking about how she and Magnus came to be expecting their first child.

Elizabeth tried to keep the sly smile from her face, but her cousin was far too perceptive.

"Beth, do you have something to share?" Deirdre giggled.

"I don't know for sure, but I suspect I might be with child. We've been married more than a moon, and my courses haven't started." Elizabeth kept her voice down. She didn't want her news to become the latest gossip, nor did she want anyone who might wish her dead to learn she might carry the king's niece or nephew. She feared that would make her an even greater target. "Don't say aught to anyone. Eddie doesn't even know."

Ceit, Deirdre, and Isabella nodded solemnly. All three married women trusted one another enough to share the pet names they had for their husbands. Only Isabella lacked a special name for her knight.

"I swear if it rains one more day, I will think God intends us to build an ark," Edward grumbled as he pushed his sopping hair out of his face. He and the other men had been sleeping under the stars and wet sky for a month, and he was ready to return home to a hearty meal and the warmth of sharing a bed with Elizabeth.

"Ye ken we can have all four seasons in a day. 'Tis the way of things in Scotland," Tavish chuckled despite looking half-drowned himself.

"That's supposed to be in the Highlands, not down here by the border," Edward continued to grumble.

"Then be glad it's only rain and nae sleet nor snow as it would be in the Highlands," Magnus reasoned.

"True enough, true enough," Edward conceded as their horses plodded through the mud. They had been scouting the border with little success, except for one short battle with the English. Besides that, there had been little of note to report. He found that if he had to be away from Elizabeth and suffering in the wilds, then he was happy to do it with Tavish and Magnus. Even the English knight proved himself trustworthy as he led the defense against the attack, preparing them by explaining the English strategy he predicted they would face. The man seemed to become more Scottish than English by the day.

"We'll be back with our wives in three days. We can survive that. As ma new sister Siùsan says, if a woman can survive carrying a bairn for nine moons, a mon should be able to survive the ague and a wee bit of bad weather. Rather difficult to argue that when she's standing there with her hand on her belly and yer wife is beside her," Tavish laughed.

While none of the men enjoyed being away from the women they loved, Tavish kept his sense of humor most of the time. He'd come to blows with the newcomer, but once they had it out, they all became friends.

"I will bear that in mind as I ring out my leggings and dump the water from my boots," Edward laughed as the thought that they would be home in a few days took root.

They had already turned away from the borderlands, headed toward the gateway to the Highlands. Stirling straddled the divide between the Highlands and Lowlands, but after the king united the Highland clans and fought with the ferocity of a Highlander, the court appeared more like it belonged to the wilds of the north despite the pomp and circumstance. Even though the Bruces were a Lowland clan, since his young days as a warrior, Edward sensed the pull of the rugged landscape. Elizabeth was from a Highland clan, and he saw the resilience in her that was needed to survive the locale. He also heard the twinges of a burr when she said particular words. He found it endearing as well as arousing. Edward shifted in his saddle; it was hardly the time for his cock to harden just thinking about his wife. He was saddle sore enough without adding to it. He commiserated with the other men who missed their women just as much as he did, the silent understanding when they slipped away from camp for longer than was needed to relieve themselves.

"I am looking forward to ma Ceit's tender ministrations when we return," Tavish waggled his eyebrows.

"Tender?" Magnus snorted. "I dinna ken how she hasnae killed ye yet. The two of ye bicker like fishwives."

"Aye, and we enjoy making up afterward." Tavish shifted in his saddle too, becoming uncomfortable while thinking of his wife.

The jesting carried on, moving to the endurance and bravery of their horses and who would last the longest if they were to challenge one another in the lists. The weather lightened up just before Stirling came into sight on the third day. The four warriors and their men spurred their horses into a gallop as they raced to be welcomed home.

CHAPTER NINETEEN

E dward watched as Elizabeth dashed outside with Deirdre, Ceit, and Isabella at her side. He catapulted himself from his horse before it had even come to a stop. He assumed a stable boy would gather the reins and lead his horse to the stables. Under normal circumstances, he would've cared for his steed himself, but nothing would keep him from enjoying Elizabeth being in his arms. He took the steps two at a time until he met her in the middle. She launched herself into his arms, and he squeezed her so tightly, he was certain he'd crush her, but he was unable to bring himself to let go. Her arms held him as close as she could around his much broader frame. Their kiss was hungry and frenzied. No one existed in that moment besides each other.

A clearing of a throat did little to keep the four couples from continuing their reunion. Robert only laughed as he observed the four warriors with their petite women, knowing that no one should underestimate the women's ferocity just because of their smaller stature. When the group was ready to enter the keep, Robert opened his mouth to command them to meet with him and the Privy Council to debrief their findings, but eight scowling faces and four *feminine* growls left him suggesting that he meet with the returning warriors in the morning. Even Robert knew not to push his luck.

"I ordered a bath as soon as Ceit brought word that you were spotted," Elizabeth explained as she stepped past the guard and into their chamber. Her halt was so abrupt Edward ran into her back, pushing her a few steps forward. He encircled her waist and pulled her back against him as he drew his dirk. It took little more than a moment for him to spot what she had. There was a dead blackbird, its wings spread apart in rigor mortis, laying on their bed, feathers strewn about the floor. Edward moved Elizabeth behind him as he inched further into the room. The brief notion of pushing Elizabeth out of the chamber came to mind, but the guards hadn't done a good enough job once; he didn't trust them now. As they neared the tub, they both gasped to see the water was red.

"Blood?" Elizabeth asked. She stopped beside Edward as they both leaned over the water. Before he could stop her, Elizabeth scooped a handful and dipped her tongue into it. She spluttered, and Edward panicked. "Beets. Ugh. I detest beets. I would rather it'd been blood. Disgusting."

"Beets?" Edward bleated. He was ready to throttle his wife. "What were you thinking? What if it was more dangerous than that? You could have poisoned yourself."

"That's why I only used the tip of my tongue. And besides, I was sure I recognized the smell. Someone did this to scare us into assuming it was blood."

"Guards!" Edward bellowed. When the door opened, both men peered inside. "Who else, besides the maids who brought the bath, has been inside this chamber?"

"No one, my lord. Only the two maids and three men who brought in the tub and buckets of water. We oversaw them ourselves to be sure there was no cheeky business." The guard nodded but caught sight of the bird on the bed. "Ay up! What's this?"

"Someone else has been in here," Edward growled the obvious.

"I swear we let no one else in here," the other guard spoke up. "And we watched them the entire time."

Elizabeth tugged on Edward's sleeve and tilted her head to the wall behind the bed. Edward remembered the secret passage and trap door behind the tapestry by their bed. It was the same tunnel Elizabeth led him through when he followed her after a visit to her siblings.

"Very well. That'll be all," Edward dismissed the guards, but one lingered.

"Should we summon someone to see to this mess, my lord?"

"No. We shall deal with it."

Once the door was closed, Elizabeth raced forward and turned the key in the lock before dropping the bar.

"Someone else knows that a passage leads here." She pushed the tapestry aside and ran her hand over the stone wall. She sensed nothing out of the ordinary; the latch felt just as it should. She pressed it and the door sprang open. She wondered if the torch she dropped when she ran before was still there. She made to take a step inside, but Edward's arm wrapped around her and lifted her off her feet.

"What do you think you're doing?" Edward bellowed, but looked over his shoulder at the door.

"I was just going to go far enough to figure out if the torch I left behind was still there."

"I'll check." Edward stooped and passed through

the doorway. With his hands out in front of him, he shuffled his feet until he kicked something. He bent down to retrieve whatever it was and discovered it was the torch. It had been resting against the wall and out of the way of the path. Whoever came to their chamber hadn't discovered it. He stepped back into the chamber and went to the roaring fire. He lit the torch before turning to Elizabeth. "I want to tell you to stay behind, but I'm sure you won't, and I need your knowledge of the tunnels to guide me. Just promise you will stay behind me, holding onto my tunic the entire time."

Elizabeth nodded but said nothing. Edward tucked the torch into a wall sconce and pulled Elizabeth into his embrace.

"I know you're scared, little one. I am too, truth be told, but we both know we must, to discover what we can find."

"I just wish for a quiet evening together rather than dealing with this. Everything seemed fine while you were away, and the moment you return--" Elizabeth broke off as she leaned back to look at Edward. "This isn't aboot me. This is aboot you," she gasped as everything began to fall into place. "When Isabella recalled what she heard the men say, it was that they hoped naught tied them back to the accident. They hoped that whoever you and Robert sent wouldn't find aught beyond the axle I guess your men brought back. They said naught that implied the attack was intended for me. What if it wasn't? What if the attackers discovered I was leaving in a hurry in a carriage and assumed we were running away? What if the ambush was aboot using me to lure you out? Oh God, Eddie. What if someone is trying to kill you?"

The notion had crossed his mind after the ambush, but he'd been certain everyone at court was aware Fraser sent his daughter away to keep her from Edward. Now he questioned whether anyone learned that *before* Elizabeth left. If this was the case, he had more than one enemy who might desire him dead. It could be anyone from Sinead in a jealous fit to a noble who sided against Robert. It didn't narrow the possibilities.

"You may be right, but as long as we are together, you are in danger."

"As long as we're together? What is that supposed to mean? We're supposed to always be together." Elizabeth felt nauseous as bile rose in the back of her throat.

"It means I'm bluidy well fucked," Edward muttered before glancing over at Elizabeth's stunned expression. "I'm sorry. I shouldn't be so crass. I don't want to leave you alone as I trust no one to protect you like I can, and we've seen how well that goes, nor do I want you harmed because you remain at my side. This makes me wonder if Mitchell intended to goad me back at Culcreuch, perhaps even draw me out into a fight."

"Eddie, I don't know that I want to lead you through the tunnels now. If Mitchell was our only trouble at Culcreuch, then maybe we should ask Robert if we can return."

"I already plan to." Edward brushed back hair from her temple before kissing the smooth skin. "We'll leave off on the tunnel, but you must promise me you won't go investigating without me."

Elizabeth swallowed, not sure if this was the right time to share her news. She took Edward's hand and looked around for somewhere to sit not near the bed nor the tub. She settled for arranging a few cushions on the floor before the fire.

"You haven't promised me, Beth."

"I know. That's what I want to talk to you aboot, or at least I do promise that I won't go exploring. I also won't gallop on Reubadair or go into Stirling without you. I won't take any chances slipping on ice by going for walks without you to brace me. I won't do any of those things that might hurt my body... or the bairn I'm carrying."

"Bairn?" Edward whispered.

Elizabeth nodded as Edward drew her into his lap. He caressed her hair before smattering kisses across her face and resting a hand over her still-flat belly.

"I realized while you were away that I hadn't had my courses since before we wed. We were at Culcreuch for a moon, and you were away for a moon. I visited the queen's midwife yesterday, and she confirmed it. She estimates me close to three moons along."

"That would mean when we were at the inn or the cottage."

"Aye. Right when we first pledged ourselves. Our handfast bairn."

Edward's kiss was slow and gentle as he marveled knowing his wife was growing another person within her womb, a person they created together.

"I love you, little one."

"And I love you, Eddie. Are you happy that it happened so soon?" Elizabeth bit her lower lip until Edward tugged it free.

"I admit I was looking forward to time alone with you once we leave all this court intrigue behind us, but I find knowing we are beginning our own family makes me happier than I ever imagined. I realized when I met you in the Great Hall and led you onto the terrace last year that you were special. You drew me to you like a moth to the flame, but you disappeared as quickly as you appeared. When I returned to Ireland, I assumed I would never meet you again. Then I spotted you in the chapel, and you drew me again like a lodestone. I was certain that day that I met my match, and I agree, you don't scamper. You're just as graceful as you appeared each Sunday as I watched you during the Advent services. I am the luckiest of men to have found you, Beth. I know you believed you would never marry, but I'm glad the good Lord saw fit to keep you unattached until I returned to you."

"You would be a splendid bard," Elizabeth murmured as she basked in the warmth of Edward's words and his embrace. "I knew when we first met that I'd made the right choice to spread that rumor, but I accepted that it was only for Ceit and Tavish's benefit. I never imagined I would leave as lasting an impression on you as you did with me. I dreamed of you, but was so certain I'd never meet you again. Even once I did, I was convinced I'd never get to marry you, never experience the happiness I've found with you. I didn't believe it would ever be possible."

"You being with child lends a new sense of urgency that we resolve this threat and find our new home. Even if I'm the target, court and everything attached to it isn't safe for you. We need to meet with Robert, and I don't want you in this chamber any longer. Someone has violated our space. Twice."

Edward eased Elizabeth to her feet before they left to speak to Robert. The king became outraged when he learned of not only the dead bird, but the bath intended to look like blood. He stormed through the passageways, Edward able to keep up but Elizabeth running, until they reached Edward and Elizabeth's chamber. The king burst through the door and took in the scene. He spotted the dead bird still on the bed where his brother and sister-by-marriage discovered it, along with the red bath water.

"I ask your forgiveness, brother. I admit I didn't

take your concerns enough to heart. I ensured the guards followed Elizabeth to appease you, but it's obvious Elizabeth was in far more danger than I accepted." Robert looked contrite as he spoke loud enough for only Elizabeth and Edward to hear. Now that they knew someone used the secret passageways to come and go from this chamber, they were cautious not to speak loudly enough for anyone who might be spying to overhear. Elizabeth's skin crawled as she realized someone may have been listening to her most intimate moments with Edward, or the confidences she shared with her friends. She recalled there were no peepholes in this part of the castle, but the walls were still thin enough for every moan and grunt to carry. Edward looked over at her, his brow creased, but she shook her head and mouthed "later." He nodded, but still laced his fingers through hers and gave her hand a squeeze.

"I accept your apology, Robert. I would rather believe they intended the attacks for me than Elizabeth, but she is my wife now and is just as vulnerable a target, if not more so." Edward looked at Elizabeth and the silent question passed between them of whether he should share their news. Elizabeth nodded once. "Robert, you shall be an uncle in aboot six moons."

"An uncle?" Robert's eyes widened as he looked between his brother and Elizabeth. "Felicitations are in order, but I can understand the renewed sense of urgency to find you a permanent home. With spring approaching, I would settle you somewhere before it becomes too arduous for Elizabeth to travel. But I doubt leaving will solve this problem."

"I agree. I want to meet with Tavish and Magnus as soon as possible. Perhaps Ceit will come up with some suggestions on where to start." Edward beamed while Robert congratulated them, but grew serious as they planned the investigation after having had to put it on hold for so long. "In the meantime, we need another chamber. Preferably one that doesn't include a hidden corridor behind it."

Both men looked to Elizabeth, who grimaced before looking apologetic.

"There are none that I'm aware of. Even the king and queen's chambers include them. I suppose most especially the royal chambers do in case the king and queen should ever need to flee, but what I mean to say is there are passageways running to and from all the bedchambers. The royal chambers and those for the royal family don't have peepholes, but most of the other chambers do. The antechamber and Privy Council along with the queen's solar and the king's library have them. The tunnels run behind the altar of the chapel and to the music room, scriptorium, the main library, all the way down to the kitchens. There is a wide passageway behind the Great Hall with a platform and a rotting latticework screen that allows someone to observe what happens below without being seen. I used to use the passageways that led from my chambers to the part of the bailey closest to the stables. It's how I slipped out for rides or to visit my siblings."

Both men stared at her as she described only a small part of the maze that existed behind the walls and out of sight.

"They will be searched," Robert declared.

"I don't think that's wise," Elizabeth murmured. At Robert's questioning look, she continued. "The passageways are meant to be secret. If ever needed, you and the queen should be assured they are safe from being used to enter the castle. If too many people discover their existence, then someone might share information that leads to an attack. Most people are under the impression Stirling is impenetrable, and it should stay that way. Besides, if more people learn aboot them, then more people can spy on you. Edward knows they are a tight fit, but I'd be able to lead him and Magnus and Tavish through the maze. With the tight confines, no one would get to me through them."

"Very well, if my brother agrees." Robert looked at Edward and was uncertain Edward would agree, but after a moment, he nodded his head. "For now, let's figure out where you can go. I plan for you to take the queen's quarters tonight."

Elizabeth blushed but didn't comment on the fact the king and queen would share a chamber that night. She'd been at court long enough to be aware it happened, but most certainly not every night. Edward nodded, but refrained from saying anything either. The three left the chamber, but only Elizabeth looked back. She sought to memorize every detail after realizing someone had breached their privacy.

CHAPTER TWENTY

T he king posted a watch on Elizabeth's parents. They seemed unlikely culprits now that they assumed the attackers intended to harm Edward. The couple knew Edward wasn't traveling in the coach with Elizabeth, so if they had arranged it, the accident would mean Elizabeth was the only intended victim. His men found Duncan, the family's longtime driver, several days after Elizabeth and Edward's return, his head bashed open but still breathing. They discovered the man unconscious, but he eventually told the story of how two men attacked him, leaving him for dead in the carriage house. He saw their faces but had no idea who they worked for. Since both men perished in the accident, that seemed like a dead end. Edward vouched for the men who accompanied them to Culcreuch. He saw how they fought to defend their party. None appeared to aid the attackers nor hide from battle. Elizabeth's mind only conjured one person who had a clear reason to be angry.

Elizabeth avoided suggesting Sinead as the culprit until it seemed like they exhausted all the other potential suspects. Edward sensed Elizabeth considered his former mistress but didn't want to speak of her. He had no desire to talk about his former lover with his wife, who at that moment carried their child. He also had to admit that Sinead looked more and more like the most likely perpetrator. Edward sent missives to his brother in Ireland asking how the campaign progressed and how Robert's blood brother fared.

A stack of folded parchments arrived one morning, and Edward recognized the handwriting as that of his brother in Ireland. Edward realized they had arrived some time ago. The first missive he opened turned his blood cold. His brother Edward described how Sinead went on a tirade when she not only realized he wouldn't be returning from Scotland, but that he was instead pursuing a woman and he intended to marry her. One reason for Edward's eagerness to leave Sinead behind was the fact that she'd hinted at them marrying. He never even considered it a possibility, despite his earlier thoughts that she might remain his mistress indefinitely. According to the missive, Sinead schemed to send her own spies to Robert's court to learn what type of woman had stolen her man. Never mind the fact that she and Edward, Robert's blood brother, had entered into their own arrangement, bedding each other every spare moment they had. Edward checked the date once more, still shaken that his brother sent it over a month before, having arrived while Edward was out scouting for Robert. He didn't understand why his brother waited so long to send the missive, since he'd been in Scotland for the entire Advent season. It made him wonder how soon Sinead discovered his new plans. Had she known for weeks before her temper got the better of her? Did she learn of his new love interest weeks into his return to Scotland and only acted shortly before his brother's missive?

The next missive, dated a fortnight after the first,

warned that Sinead had dispatched spies to Robert's court. This, too, arrived while he was scouting for Robert. Edward cursed as he counted back how many weeks it had been since not only the missive arrived, but the number of weeks Sinead's spies had to gather what she would consider incriminating evidence.

The third missive saddened him but only for a heartbeat. It was dated only a sennight ago, after he'd sent his own missives. Sinead had flown into a rage when no useful information arrived to her beyond the fact that Edward had wed but been away from court. She stormed out of the tent she shared with Edward's brother, a whisky bottle in hand, and ridden out along the coast. Even though her tantrums were well known and her sudden disappearances accepted, when she didn't return after three days, they sent a search party out. They found the horse dead, its leg and neck broken, where it fell along a craggy cliff. The searchers found Sinead's broken body washed up along the rocks, stuck among them so that the tide failed to carry her away. Edward's moment of regret was that she wasted a life with so much potential. Sinead possessed not only beauty but intelligence. If she'd been a man, she would've led an army. However, life on the run, the years-long battle between the English and Irish had embittered her, and her anger at the hand life had dealt her made her temper volatile. Edward felt guilty that her death didn't move him more, but it was as though he was learning of the death of a mere acquaintance, not of a woman he bedded for two years.

Edward sat reading the missives in the queen's chamber, where he and Elizabeth had been staying for more than a sennight. Elizabeth watched him from the corner of her eye as she sat in a window seat with her embroidery. She despised sewing, but it served as a silent pastime that gave her a chance to observe her husband and enjoy companionable silence. From the expressions that fluttered across his face, she guessed he was reading about Sinead. The page that delivered the messages announced they arrived from Edward in Ireland. She wondered if he would share any of the content. She practically pulsed with desperate curiosity but wanted to respect his privacy at the same time. She prayed he wouldn't keep secrets from her, especially about Sinead. It made her stomach twist in knots as she feared the woman still had a hold on Edward.

"She's dead."

Elizabeth jumped at the deadpan comment. She hadn't expected those words after Edward refolded the last piece of parchment. He looked squarely at Elizabeth, and she didn't see any deception or even any remorse in his gaze. She set her embroidery aside and approached tentatively. When she came close enough, Edward pulled her into his lap and opened the first missive. He handed it to Elizabeth, but she looked uncertain until he encouraged her to read it. Just as Edward had done, she reread each one twice as he handed her one after another.

"I'm so sorry for your loss, Eddie." Elizabeth tried for a soothing tone, even though a larger part of her than she cared to admit was becalmed that the woman no longer had opportunity to be part of their lives.

"Beth, I don't feel any loss."

"But you must have cared aboot her quite deeply to remain with her for two years."

"What I cared aboot was how good she was in bed." Edward regretted the words as soon as they flew out of his mouth. The pinched look on Beth's face told him his words didn't go over well. "Beth, I shouldn't have said that."

"Better to know that's all you cared aboot than to worry you are grieving a woman you loved."

"I most definitely didn't love her. I think most of the time I barely liked her. It would seem she might be behind all of this, and if that's the case, then we are well rid of her. She may have directed her vengeance toward me, but she had no qualms aboot the danger she placed you in. She was fine with it. She probably thought of it as a boon."

Elizabeth nodded as she placed the missives on the table next to them. "Your brother doesn't seem to grieve the loss either."

"I doubt he does. He's never had long-lasting tender feelings aboot any woman, nor does he care for being tied to any one woman. That's why his son, Alexander, is illegitimate. The pope gave Edward a dispensation to marry his son's mother, Isabella, but Edward claims he never did. I doubt he's lonely now either. He will have replaced Sinead."

"He sounds like a cad," Elizabeth muttered.

"He can be. But he's as dedicated to the cause as Robert and doesn't want any distractions. He's close to being the High King of Ireland, and he won't let a mistress stand in his way. He keeps his liaisons brief."

"Do you suppose Sinead's death will stop the threat? It would seem that if she coordinated this, then her spies aren't aware of her death. The bird and bath incident happened after she died, given how old your brother's last missive was. It's likely it was on the way when we discovered what they had done to our chamber. Do you think someone is still carrying out her orders, or will they stop once no new orders are issued?"

"If someone is carrying out her orders, then they've some connection to Sinead beyond coins. If it were aboot money, they'd pocket the money and not need to work anymore."

"Are you familiar with anyone at court who might have ties to Sinead? I imagine there'd be a personal connection to whoever sides with a woman set on killing the king's brother. Did she ever come here with you?"

"No. She refused to leave Ireland, and I was glad to travel alone. I can't come up with anyone other than my brother or me who is linked to her."

"Could one of her spies have some ties to you or your brothers or even someone else at court? Who could they be?"

"That's hard to say. An Irish noble, mon or woman, would stick out at court just as much as the English knight does. But an Irish servant might blend in."

"While we can't rule it out, it would seem that the timeline doesn't fit for Sinead to be to blame for this. Then again, there haven't been any more incidents since the time Sinead must have died."

"Aye. I agree though it would be nice to bring this to an end knowing that she can no longer sink her talons in me."

"What if you're not off aboot an Irish servant as a spy, but it wasn't Sinead who sent them? Maybe the Balliols who fled to Ireland? Would they strike out at you to hurt Robert?"

"Possibly. But it would gain them little. While my death might pain Robert, it would do little to weaken his reign. If aught, Edward would be a better target as he commands the forces in Ireland and will soon be named High King. Killing me wouldn't affect that or any of the power Robert has here in Scotland."

"But Robert already made you the Earl of Badenoch and Lochaber. It's known now that you want to make your home in the Highlands. Do you suppose someone wants to prevent you from gaining too much power there? Might one of the clans be after you?"

"That's certainly possible."

Edward's mind jumped to a person devious enough to plot his demise. His heart sank knowing what he'd have to share with Elizabeth. He just prayed his good intentions all those weeks ago would buy him some forgiveness.

"I can think of a clan, and I can think of someone here. The Gregors hold a deep grudge that Robert is not only king but has pushed them aside. They've been relegated to less and less land despite their clan motto 'Royal is my race.' They are being repressed by the Campbells who insist upon expanding their holdings into a small empire. Robert allows it because the Campbells remain such strong supporters of his campaigns. A sept of the Gregors are the MacAdams." This is where Edward wished his hypothesis could stop. From the hard set of Elizabeth's mouth, he predicted that she already guessed the direction his thinking was taking him. "Lady MacAdams approached me after I met you for the second time. It was the night you disappeared in the music room. She tried to seduce me, but when I realized I couldn't accept her or any other woman besides you, she sneered and claimed I would come crawling back to her. She tried one other time, but she realized I was still disinterested."

"How well acquainted with her were you?" Elizabeth bit out. She already knew the answer, but for some reason, she needed to hear it from Edward. She knew the pain would be self-inflicted.

"It has been a few years, but I had more than one encounter."

"Encounter? That's a rather innocuous word to mean you bedded her several times." Elizabeth failed to keep the bitterness from her voice. Sinead was a faceless woman, but Lady MacAdams was a woman Elizabeth saw daily. She accepted there were others. But now, to have not only a name, but a face to put with Edward, her skin crawled and she wanted to cry.

"Beth, look at me." Edward eased her head toward him, and he canted his head to be in her line of sight even as she looked down. "It's no secret there's a double standard for men to bed whoever they want, that it's expected of us. It never troubled me before. I also never imagined I would marry, so there was no one's feelings to consider but the woman I was bedding. Even then, I didn't worry much beyond making sure I satisfied them. I wish I'd made better choices, but I had no idea you would come into my life."

"I don't blame you for that. It happened before we met. But I hate seeing women fawn over you. I've heard aboot some of the women from the past, but Lady MacAdams is one of the worst. She doesn't care whether or not a mon is happily married. If she assumes a mon can pleasure her, she will pursue him tirelessly." Elizabeth accepted she had to confess, too. She leaned her head back, looking at the ceiling, unable to face Edward. "After I disappeared into the passageway, I waited while I caught my breath. You unnerved me with your looks and your persistence. I listened to your entire conversation with Lady MacAdams, I even peeked. I saw her undo the laces of your leggings, but I also saw you stop her. But then I wanted to sob when I feared you would let her take you in her mouth. I felt used and manipulated, but then you repeated that your bulge wasn't for her. I can't imagine sweeter words other than when you tell me you love me. I was horrified and hurt despite your rejection of her. I ran the entire way back to my chamber, but even then, it didn't stop my mind from returning to you, wanting you."

"I couldn't do it, Beth. Even if you never found out, I would've known. It felt like a betrayal if I was with another woman when my intentions with you were honorable." Edward feathered a kiss across her lips, and Elizabeth eased back into his embrace.

"Do you think it might be her? Either because you spurned her or because she's loyal to her clan and Clan Gregor?"

"If aught, I would assume it's the latter. She may nurse hurt pride, but she has plenty of other men she is bedding. She is far from lonely."

"She is the type to oversee her own spies here at court, and she is a powerful woman when it comes to bending people to her will," Elizabeth mused.

Edward nodded, but they both let the matter drop. They stared into the fire and enjoyed the return to companionable silence, both lost in thought. Not long after, Elizabeth relaxed enough to doze off. Edward moved her to the bed and removed her velvet slippers before removing his own boots. He settled next to her for a much-needed nap.

CHAPTER TWENTY-ONE

E dward met with Robert the next morning in the antechamber, the topic one neither wanted to give as fodder to the gossips. Edward relayed the various ideas and considerations he and Elizabeth discussed the afternoon before. Robert listened intently and agreed with the conclusions the couple had drawn; however, he was unconvinced that Lady MacAdams would work on behalf of her clan. She came to court with her late husband who was the MacAdams and remained there after he died a short time later. He fell from his horse during a hunt and broke his neck. She enjoyed life at court and stayed on. She served little purpose since she was a widow and too old to be a lady-in-waiting. Additionally, the queen didn't like her. She wasn't one of Robert's spies, nor was she someone who contributed to the royal coffers. She maintained her household at court through the gifts given to her by the men she bedded. She was a favorite among the men at court because not only was she a stunning beauty, she was lusty, too.

"Beth made an observation this morning that stuck with me. I told her I was coming to you to share what she and I discussed. She pointed out that Lady MacAdams must be one of the most well-informed, and therefore, most dangerous women at court. I didn't think much of it when Beth said it, since Lady MacAdams doesn't, or rather didn't, strike me as someone who cared much for aught beyond gossip. I realize now what Beth meant. She understood that the lady must hear things from her bedmates that they might otherwise keep secret. She doesn't seem to seduce men for their power, but she's known to take an ugly mon to her bed on occasion, so it's not merely physical attraction either. I suspect she knows enough to be far more dangerous than anyone has stopped to consider. The question is: who does she share these secrets with?"

"I've had my eye on her since she arrived. A woman that beautiful who knows it is always likely to cause a stir at court, and not in a way anyone but she appreciates. She has refused marriage proposals hand over fist, claiming her heart broke when her husband died. More likely, she doesn't want a new husband to take her away from court. She does go for powerful men, but she also goes for those who are in positions to know much even if they cannot control much. She seeks out emissaries from other countries and those sent from various clans. When she was newly widowed, I assumed she was just a lusty wench who liked a good tupping, but I noticed the pattern in who she beds. I've just never discovered what she does with the information she gathers. Either she's keeping it to herself for a rainy day, or she's passing it along from one mon to another. I've ordered her chambers searched numerous times, but no one ever finds any missives. I've arranged for her maids and grooms to be watched and followed, but noaught ever exchanges hands. I just figured she uses what she knows to manipulate men into paying for her to live in the lap of luxury here at court."

"Perhaps we should take her more seriously. After

all, she may have married into the MacAdams clan, but she's related to the Gregors through her mother's people. Many Gregors initially supported the Balliols, many of whom fled to Ireland."

"This is a tangled web of former lovers, Edward. Are you thinking Lady MacAdams, in an effort to better the Gregor cause, is funneling information to the Balliols in Ireland? Could they have bought Sinead's support through jealousy and convinced her to target you?" Robert scratched his chin.

"While the connections are possible, I doubt Sinead would ever do more than spit in the eye of a Balliol. She'd been invested in the Irish cause since she was a young girl. She was tireless in her efforts to see the English driven from Ireland, so she wasn't going to aid anyone who sided with the English. Ever. Ireland might be a coincidence, but I doubt the ties between Lady MacAdams and the Gregors and Balliols is a coincidence."

"Will they never cease? I have driven them out of Scotland and punished most of their supporters, and yet they persist. Can they not accept defeat graciously?" Robert snarled.

"Would you?" Edward teased.

"No, never. Nonetheless, they are a constant thorn in my side when I need to remain focused on Longshanks and his bluidy army."

"Perhaps they fear Edward will now take command of your army along the border." The men spun around as both Edward's wife Elizabeth and Queen Elizabeth entered the antechamber. Edward raised his eyebrows at his wife, silently asking her what else she had to say. "I would assume as much if I were the English or anyone who sympathizes with them. Many people speculated that between Edward's unexpected arrival and you sending him to the border for a moon."

"I heard the rumors but did naught to disabuse people of the idea since it seemed just as well known, if not more so, that you wanted to retire to the Highlands with your bride." Robert once again stroked his beard as he looked at his brother.

"Perhaps people think the Highland notion was a ploy and mean to keep you from taking command at the border," Queen Elizabeth offered. "They targeted you twice when they thought you were least protected and away from court. They must have thought you were in the carriage with Elizabeth, and then they had to have known you were traveling without an army to Culcreuch. After your moon at the border these people whoever they are, must have grown nervous. My guess is they thought Elizabeth would be so terrified after the accident and the attack that the mess in the chamber would be enough to push her around the bend. I think they were relying on her insisting that you leave court posthaste. They wanted to send a message that they weren't through, but they also want to chase you away, leaving you unprotected and vulnerable to the next attack."

"Have you and my wife been solving the world's problems together?" Robert bussed a kiss on his wife's temple as he looked at Elizabeth.

"Not all of the world's problems, but hopefully our most immediate one." Elizabeth came to stand next to Edward, who vacated his seat for her. He'd been overly solicitous for the past day, ever since he learned of the bairn on the way. She eased into the seat and patted the hand he rested on her shoulder. "Have you both concluded that Lady MacAdams, the Gregors, and the Balliols are the most likely culprits? That is the conclusion that the queen, Deirdre, Ceit, and I came to."

"You've been discussing this with others?" The king's tone announced his displeasure.

"Not others, Your Grace," Elizabeth fell back on the deference drilled into her since she arrived at court as an eleven-year-old. "My cousin and her sister-by-marriage are just as much a part of this as I am. It's their husbands you summoned to help Edward, and Ceit is one of your former spies tasked with keeping an eye on Balliol supporters just across the border. It seemed logical to seek their opinions."

Robert seemed mollified, and the glare his wife shot him was surely a part of it. He was accustomed to being brusque with his advisors, but he knew his manners should have been better toward his family. He was unwilling to admit out loud how much the threat to his brother troubled him. Politically, it would be troublesome if his Scottish opponents were becoming active again, especially if they conspired with the English. But it was more than that. Edward was his brother, a man he had loved and trusted since they were children. He'd already lost three of his blood brothers, and his last surviving blood brother was fighting his own war in Ireland. He couldn't stand the thought of losing one more member of his family. Their sacrifice for his claim to the throne had been a great one.

"Please. Call me Robert when we gather as family."

Elizabeth took a breath before responding. "Thank you. Robert." She looked back at Edward before returning her gaze to the royal couple. "What do we do next?"

"I've summoned Magnus and Tavish to join us. It would seem we need to learn of Lady MacAdams's connections."

"She isn't going to volunteer that information if she is a part of this," Edward stated.

"If she's exchanging information with the men she beds, then we need one on our side. I intend to ask Tavish to revisit his rakish days and see if he can seduce her into sharing what she knows."

"Absolutely nae. Ma wife would have ma bollocks. And I like them too much," a deep voice rattled through the chamber as the Sinclair brothers entered. Tavish looked fit to be tied, and Magnus's scowl looked like a thundercloud. "Even if ma wife wouldnae end ma life that day, I have nay desire to ever go near that she-devil again. I had ma fill of her and dinna want any more."

"Yer Grace," Magnus bowed, trying to show some courtesy before launching his own dissention. "Ye should've warned us that ye might suggest we commit adultery. Ye could've saved us the trip. Ye ken it will never happen."

"I didn't say he had to actually bed her. I said he should see if he could seduce her."

"One in the same, Yer Grace," Tavish snapped. "I willna do it. I willna disgrace Ceit that way, and I simply dinna want to. The woman is evil."

"We know that. We believe she's part of whomever is plotting to kill Edward." Robert broke in.

"Edward? We thought this was aboot Elizabeth," Magnus looked at his cousin-by-marriage.

"We've pieced together that there's just as strong a chance, if not greater, that this is aboot Edward instead. We think whoever is behind all of this thought he was in the carriage with me, and the attack on the way to Culcreuch wasn't aboot kidnapping me." Elizabeth glanced back at Edward.

"But ye canna be sure either way," Magnus surmised.

"Yer Grace--" Tavish began.

"Enough!" Robert slammed his hand on the table. "If I hear those two words come out of your mouth again, I shall have you mucking out horse

216

stalls just as your da had you do as a lad. You know you need not address me as such in private. You only do it when you're peeved at me."

"I am peeved, *Uncle* Robert." Tavish reverted to what the Sinclairs called the king when they were children. "Sinclairs dinna commit adultery. We dinna even consider it. If Ceit didna kill me, Da would. I willna disappoint him like that, nor will I dishonor ma clan. Ye'll have to find another way."

Tavish turned to face Edward, his eyes hard. He liked Edward well enough and had grown to respect him even more during the month they spent traveling, but he was unwilling to forsake his marriage for anyone.

"Ye should be the one climbing into bed with her if that's yer plan. Ye're the one she's taken the latest interest in. She kens neither Magnus nor I would ever try to tup her." Elizabeth stiffened, and Edward's eyes cast daggers at Tavish. "Aye. The notion doesnae sit any better with yer wife than it would mine."

Elizabeth took a deep breath, trying to unwind the coiled knot that took residence in her belly with Tavish's suggestion. She didn't think Edward would agree to such a notion, but if Robert considered ordering Tavish to bed another woman, who was to say he wouldn't issue the same order to her husband?

"Where are Ceit and Deirdre?" Elizabeth tried to change the subject. "They didn't come with you?"

Magnus and Tavish grinned.

"We don't need to hear of how exhausted your wives must be now that you've returned," the king grumbled.

"They are that, but that isnae why they havenae joined us yet. Both are a wee green aboot the gills in the mornings," Tavish's grin widened.

"Ceit didn't tell me!" Elizabeth exclaimed. "They

figured out aboot me, but neither of them said aught aboot Ceit." It stung that her cousin and friend hadn't shared Ceit's happy news when she did.

"Ceit wasna certain until a day or so ago when she couldnae overlook the nausea any longer. They've both been sick as dogs even though Deirdre seems to be over the worst of it." Magnus explained. "Deirdre told me they didna want to take away from yer happy news. Plus, Ceit wasna sure until Tavish panicked and insisted the healer examine her."

"If they can keep aught down, they will join us." Tavish's face gave a glimpse of his concern before he pushed his grin back into place.

"I'm surprised you left their sides. I would've thought you'd be hovering like nursemaids." Robert teased.

"They were, but they were driving us barmy. We were glad to send them off to answer your summons, Your Grace." Deirdre chuckled as she and Ceit entered the chamber.

"That bluidy title again. Lady Deirdre, we are among family," Robert motioned for them to take a seat beside their husbands.

Elizabeth could tell both men wished to pull their wives into their laps, but for the sake of some decorum, they settled for pulling their wives chairs next to theirs, wrapping their arms around them, and holding their hands. In turn, both women sagged against their husbands, shadows under their eyes, their skin rather sallow.

"What did we miss?" Ceit asked before swallowing several times.

They met her question with silence, making her jerk upright. She looked at the king before casting a long, hard look at Tavish. She raised one eyebrow, and Tavish looked ready to squirm.

"Before ye start buzzing at me, I refused. I absolutely refused and didna even consider it for a moment," Tavish began before casting a baleful look at the king. "Elizabeth and Edward think Lady MacAdams may be at the heart of this."

Ceit drew back and glared at her husband. There was no love lost between Ceit and Lady MacAdams after the latter tried to seduce Tavish more than once in front of Ceit. Tavish opened his arms again, and she settled back against his side before he continued.

"It was suggested that she may ken a great deal more than anyone has given her credit for. She may gather secrets from the men she beds, so Robert suggested using that to gather our own information."

"You? He suggested you bed her?" Ceit demanded, having already sensed where the conversation was going.

Tavish swiped his hand across the back of his neck before nodding. Elizabeth had witnessed Ceit's temper before, especially where it concerned Tavish. First it had been when they bickered while Tavish tried to court her, then it had been any time Ceit felt she needed to defend Tavish. She was just as protective of her husband as he was of his wife. She'd seen him badly beaten on her account and now took any threat to him as a dire need to defend him.

"Wheesh, *mo sheillean beag*." My little bee. It was Tavish's pet name for his wife since he claimed she buzzed at him like an angry bee but was sweeter than any honey. "I willna do it. I didna even consider it for a moment, and Robert kens how ridiculous it was to even suggest it."

Tavish shot his godfather a glare, daring him to contradict Tavish in front of his angry wife. Everyone's gaze shifted as Deirdre squirmed several times in her seat before rushing from her chair to the door, her hand covering her mouth.

"He didna even consider asking me," Magnus chased after her.

The queen glowered at her husband after watching all three of her former ladies-in-waiting sit in various degrees of distress.

"Well met," the queen muttered.

"Since this isn't a path that will work, what else can we try?" Elizabeth once again tried to steer the conversation onto a less fraught topic. "If Lady MacAdams is lending her support to the Gregors and possibly the Balliols, then she has to be communicating with someone. Other than her lovers."

"Who is she involved with?" Edward looked toward the queen, knowing she'd be the surest source of the romantic liaisons going on at court.

"Who isn't she?" The queen scoffed. "Between the ones she has bedded, the ones she is bedding, and the ones she intends to bed, there are few left."

"I can understand the Gregors' animosity toward me. I don't believe they'll ever forgive me ceding the land and barony around Loch Awe to the Campbells. Their only allies are Clan Grant who they helped take Grant Castle from the Comyns. But the Grants have always been loyal to the cause, first to Wallace and then to me." Robert scrubbed a hand over his face frustrated that despite uniting the Highlands, feuds kept the clans in a suffocating web of alliances and feuds. He was confident that the Comyns wouldn't rise again, so they didn't pose a threat despite their previous nefarious connections to the Balliols. While the Gregors helped rid the Grant land of Comyns, they disliked Robert, and while the Gregors sided with the Grants, the Grants sided with Robert. It was all so tangled that Robert's head throbbed whenever he considered it.

"Then is there someone besides the Balliols and

the Gregors that she might be cozy with?" Elizabeth wondered.

"I can think of several clans that aren't in Robert's favor nor is he in theirs." Queen Elizabeth rambled off names as she held up her fingers. "The Gregors, as we know; the MacDougalls and Mac-Naughtens, the Johnstones, but they sent their daughter here to serve me as a recompense; and the Comyns. The Mac-an-leistears serve the Gregors as their fletchers and they're only a small band, but they side with their overlord. The Dalziel have only recently come over to our side after years of supporting King Edward; and last but not least, Clan Baird."

"Baird?" Edward's head snapped up. "Which ones? Carnwath or Cambusnethan? I thought Baron Carnwath was someone you refused to entertain anywhere near court. You can't stand the mon. It's a great wonder to me that you trust his relatives."

"It's a fairly distant relation between the two septs, and the Cambusnethan Bairds are doing well in Fife. I don't trust Carnwath as far as I can spit. If he were drowning, I'd spit in his mouth."

"He seems like a likely bedfellow for Lady Mac-Adams," Tavish muttered.

"What is the blasted woman's first name?" Magnus asked as he and Deirdre returned. Deirdre's face had more color, and she appeared far less shaky. Magnus eased her back into her seat before taking his next to her. "For a woman everyone seems to ken so well, I've never heard her Christian name."

"I don't think many people ken it," Tavish offered. He couldn't look at his wife as he spoke because he did know. "She insists on everyone addressing her as Lady MacAdams."

"Amelia," Edward said under his breath. He felt as uncomfortable as Tavish looked. Neither wanted to think it; neither wanted to say it because saying

221

her name aloud made it too personal, too much of a reminder of a past that left little but shame and regret.

"What's that?" Robert asked.

Edward sighed, knowing he couldn't avoid repeating himself, but before he could open his mouth, Elizabeth chimed in.

"He said her name is Amelia. I've been here long enough to know even the most distasteful people's names. She is Amelia Arabella MacAdams née Grant. Her father was a distant relative of the current Grant laird, but her mother was a Gregor. The MacAdams clan has direct ties to the Gregor clan more than a few times over. They are a sept, though lately they've kept their distance from the Gregors. Now that I think aboot it, I suspect her late husband brought them to court either to ingratiate themselves into your good graces, severing ties to the Gregors and other MacAdams, or to spy." Elizabeth shrugged when everyone looked at her. "I may not be as interested in the Greeks and Romans as Deirdre, but our history fascinates me. I've read aboot the clan bloodlines and know who married whom. It wasn't difficult to tie it together once I started thinking aboot it."

"And so, we come full circle," Ceit chimed in. She'd gone quiet after her initial burst of temper. She sank into her seat when the queen listed her clan among those who opposed Robert. There was no way that she could deny she was a Comyn by birth, but she much preferred to identify as a Sinclair. Her mother, father, and siblings had suffered for their kinship to the Earl of Buchan, but her father pledged fealty to Robert. However, it didn't erase the stigma attached to the notorious family. "If she is a Gregor, and you disfavor the Bairds too, then perhaps they are in fact bedfellows. Their animosity toward you and your reign may have made them friends with a common enemy."

"That seems reasonable. This entire situation gives me a migram. I cannot keep track of the hoops you've all jumped through to go from believing Elizabeth was the intended target to Edward." The queen rubbed her temple. "You've considered the Comyns and the Balliols along with now the Gregors, MacAdams, Bairds, and who else?"

"That is where things stand now," Edward reassured. "At least we have somewhere to start."

"I feel like we need to draw a map of this web. Or at least cross off the names we've disqualified," Deirdre suggested.

They spent the next half hour making the list and map to keep everyone's mind straight on the current list of suspects. When the finished, Elizabeth felt exhausted. She wanted nothing more than to climb into bed and rest, but she had one more suggestion to make.

"None of us agree to allowing our husbands to seduce or be seduced by Amelia," Elizabeth began, feeling a sense of satisfaction when thinking of the woman by her given name. It seemed humbling after all the haughtiness Elizabeth had to endure over the years. "Then perhaps Deirdre, Ceit, and I can gain some ground. Amelia has relished reminding us of her connections to Tavish and Edward. I'm sure she's had her eye on Magnus. Perhaps if we allow her to taunt us a little, we can draw her into conversation and see if she might give something away. She has little respect for any of us, believing we're all nitwits."

"That's what I was thinking," Ceit spoke up. "She loves to crow aboot her conquests. If we can at least figure out who she's been linked to over the past few moons, that might give us an idea of who is to blame."

"I will be sure that she and the other matrons join us after the evening meal," the queen offered. "Beltane is still a few months off, but I can say that I require suggestions of how to celebrate this year. I'll say I'm in the mood for something grander than in the past. To celebrate the success of Robert's reign. If Amelia is conspiring against us, then that will be fodder for her plans."

CHAPTER TWENTY-TWO

The evening seemed to drag as Elizabeth tried not to squirm too often, but her excitement built with each bite. When the group left the royal antechamber, she felt drained and raw, but after a nap and time spent with Edward, she felt revived. Now, she anticipated retiring to the queen's solar and beginning the inquiry into Lady MacAdams's involvement. While she veritably bubbled over with eagerness, she sensed Edward grew more apprehensive as the meal progressed.

"We're just going to talk to her," Elizabeth spoke behind her goblet.

"Be sure that's all it is," Edward muttered.

"What more can we do in the queen's solar? Do you fear we'll wrestle her to the ground and thrash her until she confesses?"

"Yes." Edward didn't appreciate the mirth in her voice.

Elizabeth spluttered the sip she'd taken. Edward's abrupt answer wasn't what she expected.

"You worry we'd get into a fight with her in front of all the women at court? Don't you trust us to have any discretion?"

"I do," Edward sighed. "But I also know how

tenacious the three of you can be, and I know how much you want this resolved. I don't worry it would come to fisticuffs, but I do worry that an argument will erupt if you push too hard."

Elizabeth placed her hand on Edward's leg beneath the tablecloth. She waited to see if he'd hold it in place or move his thigh away. When his hand covered hers, she breathed easier but chided herself for having too little faith in Edward.

"We will only ask enough to get a sense for whether it might involve her. More than that would be far too nosy considering none of us have ever taken an interest in her before."

"Just be careful, Beth. If the attacks weren't intended for me but you, then you're still in imminent danger. If they intended them for me, you're still in danger because of our connection. I can't bear aaught happening to you. I'd rather we pack tonight and find somewhere up north to take refuge."

"We could always go to the Sinclairs. I doubt they would turn us down."

"And bring any unresolved threats to their doorstep?"

"No, I suppose not. But if we hid, then no one would be sure where to look."

"They would look at the Sinclairs. You're related to them now by marriage and all five of the Sinclairs are the king's and queen's godchildren. Laird Sinclair is a staunch supporter of the king."

"I'll be careful. I promise."

The music began and as the courtiers moved about to form lines for dancing, their conversation ended. Elizabeth wasn't in the mood to dance, and from the looks on Deirdre's and Ceit's faces neither were they. The two Sinclair couples welcomed Edward and Elizabeth to their table, where they observed the dancing.

"I'm too tired to even consider twirling around," Deirdre mused.

"Then let us retire," Magnus suggested, elbowing his brother as Tavish chortled.

"Yes, he plans on that too, Tavish." Deirdre shot her brother-by-marriage a pointed look. "But Magnus would rather I not meddle with Amelia." Deirdre placed a hand over her chest, the evening meal not sitting well with her.

"Tavish is one to speak," Ceit shot her husband a censuring look when he opened his mouth. "He griped at me all afternoon aboot being careful and not drawing too much attention to my questioning and not getting on Amelia's bad side. As though I haven't done this sort of thing before. He seems to have forgotten how we came to be acquainted."

"I havenae forgotten at all, *mo sheillean beag*. And that's what terrifies me." Tavish's face lost all its humor when teasing his brother morphed into worrying his wife. All three warriors found that little in life frightened them except for anything that might risk their wives' safety. Those possibilities were the makings of their nightmares.

"Edward is none too keen either as the time draws closer." Elizabeth nudged her shoulder against Edward's. "They seem to have no understanding of what our service was like. If we weren't the gossips, then we heard aboot it. Women sizing one another up based on their conquests is naught new. We, as a gender, are not so different as men. We're just not as gauche when we discuss topics that might offend our tender sensibilities."

The three women smiled like cats that got into the cream, and all three husbands stood aghast.

"Just how much talking aboot what happens behind closed doors do you do?" Magnus demanded.

"Not much since we haven't had the opportunity.

When we were unwed, well when Beth and Ceit were unwed and everyone assumed I was, we weren't privy to such conversations. We overheard them, but we never joined them. What would we have had to offer? Now that we're married, it's expected for us to join in. Especially since we are all still fairly newlywed, and it's obvious that we are all amorous with our husbands."

Magnus didn't look mollified, nor did Edward or Tavish.

"We'll be careful. We're not interested in making a scene," Elizabeth tried to sound soothing without being patronizing. "We'll just have to wait and see what comes of this conversation."

The couples had a longer wait than they would've liked. Eventually, they relented and joined the dancers. The husbands and wives were equally determined to only partner with their spouses during the slower songs. All three women turned down numerous offers, the men accepting the rejection when the ladies' husbands glowered over their shoulders. Elizabeth's feet ached and her head was pounding when the queen finally signaled it was time for the women to retire.

The queen swept into her solar and settled into her favorite chair. She cast a gimlet eye as the women filed in and gathered in their regular groups. Deirdre, Ceit, and Elizabeth noticed a group of matrons with whom they were acquainted. They wandered closer to the married women who aimed withering looks at the tittering ladies-in-waiting. Elizabeth grazed her elbow against a woman's arm.

"My apologies, my lady," Elizabeth offered as she smiled at a woman she recognized as Lady Eleanor

Gordon, a widow cast from the same mold as Lady MacAdams. In fact, they were bosom buddies.

"Ah, Lady Elizabeth," the lady gushed. Elizabeth caught the gleam in the woman's eye. She was a social climber, and the opportunity to hobnob with a countess, the queen's sister-by-marriage no less, was too fine a one to pass up. "I don't believe I have offered my felicitations on your rather unexpected marriage."

Before Elizabeth responded, the target of her mission stepped forward, offering a malicious smile.

"There was naught unexpected aboot it," Amelia MacAdams's condescension rolled off her in waves. "The earl was sniffing aboot her skirts like a lost pup scratching at the kitchen door."

Elizabeth braced herself to not let her temper get the better of her.

"My husband is very determined to get what he sets out for." Elizabeth offered the demurest smile she could.

"We know," cackled Lady Gordon. Elizabeth felt the color rise in her neck and once again, for at least the millionth time, cursed her fair coloring that would show her blush. Eleanor had just admitted she'd bedded Edward as clearly as if she said the words aloud.

"He also doesn't settle." Elizabeth's voice was hushed, but her words carried as the chamber quietened to watch Elizabeth go toe-to-toe with two of the most vindictive women at court.

"We shall see, my lady. You're still in the first blush of youth; the earl's excitement over a new toy hasn't worn off. Yet." Amelia smirked. "Then again, he has been spending quite a lot of time out of sight."

Elizabeth understood the implication but wouldn't take the bait the way Amelia wished.

"It would be rather hard to see him when we're tucked away in our chamber for so much of the day."

Amelia snapped her mouth shut, but Eleanor had more to say.

"Who would've guessed you were such a strumpet," Eleanor softened her tone making it almost sound endearing, but the words were anything but.

"My husband brings out the best in me." Elizabeth fluttered her eyelashes. "I've learned the hidden secrets you two must be experts in. Bedsport is rather divine. I understand it's even better when done with someone you care aboot."

Amelia's lips tightened into a pucker while Eleanor laughed without mirth. Ceit and Deirdre had stood quietly while Elizabeth stood her ground. Her friends pressed closer to the women who antagonized Elizabeth.

"That's what my Tavish says, too. He can't keep his hands off me, says he never realized, despite all his practice, that ravishing a woman he loves would be so much better." Ceit grinned without remorse. The most brazen of the three women, she had no qualms about gloating in front of two women who were part of her husband's past.

"Magnus can't say the same, but that's because he's wanted no one else once we got together. Turned down every offer like it was bad fish under his nose." Deirdre mused with an innocence that belied the bluntness of her words.

"We did always consider him an odd duck that way. We wondered if he was a mon for all that size and brute strength." Amelia's snarky tone caught more than one woman's attention. Elizabeth and the others were aware they didn't need anyone else listening in, so they slowly shifted their position to place their backs to the rest of the chamber. Elizabeth noticed the queen began speaking with the other women, giving instructions on her plans for the spring feast.

"He found what he liked and refused to settle for less," Deidre shrugged.

"We would apologize for taking away your favorite novelties if we weren't so sure you've already found other things to occupy you." Elizabeth tested the waters. "I heard something aboot the Earl of Atholl, but I can't remember who was mentioned." Elizabeth had heard no such thing and was aware the earl hadn't been to court in several months, but he was a powerful man both women pursued in the past.

"Good God, no," Amelia laughed. "The mon is too fickle, be it his women or his politics. Besides his daughter is the mother of the other Edward's son. It would seem incestuous to bed the father and the son-by-marriage, or rather son-by-tupping." Amelia had just admitted she bedded both of the king's brothers named Edward.

"Incestuous? Come now, Lady MacAdams," Eleanor tried not to choke as she held in her laughter. "That's not the reason. You've tupped brothers---at the same time—and not worried aboot your conscience screaming incest."

Elizabeth wondered if her own husband had been one of those sets of brothers, and from Ceit's pale face, she guessed her friend wondered the same thing. After all, Tavish had two other brothers besides Magnus.

"Be that as it may, Strathbogie is not to my taste."

"The Earl of Mar seems like a mon who might hold your interest," Deirdre suggested.

"Which one?" Eleanor didn't bother to cover her laugh this time. "Once more, Lady MacAdams, your conscience was quiet with this one. Both Domnalls and I recall Gartnait, too. Father, son, and grandson. Quite the trifecta. I wish I could claim such an accomplishment."

Amelia grew irritated, and Elizabeth noticed the woman didn't appreciate her so-called friend's teasing. Elizabeth glanced at Deirdre and Ceit before sliding her eyes to Lady Gordon and raising an eyebrow.

"Lady Gordon," Ceit moved closer to the woman, and her words trailed off as she spoke in conspiratorial tones. Elizabeth failed to make out what Ceit said. Once Ceit drew Eleanor into conversation, Elizabeth watched as Amelia stretched her neck before glaring at Elizabeth for catching her in a moment of weakness.

"I suspect you didn't have to try very hard for any of the Earls of Mar to wind up in your bed. I may detest the past you have with my husband, but I can admit you're a beautiful woman. You hold an appeal to men that is beguiling, bewitching even."

"Are you warning me away from Lord Edward?" Amelia looked down her nose at Elizabeth, even though they were the same height.

"No. I know I don't need to. I don't have to worry aboot my husband having a roaming eye, and I trust you're wise enough to recognize who not to cross." Elizabeth's tone remained soft, but the steel rang in each word. "I admit to wondering what it must be like to have so many men flock to you. Now that I am no longer a maiden, I can speak more freely. I've seen you over the years, and even men you barely glance at seem drawn to you like you're a siren of some sort."

"Entertaining." Amelia offered only one word as she looked past Elizabeth as though she grew bored with the conversation now that Eleanor wasn't at her arm.

"I would imagine having such choice must be very freeing," Deirdre spoke up. "I remember when I was being forced into a betrothal with Lord Hay, I felt trapped, but once I reunited with the mon I wanted, it was like they had released me from a cage."

Amelia paused and studied the two women before responding.

"I don't dislike either of you even if I desire your husbands. A lesson you would do well to learn with warriors for husbands is to remember you control your own lives far more than any mon wants you to believe. In all likelihood, they will leave you widows sooner rather than later, so you'll find yourself in need of protection. That doesn't come from any mon; it comes from your wits. Choose your bedmates for their looks and their prowess alone, and you will be satisfied but destitute. Choose your bedmates based on what they want to learn, and you will find security as long as you are judicious in what you share."

Amelia's revelations stunned Elizabeth and Deirdre. Neither was sure which was more shocking: the realization that Amelia had just offered them confirmation that she traded in court secrets, or the fact that she'd offered them advice that was sound.

"Thank you, Lady MacAdams. That is a notion to keep in mind. Now that I'm not much in favor with my clan, I would have to rely on the generosity of the Sinclairs if something were to happen to Magnus. I don't enjoy the idea of ever bedding a mon besides my husband, but I'm afraid the king or my parents would order me to remarry if I waited too long. Keeping my ability to choose is paramount after being manipulated for so many years. But I fear

I would be too naïve, even after my years at court, to pick the right protector."

Amelia appeared aggrieved as she considered what to say to two young women who she never guessed would ever be her tutees. She studied both women who'd lost the naivete inherent in virgins, but they still weren't worldly enough to understand why she chose some of her partners. She remembered being their age not so long ago when she was still a young wife, newly arrived at court and on the elbow of a robust husband. While they hadn't been a love match, they were well suited. She hadn't been lying when she said she was too heartbroken to marry again. The pain of having to learn to navigate through the dangers of court life, the pain of knowing there was little to return to on either Mac-Adams land or Gregor or Grant, the pain of sacrificing her body to provide for herself had all broken her heart. She refused to be so reliant on any one man ever again. However, despite knowing there was little for her if she returned to her husband's clan or those of her parents, she remained loyal to a fault. She tolerated a great deal to protect the ones she loved.

"Men come and go as easily as the weather in Scotland. Women persevere and exist like the mountains that are the heart of our land. Men want pretty women in their beds; lusty ones are all the better. But their greatest shortcoming is underestimating a woman's intelligence. They assume we're feather-brained, which I will never understand. What do they think happens with all that they tell us? In one ear and out the other? Does it fall upon our pillows while we sleep? Men love to hear themselves talk, and a woman who allows them such self-interest is one who will never fear for her next meal and will always be in demand. Squirrel away the drivel they spew for a rainy day. The knowledge may be the difference between serving men on your back in a castle rather than a tavern. For all they think you'll forget when they are the ones doing the talking, they're quick to pursue you for what someone else may have told you. These secrets are your currency. Trade them for the necessities, and I mean more than just jewels. Trade them for the clothes on your back and the table at which you dine. You can sell the jewels to pay your servants."

All that Amelia shared left Elizabeth and Deirdre agog. Neither had ever heard her speak so many words to any other woman let alone to them. Elizabeth deduced Amelia had no indication they suspected her in the attacks. It was obvious she considered them naiver and more gullible than they were. Elizabeth understood if her life had taken a different path, the thoughts Amelia proselytized would've been ones she'd remember for later use. But for now, she took them as a veiled confession to possessing secrets that might affect those at court and beyond, in particular Edward and her. She just needed some names.

"I wouldn't even know who to approach," Elizabeth murmured.

"Approach only the men you want for your own entertainment. Let the men with power and influence approach you. They always will since you're both beautiful in your own right. These are the men who want to chase, then dominate, for the sake of having what another does not, even if it's only for a night."

"But what if a mon approaches that I neither desire nor think can do me any favors?" Deirdre wondered.

"Consider what information you might gain rather than what you can offer."

"I suppose that is a favor in a way," Elizabeth mused.

"Exactly," Amelia nodded.

"But that still doesn't clarify which men to accept. I mean I understand what you're telling us, but I suppose I want to figure out which men are too dangerous to tangle with." Deirdre adopted a pensive expression as she tried to steer Amelia toward naming anyone she might have bedded who was a threat to women who supported Robert. "I mean what if the wrong person approaches?"

"They're only the wrong person if you can't make use of what you learn. Every mon can have his own use. Some men like their bedsport rough. Those are men to avoid, unless of course, you're into that." Amelia's gaze swept over Elizabeth and Deirdre before she gave a brief knowing nod. "Other men can grow angry if they doubt you've shared enough, or they realize they've shared too much. But most men are just happy to swive. The more adept you become, the more power you realize you have. Empires have been built and fallen from what a woman knows."

Elizabeth and Deirdre nodded before Deirdre offered, "I never realized all of that. That's rather profound."

"And true," Amelia looked past the cousins and appeared to grow bored once more. Neither woman wanted to push their luck after everything Lady MacAdams divulged. They watched as she glided toward the queen and Lady Gordon joined her.

"Lady Gordon is quite a wealth of information," Ceit spoke, but her lips barely moved; a skill she perfected during her days as a spy. "It thrilled her to share Lady MacAdams's extensive list of bedfellows. She painted quite the picture of a whore dressed as a lady. Seemed more like the pot calling the kettle black."

236

"You may have done better than we did if that's the case." Elizabeth murmured. "Amelia said she doesn't dislike us even if she still wants our husbands. She offered a few life lessons for women who must make their own way. She admitted she trades her body for secrets, so I'd say it's probable that she's involved in this even if she isn't the mastermind."

"Let's find the men and retire to a chamber where we can speak." Deirdre looked toward the queen who watched them from the corner of her eye. Deirdre nodded, to which the queen responded with her own nod toward the door. Ceit, Deirdre, and Elizabeth slipped from the salon and made their way to Elizabeth's chamber. It was the largest of the three couples, so it made the most sense for everyone to meet there.

CHAPTER TWENTY-THREE

"**W**here are they?" Tavish paced like a caged animal as his gaze darted to the door every few seconds.

"The queen won't release them until the woman is ready to retire for the night. I don't like it any better than you do, but we must wait." Edward fastened his own gaze on the door.

Magnus sat before the fire, neither watching his brother nor the door. Instead, he sat pensively. The only outward sign of his anxiety was the white-knuckle grip he had on the chair's armrests. He sprang from his seat at the sound of someone pressing the outside door handle. The wives entered, chattering and laughing, to find three husbands who stood with their feet hip-width apart and arms crossed. The women jerked to a stop when they saw their brooding men, but Ceit burst into laughter.

"Look, Elizabeth. Your husband has become one of them. He uses the Odin stance, too," Ceit guffawed.

"We call it the Sinclair stance at court, but aye, Edward does resemble them. Maybe a cousin with the red instead of brown hair." Elizabeth approached Edward, using his crossed arms to brace herself as she rose on her toes to give him a peck. Edward's arms snagged her against his chest as he captured her mouth in a searing kiss. If Elizabeth had looked around, she would've discovered her cousin and friend were similarly engaged with their husbands. "You need to remember that we were all ladies-in-waiting long before we came to live with our husbands. How do you think we survived before we had you to safeguard us?"

"I never doubted your ability to survive at court, but that doesn't mean I have to like you sitting in a den of vipers," Edward stroked her hair back from her cheek. "I want more than aught to get you away from here, and yet, you are still in the thick of things."

"Ye both are more than welcome to come home with us," Tavish offered. "The air is fresh and doesnae have the taint of these bastards. We can leave in the morning."

Tavish's offer brought smiles to everyone's face, but they were small and weak. They all recognized they could go nowhere until they put this situation to rest.

"We'll take you up on that offer, friend," Edward nodded at Tavish and Magnus.

"In the meantime," Ceit broke in. "We have plenty to tell you." She practically crowed as she drew Tavish toward the fireplace. Tavish sat and pulled her onto his lap. Magnus followed his older brother's lead, and Edward was only too happy to follow suit.

"Beth and I spoke to Amelia," Deirdre explained. "And while she didn't give up any names, she confirmed she trades her favors for secrets. I almost feel sorry for her, to be honest. It's clear she can't or won't return to MacAdams land nor Grant or Gregor. I don't understand why that is, but she's decided that court is her home, and she's willing to do what she must to remain."

"Eleanor had no such qualms gossiping aboot Amelia's exploits. I had to keep repeating the names in my head to make sure I didn't forget any on the long list. The woman has slept with a mon from nearly every clan! Several from some clans." Ceit cut her a husband a glare before going on. "Most recently, she attached herself to delegates from Clans Gunn, Kerr, and Hay."

"The three clans we've had the most trouble with," Tavish mused. "She obviously likes to stay abreast of the current political climate. She couldnae get aught from Magnus or me while we were here, so she went to the other side."

Laird Liam Sinclair had originally sent Magnus to court a few months earlier to resolve issues with the Gunns, Kerrs, and De Soules after his older brothers' wives' families caused strife with the Sinclairs. When Magnus reunited with Deirdre, the ensuing intrigue kept him from settling the problems and kept him away from home so long that their father sent Tavish to discover what was keeping Magnus. It was also a chance for Tavish to meet Ceit, the woman his father and the king intended him to marry. Fortune smiled upon both men because they found the women they loved. But that didn't change the tensions that existed among the clans, and Amelia MacAdams seemed to be in the thick of it.

"But there's so, so much more," Ceit responded. "Eleanor hasn't forgiven her for her dalliance with her own dead husband, who was the brother of the current Gordon laird. In fair turnaround, Eleanor bedded a Grant and a Gregor, at the same time mind you, that Amelia had her eye on. I don't think Eleanor realized it, but I would assume these were men Amelia had business with beyond the bed sheets. Amelia made them merely seem to be the object of her desire and naught more. Apparently, she's also been very cozy with her late husband's nephew, Hamish MacAdams, who's been at court for the past couple of moons. It's said he's best friends with Roy Gregor, the son of the Gregor laird."

"I suspect she's funneling information to Hamish to give to Roy and his father." Edward mused. "The Gregors won't show up here any time soon, since there are too many Campbells floating around. That said, I'm certain they'd like to be kept apprised of what is happening with the Campbells. Losing that land came as a hefty shock."

Edward hadn't agreed with Robert's choice to reward the Campbells at the Gregors' expense. The Gregors had been just as loyal as the Campbells once they came over to Robert's side, but didn't have the numbers or strength that their neighbors did. Robert needed the Campbells as a foundation for his army. The Campbells were gloating and harrying the Gregors, pushing them into smaller and smaller tracts of land, and Robert had turned a blind eye.

"That's exactly what she must be doing, because Eleanor said she was entertaining a Campbell who visited court a few months ago at aboot the same time as when Robert ceded the land to the Campbells." Ceit responded.

"How does she find the time?" Deirdre wondered aloud before blushing.

"We all ken there is plenty of time for that much bedsport." Tavish nipped at his wife's ear. "But how does she find the time to juggle so many without one growing jealous or suspicious?"

"How'd she manage her time with you?" Ceit snapped.

Tavish swallowed so deeply that his Adam's apple bobbed. He kicked himself for not keeping his mouth shut. He closed his eyes before answering his wife.

"I didna care who else she was with. I had other diversions."

Tavish opened his eyes and looked at his brother, who offered him no sympathy. He glanced at Edward, who looked just as uncomfortable. Edward was only slightly less miserable since he'd resorted to finding his diversions with servants and tavern wenches toward the end of his relationship with Sinead. Bedding ladies seemed to enrage the fiery redhead, so he avoided them.

"I'm guessing most of her lovers are the same way," Elizabeth, always the arbitrator, tried to smooth out the discomfort this conversation caused. "That's why she can have so many bedfellows, and that's why men end up sharing more than they intend. They consider their time with her a dalliance. They must say things in passing, thinking it matters little since they don't have a more lasting attachment."

"I agree. That's probably how she does it. I assume she sets them at ease with her, ah—skills--, and the pillow talk results." It embarrassed Deirdre to discuss the matter in front of her two friends, who were in turn trying not to show how much discussing their husbands' former lover bothered them. She thanked God that she never had to contend with such awkwardness and embarrassment with Magnus. She feared he'd moved on during the time they were apart. She'd never felt more relief and more cherished than she did when she discovered Magnus had been as faithful as she had, despite the years separating them.

"Who else?" Tavish asked.

"The only other name that stuck out was Baird." Ceit's tone was tart, but she relaxed against Tavish's chest as he stroked her back and whispered something in her ear that seemed to soothe her. "Eleanor discovered Amelia was entertaining a mon in secret out in town. She saw her slip out of the castle one night and sent one of her guards to follow Amelia. Thank heavens for Eleanor's nosiness; otherwise, we wouldn't have a clue that Amelia was involved with the last suspect on our list. Eleanor gloated that she seduced the mon after meeting him in the market 'by accident'. She didn't want Amelia to have something she didn't, but I suspect Amelia's reasons were very different. From what's said, the mon looks like a toad."

"You must be talking aboot Carnwarth then. He is mealy mouthed and two-faced." Edward's lip curled in disgust. "But as weak as he appears, we shouldn't underestimate him. He's not welcomed at court, but if Amelia is slipping out to see him, then she must have a good reason."

"How long ago did Eleanor say Baird was in Stirling?" Elizabeth asked.

"He's here now," Ceit grinned. "And what's more, Eleanor said she knows Amelia's had him smuggled into the castle every evening for the past sennight. She didn't mind letting him go, said he was naught to write home aboot, but I think she envies Amelia for having such an illicit affair."

"I know what I have to do," Elizabeth bit her bottom lip, waiting for her husband's explosive refusal.

"No! Absolutely not, Elizabeth." And there it was. Elizabeth looked at her husband's face as it turned into the hardened appearance of a warrior. "You're not going traipsing through those passageways. No!"

"Eddie," Elizabeth kept her voice low and reached out her hand to stroke his forearm, but he yanked it away. "I've been wandering around those tunnels for the entire time I've lived here. I did long before I met you, and I survived just fine."

"But that was before---" Edward trailed off.

"Before what? Before you cared aboot me? Or more accurately, before I was carrying your heir." Elizabeth's chest hurt to think Edward's worry had little to do with her, but more to do with the vessel carrying his child being harmed.

"Don't, Elizabeth. That's not fair, and you know it. I was aboot say before I knew you. I have tried to convince you not to go into them alone since I followed you through one. I've feared you falling or becoming ill and being lost in there forever. I had those feelings long before you got with child. You insult me, and I don't appreciate your low opinion of me." Edward's voice trailed off, so only Elizabeth heard his last words.

"I'm sorry," Elizabeth whispered before turning back to the others. "If someone will go with me, then that's the best way to discover what Amelia is up to. Many of the chambers in the royal family's suites have walls thin enough to listen through, but that isn't the case in other parts of the castle. The wing that Lady MacAdams and Lady Gordon live in, along with other unwed matrons, wasn't always used as bedchambers. All the walls are thin, and there are even gaps where you can see into some of them. The mortar is crumbling in some parts, so it wouldn't be hard to scrape some away to make it easier to hear and see."

"Not someone, me." Edward crossed his arms over his broad chest and dared his wife to disagree. Without batting an eyelash, she took up the challenge.

"That part of the castle has narrower passageways than others. Because those chambers weren't meant for anyone to hide there, the tunnels aren't wide. They are just connectors to the main parts of the keep. They weren't designed for many people to use at once like others were if the castle needed to be evacuated. You'd have a hard time fitting. Any of you men would. Ceit could come with me."

Ceit nodded, but Tavish was already shaking his head.

"Nay. Dinna even let the idea take root, Ceity. Ye arenae wandering through the bowels of this heap."

"You can't fit. You heard Elizabeth. Deirdre is too far along to be comfortable either, even if she's only showing a bit. Both Elizabeth and I can bend and stoop if we need to. The last thing Elizabeth needs is to try to unwedge one of you giants. Then she really will be up a gum tree."

Elizabeth and Ceit faced off with their husbands, an epic battle of wills the men already accepted they would lose. Tavish and Edward may have stared down enemies intent upon killing them, but both men would acknowledge their stubbornness was little match for their wives' iron wills. They also understood that logically speaking, their wives were right. But neither was willing to give up the good fight yet.

"What if someone hears you?" Edward demanded.

"Even if they did, and that's assuming I stop using the skills I've had for half my life and our former spy suddenly forgets how to be quiet, they still wouldn't know how to get into the passageways. They wouldn't even know where on the walls to search for the peepholes or the latches," Elizabeth reasoned.

"What if someone kens how to get into the passageways and they hear ye passing by? They could catch ye before ye even get to Amelia's chamber," Tavish reasoned.

"Only a few ladies-in-waiting are aware of the tunnels, and they use them to slip outside to the barracks. There's a door to the bailey from a passageway. None have any idea how it connects to the larger maze. I don't think the king even knows where all the tunnels lead. I have the entire castle memorized after all these years. I know how many steps it takes if I walk and how many it takes if I run. I know what to search for in the dark to know my way or to find an exit." Elizabeth explained, but blushed to her roots when everyone shared the same shocked expression. "I was lonely as a child. This was well before Deirdre came to court; I'd already been here for five years. I had Reubadair and rode as often as I could, but that didn't fill all my days. I took lessons with a tutor, learned to dance and play more than one instrument, but that still left large stretches of the day where my parents expected me to stay confined to my chamber. I got bored and explored. Knowing my way around allowed me to slip out to ride or to see my half-brother and half-sisters."

Elizabeth wasn't about to admit to the Sinclairs what she had to Edward: it allowed her to watch other couples.

"What if we took an hourglass with us?" Ceit offered. "We set one before we go into the tunnels and you set one from wherever we enter. If we aren't back before the glass runs out, then you search for us. Elizabeth, can you draw a map of where we enter to Amelia's chamber? That way if they get into too much of a twitch, they can find us."

"I can do that. I already have some parts of the keep drawn out. I hide the parchments in one of my chests. I used to roll them up and stored them with the clothes I wore to ride or go out into town. I had a spot under the floorboards beneath my bed."

"That's where I hid my clothes and weapons,"

Ceit giggled, but Tavish's growl cut it short. She leaned over and gave him a peck on the lips. "Aye well, you aren't the only one with a past that's less than spotless."

"If Amelia's been seeing this mon for the past sennight, then mayhap she'll see him again this evening. I'd guess she's been in the Great Hall until well after the dancing begins, but I'm not certain how long she stays since we leave early." Deirdre rubbed her belly as Magnus kissed her cheek.

"All of us retire early most nights, so it won't seem unusual if we go before most courtiers even begin their revelry. Ceit and I can slip into the passageway once we're given the sign that Amelia is in her chamber. I trust my maid enough to watch for Amelia and to inform us when she retires."

"How do you suppose she's getting him smuggled into her chamber? Do you think Amelia kens aboot the passages, too?" Magnus asked.

"It's possible since she has been here for years, but I doubt it. I've never heard anyone else and never seen traces of anyone else in the tunnels. Even when someone broke into our chamber, there was no sign of who it was. There are no additional sets of footprints other than near the ladies-in-waiting tunnel. I suspect a thick cloak and some well-greased palms." Elizabeth explained.

"Then there is not much for us to do until tomorrow eve," Deirdre offered.

The three couples said their goodnights before leaving Edward and Elizabeth alone.

"I'm sorry for what I said," Elizabeth offered. She wasn't sure where to gaze because she still felt guilty accusing Edward of using her. "I haven't accepted your past with as much aplomb as I wanted to believe. It was eating at me, and that was the moment I lashed out."

Edward cupped Elizabeth's shoulders and waited for her to glance up.

"I realize this isn't easy. I've said we can leave the past where it belongs, but now none of us have a choice but to face part of it. I would protect you from it; you know that, but it doesn't seem that fate wants to cooperate."

"If your past were filled with faceless and nameless women, then it wouldn't hurt so much." Elizabeth's voice rasped.

"I understand, little one."

"It's not even aught you've done. It's them. Their constant need to remind me is horrible." Elizabeth sank into Edward's embrace and wrapped her arms around his waist. "I mean, look at us. We're alone in our chamber. I know where you are. I know that you choose to be here with me. I know you're not going anywhere. But yet, it still bothers me." She rested her forehead against his chest before continuing. "I'm even jealous of Ceit, and I'm wretched for it. I realize this isn't any easier for her than it is for me, but she escaped it soon after she married. She told me she hasn't had to deal with any women from Tavish's past now that they are at home at Dunbeath. She accepts that there are women in the village, but none have made themselves known, and she hasn't asked. She'll escape it once again soon enough when they leave."

"Beth, I wish I figured out how to make this better for you. I would do aught."

Elizabeth looked up and pressed a long, soft kiss against his lips.

"I know you would. It's a problem of my own mind's making."

"Perhaps, but I can't imagine being in your shoes. I'd kill any mon who reminded me that he had carnal knowledge of you."

"Can I kill any woman who reminds me?" Elizabeth grinned.

"Would that you could." Edward began unlacing Elizabeth's kirtle as she rolled down her stockings and kicked off her slippers. It wasn't long before they were both undressed and climbed into bed. Other women and other men were the last things on their minds for the rest of the night.

CHAPTER TWENTY-FOUR

E lizabeth and Ceit stood by an open door in the stone wall of the music room. It was the same chamber all those weeks ago that Elizabeth slipped into to avoid Edward, and where he found himself in the clutches of Lady Amelia MacAdams. Elizabeth held a lit torch while Ceit clutched a large hourglass that had enough grains for two hours. Elizabeth soundly argued they needed that much time because it would take them at least fifteen minutes to wind their way through the tunnels each way, and Amelia might not be in the midst of a confession when they arrived. Magnus, Deirdre, Tavish, and Edward stood in a semicircle as the two women prepared to enter the passageways. Elizabeth and Ceit wore breeks and long tunics, since Elizabeth warned how tight the tunnels were. Neither wanted to trip over their skirts.

"I don't like this, but you're right that it's the only way." Edward lifted the torch out of the way as he pulled Elizabeth into his tight embrace. She absorbed the tremor that ran through him as she pressed a kiss to his neck. He tucked hair behind her ear and kissed her.

"I'm not headed off to battle," Elizabeth tried to

reassure her husband. "You look grimmer than I did when you left to go scouting."

Edward only nodded.

"You do know I'm coming back? Eddie, there may be some spiders and even a rat or two, but naught is coming to get us. There isn't a brollachan waiting for us. No shapeless nightcrawler is waiting to pounce." Elizabeth looked to Ceit and noticed she was having a similar conversation with Tavish, whose massive arms looked to hold Ceit in a vice.

Ceit pushed away from Tavish and nodded. She and Tavish flipped their hourglasses simultaneously before Ceit and Elizabeth stepped into the passageway. Ceit's voice drifted back to the others who waited for them.

"What the bluidy hell do they think we did before they came along?"

———

Elizabeth guided Ceit through the passageways, both walking on silent feet. Elizabeth held the torch aloft, so they could both see where they stepped and Ceit could watch for Elizabeth's signals. It took them the fifteen minutes Elizabeth predicted. Elizabeth held up a fist and turned to face the wall.

"This should be aboot the right place. Run your fingers along the wall at aboot forehead levels. If there is already a peephole, it was made by a mon taller than us. If not, we can try to pry some mortar away. I don't hear any voices, but this should be right." Elizabeth leaned close to Ceit to whisper.

Both women ran their hands over the wall, but neither found anything. Elizabeth handed the torch to Ceit and drew her dirk from her belt. She tested how loud it would be when she scraped the blade against the mortar. The sound rang in Elizabeth's ears, but she realized it wasn't that loud when Ceit didn't react. She pried more of the mortar out of the way until a tiny sliver of light floated through the wall. She placed her eye to the hole. It was almost too small to peer through, but she stared into the chamber. Directly across the room was a large fireplace, and above the mantle hung an enormous painting of Amelia.

"Right room," Elizabeth whispered and motioned for Ceit to peek.

"Pride is a sin," Ceit muttered.

There was no doubting they found the correct chamber. Elizabeth whittled the hole a little more, giving her enough room to observe the chamber without making the hole obvious to anyone on the other side.

"Now we wait," Elizabeth breathed. "We need to put the torch out. We can't have the light be a beacon. I have a flint to relight it later. I wish you could make a peephole, but I don't dare make two holes in the wall. The air will whistle when the door opens and closes if we do."

Elizabeth ground the torch against the ground, extinguishing it and casting them in pitch black. The two women slid down the wall behind them and sat to wait. Ceit worried that time was slipping away from them, but the hourglass wasn't visible. After what seemed like an eternity, the creak of a door and voices floated to them. Elizabeth and Ceit eased to their feet, and Elizabeth placed her eye to the hole as Ceit pressed her ear against the wall. Ceit realized Elizabeth hadn't been exaggerating about the sound carrying through the wall. It made her want to hold her breath lest she give them away.

"Come in before someone sees you," Amelia hissed to a man not yet in Elizabeth's line of sight. The spyhole limited her view to only a few feet on each side of the fireplace. Fortunately, the bed was below her, but she also realized it would mean she should not peer through the hole if they approached. She wanted neither Amelia nor the unknown man to catch her eyeball glowing white against the gray stone wall.

"You worry needlessly, my dove," came a gravelly voice. "It's not like people don't expect men to enter your chamber. They will marvel that you found one with discretion at last."

"You don't look like you have discretion. You look suspicious," Amelia snapped.

"Now, is that any way to greet your lover?" The man stepped before the fire and dropped the cowl of his cloak.

Elizabeth covered her mouth to smother her gasp. The man in Amelia's chamber wasn't Baron Baird. It was Roy Gregor. Not only was he the son of the Gregor laird, but the Campbells labeled him an outlaw for an incident involving the death of a forester and the raiding of Campbell cattle. It astonished Elizabeth that he dared come into Stirling, let alone the royal castle. She sympathized with the Gregors' plight and didn't agree with Robert's decision to give their land to the Campbells, but her sympathy ran out when it came to the cattle rustling that led to deaths. Roy Gregor risked his life to bed Amelia. There were Campbells from all parts of the country at court. They were in favor with the king, so there was little chance Roy would survive discovery.

"I would prefer not to watch your neck stretched," Amelia's voice was soft, and it surprised Elizabeth to note true emotion in it.

"My love, would you mourn for me?" Roy queried as he took Amelia's hand, but she resisted being pulled into his embrace, so he stepped forward to wrap an arm around her.

"You know I would. I don't like that jest, nor do I like you creeping aboot the castle."

"Afraid one of your other lovers will be put out because I'm stealing their time?"

Amelia pushed him away and scowled.

"It's not as though you don't benefit from my liaisons. You know you're why I do it."

"Me? I assumed it was for all Gregors." Roy grinned as he cupped her nape and pulled Amelia into a smoldering kiss. When they broke apart, Roy brushed a tear from her cheek. "What's this? Tears? You never cry."

"No one else is worth my tears." Amelia's quiet words were difficult for Elizabeth to catch, but she made them out if she strained. Amelia brushed away another tear and shook her head as though it would knock away her feelings. "Baird will be here soon. I don't want him to find you. He has expectations."

"Expectations that you will tell him the king's schedule. The mon oversteps believing he can kill Robert when so many others have failed."

Elizabeth sensed Ceit's movement, and she assumed her friend was staring at her in the dark as shocked as she was.

"That is what he wants. Do you have any idea how difficult it has been to keep him at bay long enough to gather enough information to implicate him so your father can go to the king?"

"And when do you think that will be?"

"You just want me to stop bedding the odious little mon."

"I'd like you to stop bedding any mon beside me."

"And then how would you get the information your father expects?"

"There's bound to be someone he can pay to do this. You could come home." Roy kissed Amelia once

255

more, but this was a tender kiss, and Elizabeth's heart felt pinched. It was clear there was genuine emotion between the couple.

"And how would your father pay for that? You have even less than you did a year ago. Your father won't give up my free service for someone he has to shell out coins to."

"Your service comes at a cost far greater than my father realizes. I never wanted you to spy for us. I wanted you to be by my side as we grow old together."

"Aye well, neither your father nor mine considered us an advantageous marriage. Your father argued that my mother's marriage to my father connected the Gregors and the Grants more than enough. My father wanted to ally the Grants with the MacAdams, and your father agreed, knowing marrying me off strengthened their alliances to them, too."

"Your father wasn't even in a position to form an alliance. Not as a distant cousin of Laird Grant. It was just another marriage as far as Laird Grant was concerned."

"But he was as ambitious as my husband was and your father is." Amelia looked away and closed her eyes. "My mother and I both paid for it."

"Amelia, come home with me." Roy's voice was strong, but Elizabeth didn't miss the pleading.

Amelia collapsed into his arms as he held her tightly against his bigger frame. Elizabeth watched as tears streamed down the woman's beautiful face, and Elizabeth understood Amelia's life better than she ever imagined. She sympathized with the woman who was as much a pawn as she'd been, and much like Ceit, Deirdre, Isabella, and every other woman at court.

"You know I can't," Amelia's ragged voice

choked out each word. "Your father would never allow me to stay. He'd kill me or send me back. He believes the MacAdams still owe him, and he expects me to pay that debt."

"You're not even a fucking MacAdams," Roy growled.

"But I'm able to keep your father informed. When I warned him that your land was being given to the Campbells, he realized that all my years at court were worth it. He expects me to work for my room and board here along with being his informant. He doesn't see me as useful at your home. Now he wants to ingratiate himself back into the king's good graces by being the one to warn the king of Baird's treason. But he has to realize that the king will never give that land back."

"You and I both know that, but my father refuses to see reason. His feud with the Campbells only grows worse as they push us onto less and less land. He still hopes the king will reel in Laird Campbell if he warns the Bruce of the assassination plot."

"That'll never happen."

"I no longer care. I'll be laird one day, and what will I be laird of? A clan that has starved to death because it has no land left to farm. A clan that has few members since more and more leave each day to join other clans that can provide for them. A clan others mock. If this is my future, then I would at least have the woman I love by my side. And I'd save you the indignity our families have forced you into. I was unable to protect you before, but I can now."

"How? You said yourself that you have less by the day."

"There's no one else to inherit but me. Regardless of whether I live among the clan now, I'll be laird one day. I'll take you away from here. Take you anywhere you want, and when the time comes, we can return to whatever is left of Gregor land to be laird and lady."

Amelia's laugh lacked any mirth. It crackled through the air.

"As if your people would accept a whore for their lady. They know what I am, just as I do. I've sold myself to the devil. Your people would never accept sin incarnate as the laird's wife. I can be your leman, but never your wife."

"They'll accept whatever I tell them to." Roy's frustration was betrayed through his voice, along with how he ran his hand through his hair.

"You know that isn't true. You're not narcissistic enough to believe that."

"You're not a whore," Roy whispered.

"I am. I know it as does everyone else. The only comfort is knowing that none of it has been for my pleasure. Not truly. Every mon I've bedded other than you has been for a reason."

Elizabeth was uncertain if that was a consolation as she contemplated her husband being manipulated.

"You gave away your youth and your future for what? Three clans willing to take from you and never give back. I'm ashamed on your behalf. The Grants, MacAdams, and Gregors owe you a great debt."

"The Grants owe me naught. The laird never sanctioned my father's actions. My father sold my hand hoping to be noticed. What did it gain him? Naught. Laird Grant couldn't care less, and Laird MacAdams sent my husband to court so he didn't have to deal with his slithering cousin. He was the snake his cousin accused him of being. He was the first one to make me bed men for his benefit. Your father picked up where he left off."

A knock at the door interrupted the conversation. Amelia spun toward the door, her face a picture of horror.

"He's here," she hissed. "He can't catch you here."

"How am I supposed to leave?"

"You can't. Get in my wardrobe."

"Bluidy hell," Roy snapped. "I'm not watching him fuck you."

"Then close the doors."

"No."

"Yes. Besides, I haven't bedded him. I get him sotted and unlace his breeks. He wakes believing he's had me, and I don't disabuse him of the idea. Now hush and go."

The next set of knocks was more like pounding. Amelia glanced in the looking glass and then back to ensure Roy was tucked away. She opened the door and ushered a rotund and balding man into her chamber.

"My apologies, my laird. I lay down to shut my eyes for but a moment, but I must have drifted off."

"Wanted to be well rested for me, did you?" Fergus Baird chuckled.

"Of course, my laird," Amelia gushed as she poured a chalice of whisky. She handed it to Fergus, who threw back the contents in one swallow.

"Remember for the future that I don't care to be kept waiting in a passageway. Everyone may know that you're a good ride, but I don't need anyone seeing me here. The longer you make me wait, the greater the chance someone will recognize me."

Amelia drew in a lungful of air and kept her most serene smile in place. She exchanged the empty chalice in Fergus's hand with a full one. Once again, he guzzled the contents.

"The Gregors may be a lost cause, but they make fine whisky."

"Lost cause, my laird?" Amelia infused as much innocence into her voice as she could.

"Aye. You must realize your relatives are doomed for extinction if the Campbells have their way."

"That's horrid!" Amelia exclaimed, her hand over her heart. "Won't the king do aught aboot it?"

"He won't be doing much of aught soon enough."

Amelia helped ease the portly man's doublet off his shoulders. She guided him to a chair before handing him a third chalice of whisky. It was unbelievable to Elizabeth how quickly the man consumed the whisky. She was certain there were several fingers in each chaliceful, but the man drank it like water. Fergus tipped his head back and closed his eyes, the chalice dangling from his fingers, as Amelia kneeled to remove his shoes. With his eyes closed, the man missed her expression of revulsion.

"Perhaps someone should warn the Earl of Badenoch," Amelia suggested.

"That arsehole. He should already be dead. Useless servant told me 'he must be in the carriage since he goes nowhere without Lady Elizabeth'." Fergus's voice took on a whiny sing-song tone as he quoted whoever gave him the wrong information. "Nearly killed the chit and got naught out of it. He should have died searching for her in that blizzard, but no, he has Saint Michael on his side. Two warriors who think too much of themselves."

"God's general thinks too much of himself?" Amelia once more infused innocence into her voice.

"Mayhap not, but Lordling Edward does. He didn't even have the good graces to die in the woods. No, the chit defended herself before he ran off with her to hide." The man snorted. "Pshaw, some warrior hiding among horses."

"I heard it was romantic how he saved Lady Elizabeth."

"What mon needs romance? What I need is him

dead. Even the lackwit I hired at Culcreuch failed to draw him into a fight over the chit. Then he failed to get the Galbraiths to rally against Edward. Useless. Aww of dem less." Fergus's last words slurred together, but he shook his head. "Now come here, lass."

Amelia brought yet another chalice of whisky to Fergus before she perched on the edge of the man's stumpy lap. She maintained her smile as Fergus squeezed her breast as he finished the chalice, in two gulps this time.

"You need someone you can trust, my laird. You shoulder a great burden." Amelia slipped from his lap and rounded the chair to massage his shoulders, once more hiding her grimace as she looked at the wardrobe. Elizabeth's gaze shifted to the large piece of furniture, but it was just past her view. From the way Amelia's eyes widened, Elizabeth assumed Roy had the door open a crack. "Perhaps you might enlist the support of others? Oh, but I'm sure you've already done so. Your mind is so much quicker than mine."

"Aye, my uncle and three cousins. They're lesser barons, but my uncle has his eye on Cambusnethan."

"Where it that, my laird?" Amelia murmured.

"Larkinshire, you hen wit. How can you not know where the Bairds rule?" Fergus's disgust was evident, but few were aware of where the small territory was located. The Baird name was well known enough to be recognizable, but they were not large landowners.

"But who shall rule if King Robert is dead? Edward, Earl of Carrick, is in Ireland making himself king, and Edward, Earl of Badenoch and Lochaber, can't inherit? Would you have Princess Marjorie wed and her husband put on the throne?"

"Hardwee," Fergus's words slurred once again.

Ceit nudged Elizabeth, and Elizabeth accepted their time was waning. They just needed this final piece of information.

"Anower Edward. Bluidy Balliols. Too many Edards." Fergus hiccupped as his eyes drooped.

"My laird, you have considered of everything. When do you think you will succeed at outwitting the king?" Amelia tugged on Fergus's hand and led him to the bed where he dropped like a rock. He tugged her into his lap once again, licking her neck. Amelia shuddered but pushed him back onto the bed. She tugged at the laces of his leggings as she crooned. A snore rumbled from Fergus before she was even halfway done. When another snore erupted, this one even louder than the first, Roy emerged from the dresser.

Ceit pulled on Elizabeth's arm.

"Just a little longer," Elizabeth whispered.

"No. Our husbands will come searching. I don't want them lost."

"Trust me. I can tell we need one more moment."

Ceit sighed and put her ear back to the wall. Elizabeth watched as Roy stalked toward Amelia and yanked her against him.

"I should kill him where the bastard sleeps." Roy snarled.

"I wish that you could, but that must be the king's privilege if this is all to have been worth it. All these years; everything we talked aboot. Go. Tell your father what you heard. Once your father tells the king, I'll leave with you. I can't do this any longer." Amelia looked back over her shoulder at the slumbering lump on her bed and shuddered. She'd have the maid change the sheets in the morning, and she'd sleep in the chair that night. "My only regret is I wish it were possible tell Lady Elizabeth the truth. The truth that I never wanted Edward, not for more than what I hoped to learn from him. I spoke with her and Lady Deirdre last evening. I like both of them even if they despise me. I understand how Lady Deirdre must have suffered all those years she was apart from her Magnus. At least I've been able to see you, touch you. She didn't even know he still loved her. I wish I could apologize to Lady Ceit while I'm at it. I used the Sinclair brothers as much as I did Edward. The worst of that is I never learned aught from Callum or Tavish despite how I tried and the fact they're the king's godsons. Eleanor and I were wretched to Ceit, but it was too dangerous to lower my guard."

"What is done is done. You can't take it back any more than I can."

"True as that may be, I've hurt a lot of innocent people along the way. For what? This." Amelia gestured toward Fergus. "Aye, we might save the king's life, and that's important, but it's been a long path to get this one piece of information."

"But can there be aught more important than learning of a conspiracy to commit treason? Not just treason but to murder the king."

"I suppose not. When will your father approach the king?"

"He's camped just beyond the town walls. I'll make him wait until morning, late enough for Fergus to leave. I won't let them find him here. No one will speak your name. I'll kill my father with my own hands if he brings you into this."

"There's naught of my reputation to save. The king knows I trade in secrets. How could he and the queen not? I've lasted here too long not to be doing more than bedding every mon with a pulse."

Roy once more pulled Amelia into his embrace

before cupping her nape to angle her head for his demanding kiss.

"Pack your essentials and prepare to leave before the noon meal. I'm not chancing you changing your mind."

"I don't know where we'll go, but tonight was the final nail in the coffin. I can't do this anymore. It very nearly killed me knowing you watched everything. I'm so sorry."

"Shh, my dove. I'm as much to blame as my father. I've failed you too many times. How you still love me is one of God's greatest mysteries, or perhaps the Lord's greatest miracle."

"Go now before he wakes. I love you, Roy."

"And I love you."

Amelia peered into the passageway before Roy stepped through the door. Roy counted to twenty before slipping away. Elizabeth tapped Ceit, and the two women walked the way they came until Elizabeth stopped them and lit the torch again. They wound their way through the labyrinth. Before they reached the door, Elizabeth whispered to Ceit.

"Do we tell our husbands the part aboot them being used? Do we remain satisfied knowing that she never really wanted them and that the coupling was aboot leverage? Or do we confess all?"

"I was wondering the same thing. I don't know. I —I think they might feel better for knowing," Ceit drew out her words as she tried to work it out as she answered. "Perhaps they will feel less guilty if they understand that it was more aboot business than pleasure."

"But it was aboot pleasure for them. That's the part that still sticks in my throat."

"Me, too," Ceit sighed.

"I don't know that I can avoid telling Edward. He's the king's brother, and that's the reason she got involved with him. I always assumed it was for his looks. He's virile and," Elizabeth's neck heated, a telling sign she was blushing and could only whisper the next word. "Talented."

"It's the same with Tavish. He's just not the king's brother. Nay, he would have to be the king's godson. But hearing her with Roy makes me realize that she would've approached our husbands even if they were like Fergus. It hurts because they are both exceptionally handsome."

"I agree. So, do we tell them?"

"I think we have to. It's rather important, at least in making them understand the trap Amelia found herself in. My heart aches for her. I never imagined I'd sympathize with that woman, but I do."

"Me, too. I can't decide which is worse: having seen her sadness as Roy held her or being in your position and only hearing it and imagining her pain."

"I wish there were a means to help her. She may love Roy, but I can't stomach her having to go to the Gregors. It sounds like a rough survival for them, and Laird Gregor will find another way to manipulate her and his son."

"I know, but I don't have any solutions either," Elizabeth responded before continuing along the path. They rounded the last bend and heard heavy footsteps coming toward them.

CHAPTER TWENTY-FIVE

"**B**eth!" Edward called.

"Ceity!" Tavish bellowed.

"Haud yer wheest, silly mon!" Ceit called back, her courtly accent slipping back to her Highland burr. It was the first time Elizabeth heard it since Ceit returned to court.

"We're coming, Eddie." Elizabeth called back as she and Ceit scrambled to reach the men before their voices carried too far.

The two men lumbered back to the door as the women followed. All four eased through the small stone doorway.

"There's nay way ye would fit, ye behemoth," Tavish elbowed his brother in the stomach as he pushed past Magnus who held a torch toward the entrance. He spun around to face Ceit. He stood, feet spread hip-width apart and his arms crossed. "Ye were gone too long."

"It was impossible to see the hourglass in the dark," Ceit purred as she stood on her tiptoes to kiss his cheek. "I like it when you worry aboot me. Now you know how I feel every time you ride out on a sortie. Doesn't feel good, does it?"

"Nay," Tavish snapped before turning into pudding and embracing Ceit, his face buried in her hair.

"We heard everything we need," Elizabeth took Edward's hands and squeezed them before launching herself into his arms. "There's so much to tell you."

"First off, I feel sorry for Amelia. She isn't at all what we believed," Ceit insisted as four skeptical faces looked at her as if she lost her mind. Deirdre and Magnus looked doubtful, but Edward and Tavish shook their heads. "Hear us out."

"She came to court much like Deirdre, Ceit, and I did. She didn't have any choice. Her husband came as an informant for his clan. He hoped he'd improve his standing if he gathered useful information and sent it back to his cousin, the laird. He pimped Amelia and made her bed men for that information. After he died, it was the Gregor laird who forced her to continue. Returning to the Grants wasn't an option. Her connection is too far from the laird to rely on kinship and her reputation's too sullied to rely on the clan's acceptance." Elizabeth led the others to the chairs in the room. They pulled them close to continue speaking in hushed tones.

"She's in love with Roy Gregor, and he loves her, too." Ceit held up her hand when others opened their mouths to interrupt. "He knows what her late husband and his father forced her to do. It's all been business for her. Where would she go if she left court? No clan wanted her back all because of how her husband used her. The MacAdams weren't her people. The Grants didn't want her as Elizabeth explained, and the Gregors wouldn't take her as long as she was useful here."

"Wait. How did you learn aboot Roy Gregor? Did she tell Baird all of this?" Edward wondered.

"No," Elizabeth shook her head. "He was there. Before Baird arrived."

"He risked his head on a pike?" Magnus asked. "He must love her."

"He does. I saw them. He hid in the wardrobe when Baird arrived. It turns out that Amelia doesn't bed all the men as she's led us to believe. She gets some too drunk to remember that they passed out before doing aught. She unlaces their breeks and makes it look like they coupled, but in actual fact, she just learns what she needs."

Tavish and Edward exchanged a look as they both tried to remember back to their encounters with Amelia. Both shook their heads, knowing that hadn't been the case with them. They had done the deed with the woman.

"How much can Roy love her if he knows she's bedding other men?" Deirdre asked.

"I wondered the same. It's hard to explain, but they know their hands are tied. Like I said before, where would she go?" Ceit reminded them. "Unless she remarried, there wouldn't be anywhere to go. If she remarried, it would have been to someone Laird Gregor agreed to since he's pulling her strings. He wants her here as an informant and not as another mouth to feed in his clan. That leaves being a tavern wench or being hidden away as some laird's leman. Both are hard lives, and women don't last long working in taverns."

"I still don't see how Roy can be convinced she bedded all those men just for the sake of the clan. She has taken some handsome men to her bed, some accomplished lovers. It couldn't have all been a chore," Deirdre gave a pointed look to both Tavish and Edward, which made them shift uncomfortably.

"I don't know if being pleasured is a consolation for what she had to do, but the men she bedded served a purpose." Elizabeth looked at Edward as she continued. "She chooses men who get her infor-

269

mation aboot the king or who are influential, like the king's brother or the king's godsons. Why else would she choose a toad like Fergus Baird?"

"I feel rather filthy now," Tavish muttered. "As though I didna already feel guilty enough. Now I ken she used me."

"Mayhap, but I think Elizabeth and I are better for knowing it. If you had been ugly but still the king's godson, she still would have pursued you. I can't explain it but knowing the reason she wanted you wasn't your looks or your character makes it a wee easier to accept."

Elizabeth nodded as the three men looked at her and Ceit as if they were insane, but Deirdre nodded too. She understood her friends' feelings.

"What did you learn beyond her relationship with Roy Gregor?" Magnus'd had his fill of hearing about the woman's love life.

"When Baird arrived, she plied him with whisky. The mon is a sieve. I can't get over how he drank four full chalices of whisky without batting an eyelash. I mean if it had been one of you," Elizabeth gestured to the men. "I'd understand. You're huge. But the mon is short and portly. He must drink a lot and often. He began sharing his secrets after the second one. Fergus even called Amelia a hen wit when she pretended to be unsure where Baird land is."

"He and his uncle and three cousins are conspiring against the king," Ceit picked up the story. "I couldn't see aught, but I listened. He orchestrated the carriage accident and the attack as we suspected. His source gave him the wrong information, assuming Edward would be in the carriage."

"That explains why I didn't recognize the driver or coachman, but I still wonder aboot the axle. I mean, my parents herded me into the carriage so quickly that I barely had time to pack. My father demanded I leave within fifteen minutes of his mon telling me his plans. How was there time to tamper with the axle?"

"There wasn't. That's why you made it so far north before the accident. Someone attempted to weaken it but didn't have time to saw through the axle," Edward mused.

"He wished you'd died in the blizzard since you weren't in the carriage." Elizabeth bit her lip before telling them more since the next part didn't paint Edward in a good light. "He was angry that the attack in the woods didn't work. It frustrated him that you didn't fight and hid me instead. He claimed you're a coward."

"He can sod off. I can imagine him questioning my manhood, but I don't give a bluidy damn. I'd do the same all over again. I'm not ashamed of making sure you lived."

"I would have done the same thing," Tavish spoke up.

"Me, three," Magnus nodded as he squeezed Deirdre's hand before placing his hand on her belly.

"He mentioned something aboot a mon he hired at Culcreuch," Ceit continued. "He wanted the mon to lure you into a fight, and when that didn't work, he wanted the mon to create an uprising."

"That seems incredibly naïve, or perhaps hamhanded, to rely on an uprising against a mon who wasn't laird and who was a gracious guest," Elizabeth mused. "But that does explain Mitchell's behavior."

"Did you catch aught aboot when he plans to carry out this plan to kill Robert or how he intends to do it?" Edward asked.

"No. He passed out before the conversation got that far, but Roy said his father is camped outside the wall. He was to report back to his father, and Domnall Gregor is to go to the king in the morning. Roy promised to give Amelia enough time to shoo Fergus out before the king's men seize him."

"Roy can't guarantee Fergus will remain in the castle through the night. That's a mighty risk he's taking, since his father may come to report a plot where the perpetrator isn't even nearby." Edward reasoned.

"I thought the same thing," Ceit mused. "I imagine Domnall has lookouts throughout the town and posted near the gates."

"Edward, what do we do?" Elizabeth looked to her husband. "Do we tell Robert right now and have Baird seized in Amelia's chamber or at least have the king post guards to seize him when he exits? Or do we remain quiet and let the Gregors follow through with their plan? Or do we do both? Warn Robert but urge him to allow the Gregors to have their shining moment?"

"We must warn Robert, and while we can encourage him to allow the Gregors to do something valiant, it won't do them any good. It's likely to get Roy captured and killed with Fergus right next to him." Edward warned.

"Amelia wants to leave with him." Ceit shook her head. "They don't know where they'll go. Roy said he'd find somewhere other than Gregor land if need be. There aren't any other heirs, so they would return once Domnall dies. But Amelia was right when she warned Roy that the clan would never accept her after her reputation here."

"Maybe the Grants would take them in," Deirdre suggested.

"Nae as long as Roy is an outlaw. They may be allies to the Gregors, they're also loyal to Robert and willna go against the Campbells even if they canna stand them," Magnus reasoned.

"Then we make Roy's reprieve part of the deal to tell Robert the plot." Ceit shrugged.

"Ceit, I can't blackmail my brother," Edward snapped.

"Then we suggest Robert acquit him of the charges as thanks for his loyalty to the crown," Ceit offered.

"That's reasonable," Edward agreed.

"We should go now then." Elizabeth rose. "If we wait, Baird might get away."

"Wait," Edward's brow furrowed. "You never said who they wanted to take Robert's place."

"They still want you dead, Eddie. Your brother is busy in Ireland, and that didn't seem to bother them. Marjorie was out of the question." Elizabeth cringed. "They want Edward Balliol to take the throne."

"And they imagine my brother Edward would ignore that? The whole purpose of him being in Ireland is to solidify our power with Gaelic kings rather than the bluidy British." Edward's face flushed red as his temper rose.

"All the more reason they're bampots for assuming this plan would work." Magnus led the way to the door.

CHAPTER TWENTY-SIX

Robert glared at the six faces that stood awaiting him in his private solar that connected to his bedchamber. He pulled his robe snugger around his muscular frame.

"Rouse the queen," he demanded of no one in particular. "This better be as urgent as you claim. And this better not have even a hint to do with any of your marriages."

"Robert, we wouldn't have roused you or asked that you have Elizabeth join us if it weren't in earnest. We discovered why someone sabotaged Beth's carriage and aboot who was behind the attack in the woods." Edward stood next to his brother; his voice low so none of the guards were able to listen.

It was only a few minutes later that the queen joined them. It was clear she had no intention of looking less than presentable, even before family members. She swept into the chamber and surveyed Robert and the others. She paused before going to Robert's side.

"What's happened?" she asked.

"We've learned of a plot against Robert's life and mine. We figured out who is behind it, and it's linked to the attacks on Beth and me," Edward explained.

"What the devil?" Robert exclaimed. "Who now?" Robert didn't sound surprised that someone was plotting his death; instead, he seemed annoyed that he had one more issue to resolve.

"The Bairds," Elizabeth spoke up. "Ceit and I used the hidden passageways to spy on Lady Mac-Adams. We learned a great deal while we were there. Fergus Baird intends to kill you and Edward with help from his uncle and three cousins. We didn't overhear how or when because he passed out drunk as a skunk before he shared that information with Lady MacAdams. We also discovered the Gregors intend to be the ones to tell you."

"What do they have to do with this bluidy mess?" Robert demanded before closing his eyes and tilting his head from one side to the other. "I mean how are they involved? I don't mean to snap, lass."

"We understand," Elizabeth glanced at the others before continuing. "Lady MacAdams's connection is tighter to the Gregors than we imagined. Domnall is controlling her and demanding she be his informant. He wants to be the one to warn you, hoping it will restore some of his status. I suppose he hopes you'll intervene on his behalf with the Campbells. They're harrying the Gregors off their land."

"Lady MacAdams admitted all of that to Fergus?"

"That's what I heard once she entered her chamber," Ceit spoke up, hedging their bets. "I didn't have a peephole to see through, but I listened to what she said.

"Is Fergus still there?" The queen asked.

"I assume so," Elizabeth nodded. "He drank quite a lot of whisky."

Robert stroked his chin as he considered what he was told, alternating between pursing his lips and flattening them into a thin line.

"Robert, no matter what you decide, is it possible to keep Amelia's name out of it?" Elizabeth asked, but her eyes pleaded.

"You would protect such a woman?" The queen looked astounded.

"I would," Elizabeth nodded. "I understand her position now. I could have just as easily been in her position if I were a widow. Her husband brought her to court for political gain, and not her own. I'm familiar with how that works."

Elizabeth didn't hide from the admission. She didn't see any reason to. She wasn't ashamed of her actions while at court, and there was little point in denying what everyone already knew: she was a political pawn. So were Ceit and Deirdre.

"But she remained of her own volition," the queen pressed.

"But she didn't," Elizabeth countered. "She had nowhere else to go, and Domnall has been manipulating her for years. She wants to leave but has felt caught in a web from which she can't escape."

"Where would she go now that she wants to leave all of a sudden?" Robert crossed his arms.

"It's not really all of a sudden. There's someone she'd make a life with if she could." Ceit paused before plunging on. "The problem is the mon would need a royal pardon before it would be safe for Amelia to join him."

"You'll need to be more specific than that. The list is far too long."

"Roy Gregor. He's the one who has been carrying information to his father. They're camped outside the city and will want an audience with you in the morning," Edward looked to his brother and tried to decipher his expression. He could tell Robert was considering the request. Edward shot everyone else a glance to remain quiet. Robert needed to reason through it with no further prodding, or he'd refuse out of stubbornness.

"Very well. Roy has his pardon. Amelia leaves in the morning, but she's not to return to court." Robert uncrossed his arms.

"I doubt she'll want to be back if her time here has been as miserable as it would seem." The queen looked sympathetic. She was another woman who had been a political pawn her entire life. Her father, a confidante of King Edward, betrothed her to Robert hoping she would spy on him. Longshanks had placed her under house arrest as a way to punish Robert for having the gall to fight for Scottish independence.

"Will you seize Fergus now?" Elizabeth queried. "It's still late enough that it's unlikely for anyone to see him being dragged from her chamber. You'd have him in custody before he can slip away, then allow the Gregors a little pride by appearing to be the ones to inform you of the conspiracy. You'll need to capture Baird's fellow conspirators. You might offer Roy a writ of pardon, or at least arrange for Amelia or Domnall to receive it on his behalf."

"Fergus Baird will be a guest of my dungeon within the next quarter hour," Robert announced. "Do you ladies want to be the ones to explain all of this to Amelia?"

"Nay," Tavish interrupted. "Ma wife's returning to our chamber to help me pack. We ride out at dawn."

"As will ma wife," Magnus chimed in.

The queen arched her eyebrow and stepped forward to stand toe-to-toe with the men who stood a foot taller than her. She'd wiped each of their noses.

"You would have your pregnant wives ride out after receiving only an hour or two of sleep, if they're lucky. What would your father say?"

Tavish and Magnus appeared appropriately cha-grined. They glanced at their wives apologetically.

"Perhaps we dinna need to leave right at sunrise," Tavish conceded.

"And they can sleep while we assist the maids in packing," Magnus ducked his head, too embarrassed to glance at the queen.

"That's much better, lads." The queen patted them both on their chest.

"I'll speak to Amelia," Elizabeth offered.

"I would go with you," Ceit spoke up.

"Me, too," Deirdre added.

"Very well. I can't have you all traipsing through the passageways if we're to make this discreet. Edward, you accompany the women while Tavish and Magnus come with me to the dungeon. We shall see Fergus well settled in." With the king's decision made, the queen retired to her chamber while the others separated into two groups.

CHAPTER TWENTY-SEVEN

E lizabeth knocked on Amelia's door, but when no one answered, she feared they were too late. Ceit pulled a pin from her hair and slipped it into the lock. It only took two jiggles and a twist before the lock clicked. She pressed the door open, Elizabeth peering around her shoulder.

"Wait here," Elizabeth murmured while Edward shook his head. "You don't want to alert Fergus or scare Amelia into screaming."

Edward took a deep breath, offering her a stern look before relenting. Elizabeth and Ceit slipped into the chamber, but Edward remained in the doorway where he observed the entire chamber. Deirdre remained with him. Fergus continued to snore on the bed, but Amelia slumped in a chair, a Gregor plaid over her shoulders and lap. Elizabeth crept forward and squatted before Amelia's chair. She put a gentle hand on the woman's arm and shook it. Amelia jerked awake and was ready to scream when Ceit put a finger to her lips and nodded toward Fergus. Elizabeth waved her to come with them. No one spoke until the five of them were in the passageway.

"What are you doing here?" Amelia demanded.

"Shh," Elizabeth peeked past the door. "We can

give you a more detailed explanation later, but Ceit and I know aboot your conversation with Roy and with Fergus."

Amelia shied away, horror and fear registering on her face.

"We know aboot Fergus's plan and Roy's. We're here to ensure Fergus's arrest, but the king will let Domnall present the news of the conspiracy," Ceit rushed to explain. "Amelia, Roy will get the pardon. You can leave with him in the morning."

"Leave Stirling as soon as you can. You and Roy can figure out where to go once you're away." Edward motioned for four guards to step forward. "Let us get Fergus out before anyone notices your involvement."

"Why're you doing this? Why would you, any of you, help me?" Amelia's suspicion was clear.

"We needed to discover why someone tampered with my carriage and the reason for the attack on the way to Culcreuch. We worked it out that you might know because there's no way that you aren't well informed considering your— er— connections. We had no idea of Domnall's role in what you did or that you're in love with Roy." Elizabeth reached a tentative hand out, and when Amelia didn't pull away, she placed it on the woman's arm. "Ceit and I admit we spied on you tonight, but we want to help you. I doubt there's a lady in this castle who hasn't been forced into doing the bidding of the men in their family. You've just suffered more than most. Ceit, Deirdre, and I have been lucky enough to marry men who love us and protect us, men willing to get us away from court. You deserve no less. If Roy can find somewhere safe for you, then you may get that chance, too. With his pardon, you won't need to hide."

Amelia shook her head as tears slid from her

eyes. She opened her mouth twice before she produced a sound. "Even if I can leave with him, there's no future for us."

"I heard why you assume that. Can you not give the Gregor clan more credit that they might understand your sacrifices on their behalf? Could they not appreciate what you've done for their safety and well-being?" Elizabeth placed her other hand on Amelia's arm, guiding her away from the door as Edward and the four guards entered the chamber. "Perhaps a little faith might go a long way. And if not, Roy swore to protect you and take you away."

A commotion in the chamber interrupted the conversation. Something crashed to the floor while angry voices exchanged colorful oaths. Fergus's voice rose above the others despite his words being hard to decipher, a result of the lasting effects of the whisky.

"Get the bluidy hell off me! What're you aboot? Do you recognize who I am? I'm Baron Baird." Fergus bellowed as the four guards struggled to restrain him. He was a great deal more agile and stronger than his appearance hinted.

"I am the king's messenger and an earl. I am placing you under arrest for conspiracy to commit treason, plotting the death of the king and his brother. Me."

"What'd that bitch say? I'll kill 'er!"

"So now you're admitting to a third planned death. You are adding to the charges, *Fergus*." Edward stressed the man's given name rather than title as he nodded his head for the guards to remove him. Fergus continued to writhe and struggle as he attempted to shake the guards off him. He sank his teeth into the hand of one guard while kicking out, aiming for another guard's bollocks. Only the guard who stood doubled over released him, but Edward's patience had expired. He was holding onto a fine line of self-control, wanting to kill the man who endangered Elizabeth more than once. He wanted to end the man's life right then and there, but he accepted that he had to let justice prevail with Robert as the man's judge and jury rather than himself.

Fergus fought like a stuck boar, thrashing and flailing, attempting to ram his head into the chest of one guard. Edward drew his dirk from his belt and held it up for Fergus to see.

"I can say you attacked me, and I defended myself," Edward mused. "Perhaps you attempted to flee, and it was the only way to keep you in custody. Mayhap you fell upon your sword, or at least my dirk, rather than give yourself up—the final act of a coward."

Edward held the sharp blade in the air to catch the light from the fireplace. It made the blade appear as though it glowed. He ran the pad of his finger over the tip and along part of the edge before showing Fergus the blood on his finger. The prospect of imminent death and the sight of blood made the man panic, a wild look replacing the glassiness from the alcohol. Edward raised his hand and brought the dirk toward Fergus's head, the captive screeching over and over until the hilt of Edward's knife landed against Fergus's temple, and the man crumpled. The four guards, the injured one having recovered, maneuvered Fergus from the chamber after binding his hands behind his back.

Elizabeth pulled Amelia out of the way, the woman too shocked to react on her own.

"I hated him more than most," Amelia whispered. "Odious mon. I know treason results in death, but I wish he'd rot away in a dank cell for the rest of his days. Once he's dead, he can't suffer. It'll be over. He deserves agony after all that he's done to his clan —and to me. Thank the blessed Lord I always got him soused before he tried to bed me, but not always before he took liberties I never wanted to offer."

"I understand that sentiment," Ceit stepped before Amelia and squeezed her hand. "I wanted that very thing for my uncle. But I find knowing he can never escape, never come after me, never hurt anyone again brings me more relief than letting him rot would have done."

Amelia nodded before she exhaled a long breath, her shoulders slumping. She shook her head as she looked at the three women.

"I still don't understand why you would help me of all people. Not after the way I treated you and what I've done with your husbands, what I tried to tempt them to do."

"My parents kept me from Magnus for seven years because they argued his clan wasn't good enough, despite them being one of the most powerful in the country. They tried to betroth me to a mon who would have raped me had Magnus not saved me. This was the same mon who tried to kill Magnus and had me kidnapped. All of this for my parents' and Lord Hay's ambition." Deirdre rubbed her belly before continuing. "Without Magnus and his steadfast love for me, I'd be another political pawn and likely dead."

"My uncle was one of the most loathed men in Scotland, and the entire country finds my clan's name repugnant. My clan sent me here as a peace offering. *Me*, a person, a woman was the peace offering. Not coin. Not jewels. Not men sworn to serve. No. *Me*." Ceit stabbed a finger at her chest. "My father did that for the sake of bringing peace to the clan, but he realized my uncle intended to coerce me into spying. My uncle had my brother beaten nearly to death to convince me to serve him. I spent weeks traveling at night on my own to pass messages. I had my uncle's mercenaries lurking in dark corners of the castle. The king demanded I provide him information on my uncle's schemes." Ceit paused to take a deep breath. She trembled as she admitted her secret to someone outside of her family. "If it hadn't been for Tavish's refusal to give up on me and refusal to accept the danger I faced, I, too, would most likely be dead. If I survived, and the king hadn't planned a betrothal to Tavish, my father would have arranged my marriage to a mon that benefited him. Tavish understands me and respects me, never making me ashamed for what I did to survive, to ensure my family survived."

Amelia looked at the two women in awe. She was familiar with the rumors and the bits and pieces of fact that had trickled out. She never considered how these women's lives paralleled hers. She labeled them as insipid and innocent. She looked at Elizabeth, the woman who most recently suffered from Amelia's machinations. Amelia was still surprised by the smile Elizabeth offered her, the patience and acceptance in her eyes.

"My father may not be as ambitious as his older brother, but he betrothed me four times and broke each one in hopes of a better match." Tears stung the back of Elizabeth's eyelids. "He would've continued to do so if Edward hadn't taken notice of me. I was prepared to remain a spinster here for the rest of my life. I never thought to find love or have a family. I was certain my destiny was to remain alone and on the shelf, only being considered as a potential mistress but never a wife. My father rejected Edward because he couldn't manipulate him, and that meant Edward wouldn't bring my father any gains. He was so set upon keeping me from marrying Edward that he was willing to send me to the very northernmost point in Scotland to hide me with the Sinclairs. In

December. Instead of showing Edward gratitude for rescuing me, he accused Edward of defiling me and demanded the king annul our handfast. Without Edward's determination and love, I'd have either died or still be pining for love."

"So, see, our stories aren't so terribly different from yours, Amelia. You were brought to court as a pretty bobble on the arm of a mon and expected to do his bidding for his ambition." Deirdre's soothing tones eased some tension from Amelia's rigid frame. The creases in her brow relaxed, and the lines around Amelia's mouth and eyes softened. "You were forced to do things you objected to, but you knew refusal was too dangerous. Even once you became a widow, there was no freedom. People may assume you're a merry widow, but we understand now that you were just surviving. With no place to go and no other means to support yourself, you fell back on the currency so many women must trade in. What else do we have that's our own? But are our bodies ever really truly ours?"

"You've found a mon who'll allow you the freedom we've found with our husbands. Love has the power to build and destroy." Elizabeth gazed into Amelia's eyes. "It's time for love to build you up, build your future. Go to Roy and make a life with him. If the Gregors won't accept you, Roy offered to leave the clan until he inherits the lairdship. I believe he'd give that up if it meant keeping you safe. There's bound to be other clans that would allow you to make a home among them. It might be a croft instead of a keep, but it would be a life with Roy."

Amelia's tears trailed down her cheeks. While they had removed a tremendous weight, she felt exhausted and aged after carrying it for so long. She prayed these young women, ones who weren't that much younger than her but still seemed sheltered, were right. She prayed Roy never came to resent her for her past. She prayed they would find somewhere safe. Amelia would gladly never see a silk garment again. Gold chalices and plates were the last things she ever wanted to eat from again. A croft with Roy sounded like bliss.

"You should pack, Amelia. Roy will receive his pardon in a few hours. You must be ready to leave when he does. You may need to deliver it to him if he doesn't come to the castle." Ceit guided her back into her chamber. "Would you like help?"

Amelia nodded, and the women worked in silence. Everything that could be said had already been shared.

CHAPTER TWENTY-EIGHT

E dward searched for Elizabeth among the crowd gathered in the bailey. He spotted her standing beside his sister-by-marriage. He thought his wife looked as regal and elegant as the queen who stood to her right. He was late because one of the prisoners attempted to escape despite the heavily armed escort that would lead them from the dungeon to the gallows. Edward joined Elizabeth, and they stepped behind the king and queen. It had taken three sennights to round up and try the three co-conspirators along with Fergus Baird.

Edward was aware Elizabeth wished to leave court, as the Sinclairs had. However, she understood duty took precedence. He also recognized a part of her needed to see for herself that the threat to them was coming to a definitive, unalterable end. Elizabeth leaned against Edward as he wrapped his arm around her waist. Their heads tilted to rest against one another as Robert announced the verdict that all four Baird men were guilty of conspiring to commit treason and were, therefore, sentenced to death by hanging before being drawn and quartered. Their limbs were to be sent to the four corners of the realm.

The guards brought men onto the platform, placing them over the trapdoor, and the hangman thrust black sacks over their heads before fitting the noose around their necks. Robert nodded, and the trap doors swung open, the men dropping with the force of gravity. Elizabeth shut her eyes, but not before seeing them convulse and twitch. She heard the order for the convicted to be cut down and taken to the wooden pallets that awaited them. She watched as they forced the men onto their backs as they tied their limbs to the saddles of four jostling horses. Elizabeth turned her head into Edward's chest and shuddered as his arms came around her. She felt him rest his forehead on her crown and sensed he wasn't watching either as the executioners disemboweled the four men, who were still alive. They tossed their entrails into a fire stoked for that purpose. The stench and howls of agony were more than Elizabeth could withstand. Edward caught her as her legs gave up trying to support her.

"Close your eyes, Beth," Edward murmured against her hair. "I'm taking you inside."

Edward lifted her into his arms as the first thud of the headsman's axe severed a head. Elizabeth whimpered as she squeezed her eyes shut and held a hand over her mouth. She was already suffering from morning sickness well into the afternoon, and this was more than her fragile stomach could bear. The crowd was dense, making Edward's path difficult to navigate. They failed to avoid hearing three more similar thuds then the whistle that signaled the riders to spur their horses, each tethered to a limb of the dead men.

"Put me down, Eddie."

"What? This isn't a good place."

"Now, or I will retch down the front of you."

Edward eased her to her feet, and she stumbled

a couple paces away before doubling over to cast up her accounts. Edward kept her hair out of the way while rubbing soft circles along her back. When they were sure Elizabeth's stomach was empty, Edward hurried to lift her into his arms again. The cacophony of noise from the crowd as they cheered the brutal ripping of limbs from torsos was overwhelming even to Edward, who'd seen even worse violence and heard far louder noises on a battlefield. He rushed up the castle steps, a guard scurrying to open the door in time. It was easy for Edward to find an empty chamber considering much of the court was watching the spectacle in the bailey. The prisoners had been hanged, gutted, beheaded, then drawn and quartered. Edward made sure the chamber was on the side of the castle that didn't face the bailey. He found a chaise to lay Elizabeth upon, unlacing the top of her kirtle, giving her lungs more room to expand. Her pallor and the perspiration that dotted she brow shook him.

"I'll be fine in just a few moments. The smell was overpowering."

"Are you sure? Should I fetch a physician? Beth, you don't look well."

"Of course I don't. I just revisited my breakfast with the stench of death seeping into my nose and mouth," Elizabeth snapped. She covered her forehead and eyes to block the light. Her other hand struck out in search of Edward's. "I apologize. I know you're worried, and I suspect I appear rather wretched right now. I just need a little time to come around. I've witnessed that more than once and never had this adverse a reaction. I think our wee one doesn't agree with such theatrics."

"Can I fetch you some water or ale at least?"

"No. Stay with me." Elizabeth squeezed the hand

she found. "Naught will make me feel better other than having you with me."

Edward kneeled at her side and stroked her hair from her damp brow. He found it disconcerting to see his stalwart wife brought low, even if it was from a weak stomach during pregnancy. He longed to ease her symptoms and relieve the discomfort. He placed a kiss on her forehead, and she sighed.

"Eddie?"

"Yes, little one."

"I want to go home." Elizabeth moved her hand from over her eyes and gazed at her husband's worried expression. "I don't know where that is, but can we go soon?"

"Yes, *mo ghaol.* Just as soon as we can, we'll leave. If you never want to return to court, you don't have to."

Elizabeth snorted before rolling her eyes. "You know that's impossible. Of course, I'll have to come back. I'm the wife of the king's brother. And besides, who will protect you from all the merry widows and bored wives?"

"I didn't realize there were any. I have eyes only for my beautiful wife. I love her to distraction."

"I think *I'm* ready for some distraction."

Edward chuckled. Elizabeth's pregnancy hadn't made her interest in coupling wane. If possible, it made her even more voracious. He lifted her into his arms again.

"I can walk. I'm sure I'm well enough."

"Mayhap, but your legs are too short to keep up with mine."

Elizabeth's peel of laughter filled the chamber and spilled into the passageway as Edward sprinted through the castle to arrive at their chamber. They stripped one another and fell into bed in a tangle of arms and legs. It was dusk by the time they remembered there was a world beyond their chamber door.

———————

Edward and Elizabeth dressed that evening and appeared at the door to the Privy Council in response to a summons a page delivered. They preferred to take a tray in their chambers, but they weren't to be so fortunate that night. Unlike people who spent the entire day waiting for admittance only to be denied, the chamberlain granted Edward and Elizabeth immediate entry. Edward was used to the mutterings and crude comments, but Elizabeth's fair skin resembled a ripe strawberry.

"You'll get used to it. Even if Robert wanted to see everyone who requests an audience, there aren't enough minutes in the day to accommodate the entire queue. Even I've entered and been kept waiting for hours. I simply had a slightly better holding pen."

Edward and Elizabeth approached Robert, who sat at the table with all the members of the Privy Council. It was rare that Robert convened them all; it was also uncommon for them all to be seated. His gaze swept over a few of the members, in particular James Douglas and Walter Stewart, the sixth High Steward of Scotland, who sat on the left and right side of Robert, respectively. Further down the table were Laird Fraser, Elizabeth's uncle; Gilbert Hay; and Neill Campbell. Thomas Randolph, David de Lindsay, and Roger de Kirkpatrick, three of Robert's most trusted statesmen, sat at the opposite end of the table from Robert. A tightening in his belly forewarned Edward that whatever Robert intended to discuss wasn't only significant, but bound to affect his and Elizabeth's life. He was uncertain if he wanted to hear whatever it was. He definitely was uncertain if he wanted to hear the news before he prepared Elizabeth.

"Elizabeth, Edward, thank you for joining us. Elizabeth, I noticed you were unwell this morning. I wish I could have stepped aside to inquire at the time."

Edward had already made his bow just as Elizabeth had made her curtsy, but she dipped her head before answering.

"It was a little overwhelming to my system, as my sense of smell has become sensitive." Elizabeth wouldn't say more. There had been no announcement about them expecting a child, nor did Elizabeth want one. At least she hadn't wanted it until they eliminated the threats. She noticed some men understood her meaning and beamed at her while others looked baffled. Her father, who stood behind her uncle, was one of the latter. She'd set aside time to speak with her mother and father to share the good news.

"I summoned you both here because there is the matter of where you will live since you no longer wish to remain at court. With the Privy Council's agreement, we present you with two choices for your future home. While both were keeps under the former control of the Comyns, they have reverted to the crown. Since you are the Earl of Badenoch *and* Lochaber, you shall have your choice between keeps in either earldom. Within Lochaber, Inverlochy Castle has been under the care of the MacDonalds in recent years, but I believe there could be an understanding that you shall accept the castle without expecting to become laird of the clan." Robert raised an eyebrow at Edward.

"I have no intention of being the laird to any clan. I will forever serve you and will always pick up my sword on your behalf, but I desire a home for

Elizabeth and any children the Lord blesses us with."
Edward nodded his head, and Robert grinned at his
brother's diplomacy since the MacDonalds wouldn't
appreciate losing an important keep such as Inverlochy.

"The other option is Dunachton, which the Mac-
Nivens oversee. As you're aware, they're a sept of the
MacNaughtons. I would give the same stipulation
that you would be in possession of the keep and surrounding land, but not a usurper to the MacNiven
lairdship."

"Those are reasonable terms. I've no need for a
lairdship when you've already made me an earl twice
over," Edward emphasized that he had no need for
clan hierarchy when his station was already well
above most local leaders. "I'd like a moment to
confer with my wife."

Edward's statement made several sets of eyebrows shoot toward their owner's hairline, but he
wasn't interested in their judgment. He wanted Elizabeth to share where she believed she'd be happiest.
He drew her aside and placed his broad back to the
table, shielding Elizabeth from their view.

"What shall it be, little one? The coast or the
mountains?"

"Isabella Dunbar and her husband are now living
with the Sinclairs. She'd be beside herself for a
chance to visit us at Dunachton. She could visit actual Pictish ruins rather than having to rely on her
dusty tombs from the Romans and Britons. That
said, Inverlochy is near to Glencoe. We could open
our doors to Amelia and Roy if the need arose."
Elizabeth looked thoughtful, tapping a finger against
her lips, but Edward recognized that while she spoke
the truth, she was teasing him. She wouldn't decide
based on their potential houseguests. But she grew
serious as her own question arose. "Eddie, would we

still be able to bring my brother and sisters? I haven't seen them enough lately, but we could offer them so much."

"Wherever you choose, their home is already there."

"In that case, I believe Inverlochy is where I'd like to make our home. I would have both the coast and mountains with Loch Linnhe and Ben Nevis so nearby. I'm sure we can find something of interest for Isabella."

"*You* will interest Isabella. It wouldn't surprise me if she is with child soon, too. She and her husband are just as--- energetic as we are." Edward waggled his brow. "Besides you and Ceit shall have bairns, as will Deirdre. After our bairn comes, I will take you to the Sinclairs if you wish."

"I do."

Edward chuckled as he nudged Elizabeth's jaw up with the crook of his finger. He gazed into her emerald eyes and asked, "Are you certain that Inverlochy is what you want?"

"Aye." Elizabeth beamed, and Edward kissed her, uncaring about their audience. Let the men be jealous and let the Frasers see he loved her well. Edward turned back to Robert, an arm around Elizabeth's waist, his other hand clasped with hers. He smiled at Elizabeth and encouraged her to make their declaration.

"Inverlochy, Your Grace. We would like Inverlochy to be our new home."

"Well met. I believe that shall be a fine choice for you. Plenty of space for bairns to run and grow. The Highland air and all." Robert covered his grin by leaning over a parchment and signing it before affixing his seal. "It is done. You may be underway as soon as you are ready."

"We're already packed," Edward's voice was

clear but soft. He expected Robert's look of surprise, but his brother accepted their departure was inevitable. Robert gestured with his hand, and the meeting was adjourned.

"You really are leaving, little brother." Robert stepped around the table and pulled Edward into a tight embrace once the others cleared the chamber. "I will look for your missives. Don't forget to write in between chasing your wife aboot your castle."

"I wouldn't dream of it. I shall capture my bride and insist she keep me company."

Elizabeth cleared her throat, making a feminine but distinct sound. Both men turned to stare at her.

"And what if it is I who does the chasing, and my husband is too exhausted to write? May I send missives to the queen in lieu of my husband?" Her expression of innocence only made the two men laugh harder.

Edward kissed her temple, and his soft breath whispered across her ear as he murmured, "You won't have to chase me. I surrender."

Elizabeth's fair skin once again blushed, but she wouldn't deny her husband his willing capitulation.

"When will you depart?" Robert brought their attention back to the conversation.

"I'd like for us to ride out tomorrow morning if I can arrange things. Chests and trunks can be sent along on wagons later."

"Perhaps you could give the MacDonalds a sennight to adjust to losing the keep. You would arrive before my messenger if I agreed to your departure tomorrow."

Edward and Elizabeth chuckled at the exaggeration, but they would arrive within hours of the messenger if they left in the morning. They conceded that wouldn't ingratiate them to their new tenants.

"Very well. But I would like to take Beth to Culcreuch then."

Edward didn't miss the pain that flashed in Robert's eyes as he suggested an alternative to them remaining at court. He knew his brother understood his desire to be away from court, but it would be the first time that Edward struck out on his own in truth, with no intention of returning to either of his brothers' side. He wouldn't remain at court, nor was he going to their brother Edward's camp in Ireland. He'd be independent, and it was an unsettling notion to both of them.

"Perhaps you and Her Grace might visit," Elizabeth offered. "Laird and Lady Galbraith have a beautiful home."

"You would have the entire court repair to their keep so soon after you arrive?" Robert questioned.

"Beth said you and Elizabeth. She didn't invite your circling flock of vultures," Edward clarified. "We'd love to host you and our sister-by-marriage. We have no intention of having the court eat the Galbraiths out of house and home."

"Perhaps the queen and I are overdue a long ride together. If we end up at Culcreuch for the midday meal or supper, then what a happy coincidence."

"Thank you," Elizabeth beamed.

"Then we depart for Culcreuch in the morning and from there Inverlochy when you deem the MacDonalds are ready to welcome us." Edward clapped a hand on Robert's shoulder now that the Privy Council chamber was empty but for them and a couple of guards. Robert gripped Edward in a tight embrace.

"Go with God's grace, little brother. You have a fine life ahead of you." Robert whispered to Edward as they continued to cling to one another. Eventually, Robert released Edward in exchange for embracing

Elizabeth. "You're a good lass, and I'm grateful you agreed to take on my brother. He is better for having you as his wife."

"And I am better for having him as my husband." Elizabeth's smile was so brilliant Edward was certain his heart would beat out of his chest as he absorbed its warmth.

"Eddie," Elizabeth looked over her shoulder to where her husband watched her from beside the fireplace. She pushed her kirtle over her hips before scooping it up and placing it on a hook. "There's something that I've been wondering aboot for some time but haven't gotten around to asking you."

Edward wandered away from the fireplace until he stood behind Elizabeth. He plucked the ribbons from her shoulders, letting her chemise fall to the floor before cupping her breasts. They were even fuller than before, and he enjoyed the feel of them overflowing from his fingers. He brushed his thumbs over her nipples, eliciting a low moan as Elizabeth's head dropped back against his chest.

"What are you wondering?" Edward's breath beside her ear made her shiver, and she moaned once more when he nibbled on her earlobe.

"Do you remember that day in the woods?"

Edward stiffened. Of course, he remembered the day she mentioned. Curiosity consumed him when he saw her ride out of the stable. The emotion morphed as he was possessed by fear while he chased her across hill and dale at a breakneck pace and overwhelmed with anger when he found her among the trees. It was also the first time her entire body had pressed against his, and the first time he tasted her lips.

299

"I do," he replied slowly.

"Do you remember our conversation and what you promised me?" Edward's mind snapped back to having Elizabeth in his lap, and how she admitted to her scandalous behavior when she thought about him. He also recalled what she admitted she wanted from him. "Do you remember our night at the inn and what happened when I wouldn't let go of your--"

Edward spun Elizabeth around and grasped her backside, pulling her onto her toes to rub his rod against her mons. His hand drew back and landed on her right globe with a resounding smack.

"Is this what you're referring to?" Edward growled, and Elizabeth's moan reassured him it was. "Is this what you want?"

Edward rained down two more swats as Elizabeth clung to him. She tucked her head into the crook of his neck and nodded. Edward continued, alternating sides, but the pressure remained light and playful.

"Eddie," Elizabeth mewled. "This is exactly what I want. I thought maybe you forgot or weren't interested anymore."

Edward paused before leading Elizabeth to sit beside him on the edge of the bed. Dissatisfied with her sitting next to him, he lifted her into his lap. His hand glided over her bare skin while he remained clothed. The contrast and Elizabeth's vulnerability didn't go unnoticed, rather heightening the tension between them.

"There has been much going on since that night. Between the threats and learning you're with child, I feared scaring you. Or worse, harming you or the bairn if I tried spanking you again."

"Eddie, you don't scare me. Even when I've seen you furious, you don't scare me. I know you'd never harm me or our bairn. I have a healthy respect for your physical strength, but I never fear you turning it on me." Elizabeth ran her fingers through his hair as she nestled closer. "I wish---I'd like—um, rather would you--"

"Are you suddenly too shy to ask?" Edward teased.

Elizabeth nodded and slid off Edward's lap. He reached for her, but she stepped around his knee, so she could position herself and lay across his lap. Her upturned backside was stretched beneath his nose, and his eyes feasted on the sight his wife presented. It was only moments later that Elizabeth's moans filled the chamber as her backside heated to a deep shade of pink. When Edward worried she couldn't bear much more, he lifted her to move further back on the bed. He arranged her so that she straddled his hips before she sheathed herself onto his throbbing sword. Their coupling had a wildness and closeness that reminded them of their first night together, and both were certain they had created a new bond within their relationship.

CHAPTER TWENTY-NINE

"I can't believe that after nearly a moon at Culcreuch, I'm *finally* aboot to see Inverlochy for the first time."

Elizabeth's giddiness made Edward smile. Their sennight layover in Culcreuch turned into a month once Robert and the queen arrived. The royal couple found they enjoyed the reprieve from court so much that they remained for a fortnight. Between time needed for missives to travel to and from Inverlochy announcing the change in ownership, along with giving the clan time to prepare the castle, the days flew by. The keep had once belonged to John "the Black" Comyn, Edward's predecessor as Earl of Badenoch and Lochaber, but the king gave the castle to the MacDonalds for safekeeping. Since it no longer had any noble occupants, the queen deemed the keep needed spring cleaning to bring it to royal standards. Elizabeth stood her ground when the queen suggested the castle might not be ready until summer. Elizabeth was adamant that she'd oversee any major restoration or projects. She was certain there was little possibility for the castle to be in much disrepair after only a few years. People still lived in and around the keep, and she wanted her home to match her taste and Edward's, not that of the king and queen.

"You shall find your new home just over the next rise." Edward had visited a sennight earlier to ensure it was ready for Elizabeth's arrival. He was pleased with the keep, realizing Elizabeth's prediction that the MacDonalds had kept it in good repair was accurate. The tenants and servants offered a warm welcome despite the land changing hands twice in a short time. There were still a number of members of the Comyn clan who received amnesty and remained. They had been farmers and servants with no say in the Black Comyn's political choices. Robert gave the people the choice to renounce Comyn and swear their fealty to him or be put to death. It was a simple choice for most of them, and they lived better for it. The MacDonalds ensured the lands prospered and peace existed where it hadn't for many years.

"Is that it?" Elizabeth pointed to the horizon where she spotted the tips of a brick tower.

"Aye, that's our new home."

"Race you!" Elizabeth didn't wait before spurring Reubadair into a gallop. While she didn't ride pellmell now that she was expecting, she still liked to give Reubadair his head. Elizabeth knew she could have outpaced Edward and his horse, but for her own safety and to not terrify Edward, she kept Reubadair even with Edward's horse. They heard the bells ring as the guards on the wall walk recognized Edward's standard, and they raised the portcullis for them. They clattered into the bailey, but Elizabeth waited until Edward lifted her from the saddle. She knew he was guarded about her coming to live at Inverlochy since there were still members of the Comyn clan living in and around the keep. She offered a silent agreement to follow his lead upon their arrival.

An older woman by the name of Eithne greeted them and introduced herself as the head of household and chatelaine. However, once the couple stepped into the Great Hall, Eithne handed over her large ring of keys to Elizabeth with a noticeable look of relief.

"I'm a housekeeper nae a chatelaine, ma lady." Elizabeth smiled at the burr in the woman's accent.

"Thank you for entrusting me with these so soon upon my arrival," Elizabeth dipped a shallow curtsy.

"Aye well, ma lady, I've heard good things aboot ye. Yer mon is fond of ye." Eithne grinned at Edward as though he were a lad rather than a battle-hardened warrior now in possession of a keep and its surrounding land. "If ye'll follow me, ma lady, I had a bath ordered to yer chamber when the scouts announced yer approach. I figure ye'll feel a mite better once ye're refreshed. Ye can have a lie down after, or I can give ye a tour of the keep. Whatever ye wish. The evening meal willna be for a few hours."

"Thank you, Eithne. A bath sounds lovely. I think I would like that tour afterwards."

"Vera well. I'll find yer maid and have her assist ye."

"My lady wife doesn't have a maid," Edward grinned, and Elizabeth's face went up in flames. "She has me."

Eithne's step faltered before she doubled over in gales of laughter. She laughed so hard she drew attention from the other people in the hall. Her serious face creased into deep laugh lines that showed she wasn't always stern.

"Ye'll do well in the Highlands, the two of ye. If there isnae a bairn on the way already, there will be before the season changes. Mark ma word." Eithne turned and continued toward the stairs. Elizabeth shot Edward a glare, but that only provoked him into being even more outrageous. He scooped his wife into his arms and followed Eithne. Elizabeth buried her face as the people below went from stunned silence to cheers.

"You're incorrigible," she hissed.

"That and impatient. I haven't seen you alone and naked in days."

"I was trying not to think aboot the fact that I haven't seen you naked in days either, but now that you've said it, I'm rather impatient, too."

Edward walked into the chamber that Eithne showed them. The tub was before the hearth with steam rising from it. Edward set Elizabeth on her feet and spoke before Eithne could.

"Lady Bruce will call for you when she is ready for that tour. Thank you." Edward crossed the floor, gently but firmly closing the door with Eithne on the other side.

"Lady Bruce. I'm still not used to that."

"Sound rather nice though."

"It does." Elizabeth wrapped her arms around Edward's neck and lifted her chin to accept his kiss. The kiss was just as they always were, passionate and explosive even in its tenderness. Clothes soon littered the floor, and just like the night they handfasted, Edward lifted Elizabeth to slide into her before lowering them into the bath together. "I wish we could stay like this the entire rest of the day."

"Who says we won't?" Edward leaned Elizabeth back to wet her shoulders and hair before cradling her against his chest.

"The water won't stay hot."

"Then we keep summoning more," Edward chuckled.

"You want some of the male servants to see me naked, impaled on your rod? I refuse to allow any of the women to even glance at you in the bath."

"Perhaps not," Edward grinned.

"Besides, weren't you supposed to send Robert a missive once we arrived?"

"I intend to be too busy chasing my wife around this chamber to send any missives today."

"Promise?"

"Promise."

The evening meal was about to be served when Elizabeth and Edward emerged from their chamber at last. Eithne graciously mentioned nothing about the missed tour while the rest of the staff brought out platter upon platter of food for the welcome feast. When the meal concluded, and amid many mugs of ale, each member of the MacDonald and Comyn clans who lived and worked within the castle walls came forward to bow and pledge their fealty to Edward and Elizabeth. As they sat upon the dais, their hands clasped while watching men and women kneel to swear their loyalty, Edward and Elizabeth knew they were finally home.

EPILOGUE

T*en years later...*

"Edward," Elizabeth's aggrieved voice reached Edward as he wiped his face on his leine and stepped away from the lists. "Tell your sons that if they insist upon sparring like real men that they must tend their wounds like real men."

Edward looked at the three boys Elizabeth herded toward him; his youngest, Thomas, being led by the collar Elizabeth gripped. He took in the three dirty faces and three sets of dirty hands along with a bloody nose, a nasty cut over one eyebrow, and what looked like a broken little finger. There wasn't a tear in sight. Instead, there was his aggravated wife and his three rambunctious sons, Neill, Alexander, and Thomas. They were steppingstones in age: Neill at nine, Alexander was seven, and Thomas was five. A cooing sound and kicking legs peaked from behind Elizabeth's back as their youngest son, three-year-old Robert, grabbed a fistful of his mother's hair. Elizabeth reached back and eased the strands from their toddler's chubby fingers.

"Lads, I didn't give you your wooden swords to create more work for your mother. You look like a lot of scruff pups. Come with me, and you can explain your war wounds while you get cleaned up." Edward shooed his sons ahead of him to the buckets of water kept near the training field for the purpose of cleaning wounds and washing mud off faces. He leaned around Elizabeth to muss Robert's hair before giving Elizabeth a kiss. He rested his hand on her swollen belly as her fingers fisted his leine. Despite having four children and one on the way, their kisses had lost none of their fire. Just the opposite, their love and desire for one another was so obvious that it never surprised their people when they announced Elizabeth was expecting. It just surprised people that more than ten moons went in between births.

"Are you certain you aren't wishing for a lass?"

"What on earth would I know to do with a lass at this point?" Elizabeth laughed.

"She might turn out to be like Mairghread Mac-Kay." Edward pointed out.

"Aye, I would be proud of a lass like her. She is still quicker witted and more cunning than any of her four older brothers, and I would wager my last coin that she is even more deadly than those four Sinclairs."

"I would too, but don't let Callum, Alex, Tavish, or Magnus hear you say that. Or Tristan for that matter. Poor mon has his hands full with his wife."

"And what's that supposed to mean? They have as many bairns as we do. I think she's the one with her hands full."

Edward leaned forward and kissed his wife again before nuzzling behind her ear. "When the younger lads go down for their nap, I can think of what I want to keep my hands full."

Elizabeth giggled, and Edward's breeks tightened. "And that's why we're aboot to have our fifth bairn."

"Perhaps it should be a lass since we're running out of names for lads."

"There's still the name Edward." Elizabeth offered.

They had named each of their sons for one of Edward's brothers. His brothers Neill, Thomas, and Alexander were slain before Elizabeth met Edward. However, when their youngest son had been born, it was only months after the English killed Edward, the former Earl of Carrick and High King of Ireland. The pain had been too fresh to consider that name, so they chose Robert instead. It seemed fitting that if this fifth child was a son, they would name him Edward.

"Aye, there is. At least if you bellow that name in the future, at least one person is likely to answer. Better odds than you have now, my love." Edward danced out of her reach.

"That's because they're all so dazzled by their da they aren't listening to my voice."

Both knew that was untrue. While Elizabeth was a kind and doting mother, she ruled with an iron hand, as it was the only way to maintain control once her children outnumbered her. Edward looked back at his men training and nodded his head to his second. He walked back to the keep with Elizabeth and their brood, helping her steer the children abovestairs. He settled the two older boys in the nursery where they could read or play quietly while Elizabeth put the younger two down for naps.

"You know Thomas won't nap for much longer. Then I won't be able to sneak away with you like this," Elizabeth laughed as they entered their chamber. "I'll have to keep him and Niall and Alexander entertained so they'll be quiet enough for Robert and the bairn to nap."

"Eithne will be more than happy to keep the boys entertained, so you might have a rest in the afternoons." Edward began unlacing Elizabeth's kirtle.

"Eithne is more than happy to see me with a bairn in my belly every year. She's the most disappointed when I'm not expecting! She'll help you make time to bed me." Elizabeth finished pushing her gown to the floor and turned to spy Edward removing his leine. He'd taken to wearing a breacan feile, or great plaid, rather than the breeks or leggings he favored at court. Her husband's body still took her breath away even after more than a decade. He was broader, stronger, and leaner than when they met. His powerful frame made her mouth water.

"Looking at me like that, little one, is what keeps getting you with child." Edward flexed his chest, knowing she wouldn't resist reaching out to touch him. He captured her fingers and drew her closer as he kissed her fingertips. She reached out the other hand and stroked his length.

"Is that what does it? I could have sworn it was this." She squeezed.

Edward and Elizabeth melted into one another's embrace as they stumbled to their bed. In a tangle of arms and legs, the couple found the rhythm they developed many years ago and still delighted in. Edward watched as pleasure blossomed across his wife's face, and she caressed the rugged plains of his cheeks and jaw.

"I love you, *mo ghaol*," Edward's breath wafted across her lips.

"And I love you, *mo chridhe*," Elizabeth answered before they sank into another kiss that bound them, body and soul.

THANK YOU FOR READING A SPINSTER AT THE HIGHLAND COURT

Celeste Barclay, a nom de plume, lives near the Southern California coast with her husband and sons. Growing up in the Midwest, Celeste enjoyed spending as much time in and on the water as she could. Now she lives near the beach. She's an avid swimmer, a hopeful future surfer, and a former rower. When she's not writing, she's working or being a mom.

Visit Celeste's website, www.celestebarclay.com, for regular updates on works in progress, new releases, and her blog where she features posts about her experiences as an author and recommendations of her favorite reads.

Are you an author who would like to guest blog or be featured in her recommendations? Visit her website for an opportunity to share your insights and experiences.

Have you read *Their Highland Beginning, The Clan*

Sinclair Prequel? Learn how the saga begins! This FREE novella is available to all new subscribers to Celeste's monthly newsletter. Subscribe on her website.

www.celestebarclay.com

Join the fun and get exclusive insider giveaways, sneak peeks, and new release announcements in

Celeste Barclay's Facebook Ladies of Yore Group

THE HIGHLAND LADIES

A Spy at the Highland Court
BOOK 2 SNEAK PEEK

Dedric Hartley watched as the English king continued his royal rage as courtiers and advisors eased away from their irate sovereign. His Majesty's face was mottled with red splotches that only accentuated his fair complexion, and spittle formed at the corners of his mouth as his rant amplified. King Edward stalked about the chamber on the long legs that earned him the moniker "Longshanks."

"I don't give a bloody damn who oversaw the attack. It failed!" He railed against the last advisor who tried to reassure him that the recent loss was not the end of his campaign against the Scots. "Failure is failure. That usurper believes he's gotten the upper hand, and he will continue worming his way further into England now that he thinks he has outsmarted me. I should have killed him when I had the chance."

King Edward muttered his final comments as he sank back into the engraved and carved chair that sat on a dais. His bile spewed the king retreated into his own thoughts as the rest of the chamber was left wondering what to do next.

Dedric had seen this pattern countless times over the course of his life. He was all too familiar with the king's mercurial temper and unpredictable outbursts, but he also knew Edward was one of the best strategists and logisticians to have every lived. While he might not like the man, he respected him. At times. Ric watched as the king scanned the crowd, assessing each knight present until his eyes settled on rich, who wished he could melt into the curtains and watch the people in the gardens below.

"Sir Dedric, approach."

A Wallflower at the Highland Court **BOOK 3**

THE CLAN SINCLAIR

His Highland Lass **BOOK 1 SNEAK PEEK**

She entered the great hall like a strong spring storm in the northern most Highlands. Tristan Mackay felt like he had been blown hither and yon. As the storm settled, she left him with the sweet scents of heather and lavender wafting towards him as she approached. She was not a classic beauty, tall and willowy like the women at court. Her face and form were not what legends were made of. But she held a unique appeal unlike any he had seen before. He could not take his eyes off of her long chestnut hair that had strands of fire and burnt copper running through them. Unlike the waves or curls he was used to, her hair was unusually straight and fine. It looked like a waterfall cascading down her back. While she was not tall, neither was she short. She had a figure that was meant for a man to grasp and hold onto, whether from the front or from behind. She had an aura of confidence and charm, but not arrogance or conceit like many good looking women he had met. She did not seem to know her own appeal. He could tell that she was many things, but one thing she was not was his.

His Bonnie Highland Temptation **BOOK 2**

His Highland Prize **BOOK 3**

His Highland Pledge **BOOK 4**

His Highland Surprise **BOOK 5**

Their Highland Beginning **BOOK 6**

PIRATES OF THE ISLES

The Blond Devil of the Sea **BOOK 1 SNEAK PEEK**

Caragh lifted her torch into the air as she made her way down the precarious Cornish cliffside. She made out the hulking shape of a ship, but the dead of night made it impossible to see who was there. She and the fishermen of Bedruthan Steps weren't expecting any shipments that night. But her younger brother Eddie, who stood watch at the entrance to their hiding place, had spotted the ship and signaled up to the village watchman, who alerted Caragh.

As her boot slid along the dirt and sand, she cursed having to carry the torch and wished she could have sunlight to guide her. She knew these cliffs well, and it was for that reason it was better that she moved slowly than stop moving once and for all. Caragh feared the light from her torch would carry out to the boat. Despite her efforts to keep the flame small, the solitary light would be a beacon.

When Caragh came to the final twist in the path before the sand, she snuffed out her torch and started to run to the cave where the main source of the village's income lay in hiding. She heard movement along the trail above her head and knew the local fishermen would soon join her on the beach. These men, both young and old, were strong from days spent pulling in the full trawling nets and hoisting the larger catches onto their boats. However, these men weren't well-trained swordsmen, and the fear of pirate raids was ever-present. Caragh feared that was who the villagers would face that night.

The Dark Heart of the Sea **BOOK 2**
The Red Drifter of the Sea **BOOK3**
The Scarlet Blade of the Sea **BOOK 4**

Leif **BOOK 1 SNEAK PEEK**

Leif looked around his chambers within his father's longhouse and breathed a sigh of relief. He noticed the large fur rugs spread throughout the chamber. His two favorites placed strategically before the fire and the bedside he preferred. He looked at his shield that hung on the wall near the door in a symbolic position but waiting at the ready. The chests that held his clothes and some of his finer acquisitions from voyages near and far sat beside his bed and along the far wall. And in the center was his most favorite possession. His oversized bed was one of the few that could accommodate his long and broad frame. He shook his head at his longing to climb under the pile of furs and on the stuffed mattress that beckoned him. He took in the chair placed before the fire where he longed to sit now with a cup of warm mead. It had been two months since he slept in his own bed, and he looked forward to nothing more than pulling the furs over his head and sleeping until he could no longer ignore his hunger. Alas, he would not be crawling into his bed again for several more hours. A feast awaited him to celebrate his and his crew's return from their latest expedition to explore the isle of Britannia. He bathed and wore fresh clothes, so he had no excuse for lingering other than a bone weariness that set in during the last storm at sea. He was eager to spend time at home no matter how much he loved sailing. Their last expedition had been profitable with several raids of monasteries that yielded jewels and both silver and gold, but he was ready for respite.

Leif left his chambers and knocked on the door next to his. He heard movement on the other side, but it was only moments before his sister, Freya, opened her door. She, too, looked tired but clean. A few pieces of jewelry she confiscated from the holy houses that allegedly swore to a life of poverty and deprivation adorned her trim frame.

"That armband suits you well. It compliments your muscles," Leif smirked and dodged a strike from one of those muscular arms.

Only a year younger than he, his sister was a well-known and feared shield maiden. Her lithe form was strong and agile making her a ferocious and competent opponent to any man. Freya's beauty was stunning, but Leif had taken every opportunity since they were children to tease her about her unusual strength even among the female warriors.

"At least one of us inherited our father's prowess. Such a shame it wasn't you."

www.ingramcontent.com/pod-product-compliance
Lightning Source LLC
Chambersburg PA
CBHW011448100726
47899CB00010BB/3214